The
CATCH

BOOK TWO IN
THE PLAYER duet

K. BROMBERG

The Catch
By K. Bromberg

Copyright © 2017 K. Bromberg

ISBN: 978-1-942832-06-5

Published by JKB Publishing, LLC

This is a work of fiction. Names, places, characters and incidents are the product of the author's imagination and are fictitious. Any resemblance to actual persons, living or dead, events or establishments is solely coincidental.

OTHER BOOKS BY K. BROMBERG

DEDICATION

To the hopeless romantics:
Someday you'll find someone who will love the parts
of you that no one else knows how to love.

CHAPTER ONE

Scout

What did I just do?
  My hands tremble.
  Not only to Easton, but to me too.
I clasp them to hide it from the men before me.
To the promise I made my dad.

 Chills tighten my scalp. Pull on my hair. Twist my heart. My stomach churns and bile claws its way up my throat.

 The clock. The hand keeps moving. Minutes pass by. But I feel like time stopped with my heart when I spoke those words. *Easton isn't one hundred percent ready to return and be reinstated to the line-up. He's not going to meet your deadline.*

 The shocked expressions. The wide eyes. The sudden scooting out of Cory's chair as he left the room, fingers dialing his cell, leaving me with nothing but hope that I did the right thing when every part within me riled against it. Told me I was wrong. That I misinterpreted what I saw.

 And yet I knew what I saw.
 Then the questions began.

Each minute that passes causing more doubt to break through and crack my certainty.

The damn unending questions.

The list of people I'm letting down growing with each passing moment.

Having to talk about Easton when all I want to do is get *to* him. See him. Explain to him. Touch him so I could soothe the discord.

Having to explain why I failed. Why Doc Dalton's *team* failed.

The hands on the clock continue to tick. Seconds turns into minutes. Minutes I want to take back.

Minutes I can't get back.

Cory, back in the room now, whispers with the man next to him while the others around the table stare at me. Waiting. Gauging. Wondering.

The door shoves open. The sound of it banging against the wall ricochets around the room but has nothing on the slamming of my heart against my rib cage.

He already knows.

For a split second our eyes meet. I see the hurt. The anger. The questions.

And he doesn't even know I'm the one who caused this to happen.

"Easton." His name is a shocked plea asking for forgiveness when my guilty conscience screams at him that it's my fault, but just as soon as our eyes meet, he shakes his head.

"Don't." It's all he says, the warning is as clear as the disgust in his expression.

I'm shell-shocked. From the events. From seeing him. From having to face what I just did. And before I can process what to say to him in front of these men, he speaks.

"A trade? A fucking trade?" His voice reverberates in the small space and commands the attention of the men sitting at the table. He's standing there, his warm-up gear still on, and his expression a mask of disbelief. "I gave my career to this organization. I've turned down bigger deals, flashier contracts to go to other teams, and this is how you repay my loyalty?" His laugh holds anything but amusement. "Well, *fuck you*, Cory. Fuck you and whatever you're trying to do here."

"I'm just trying to run a team, Mr. Wylder." Cory's voice is calm and even but the hint of condescension in it scrapes over my skin.

"Run a team . . . or ruin a team?" Easton takes a step closer, shoulders square, posture threatening. His finger pounds on the desk with each word he speaks. "You think this is how you treat players and then expect them to win a World Series so you can collect your nice little bonus? Think again."

"Good luck with your future team." Cory gives him a dismissing nod.

Easton seethes. *Understandably.* His anger so palpable it suffocates the room.

I wait with blood on my hands and guilt in my heart.

"You're a heartless son of a bitch, you know that?" Easton sneers as his hands fist at his sides.

"Then you'll be happy you won't have to work for me anymore. Good day, Mr. Wylder."

No one in the room moves as the two men glare at each other. One a picture of calm arrogance and the other a ball of restrained fury.

Several tense seconds pass where I question whether Easton is going to unleash that fury on Cory. Just when I'm convinced he will, Easton shakes his head ever so slowly as he meets the eyes of everyone else in the room but mine, before he turns on his heel and stalks from the room.

My heart leaves with him.

My feet desperately want to as well. I fight the urge to do just that—get up, run after him, explain—but I can't. I have to be a professional—one who is the face of a business and not a woman who fears she just screwed over the man she loves.

Loves?

Loves.

Holy shit. I really do love him.

"Sorry about the interruption, Ms. Dalton," Cory says distracting me from my revelation and pulling my attention back to the matter at hand. In their eyes I didn't fulfill my contract and therefore failed to achieve my father's final wish.

Cory keeps talking but I don't hear him.

I see the hurt in Easton's eyes.

I hear his voice in my ears.

What. Would. You. Do. Scout?

The answer, Easton?

I'd sacrifice me to save you.

I just did.

I can only hope he sees it the same way.

CHAPTER TWO

Easton

The opening notes of Guns N' Roses fill the stadium above me and the song's introduction—the music I've heard every time I've hit this field during my career—are like salt in the wound.

Welcome to the jungle . . .

What the hell is happening?

I need to get the fuck out of here.

I can't breathe.

I want to punch something.

I can't think with the song reminding me where I should be right now—*on the field*—or of the team's jersey I've worn since I was a kid that I won't be wearing anymore.

I jog down the empty corridors desperate to be free of what suddenly feels like a concrete prison trying to hold me back and deny me the things I love.

"It's true then."

His words stop me in my tracks. "Did you know?" Accusation owns my voice and I don't give a fuck, because every part of me is begging him to say no and for me to believe him.

"No."

I got the answer I wanted. I stare at him, wanting to believe him. Needing to know that for once I was bigger than the game to him, and yet I ask him again. "*No?*"

"You don't believe me?" The pitch of his voice escalates.

"Yes. No. *Fuck.*" I walk a few feet from him, lift my hat to run a hand through my hair, and exhale for what feels like the first time in the last hour. I turn around to face him, hands out, eyes pleading. "What the hell, Dad?"

It's an open-ended question asking how this happened. I know it and yet I want him to answer it because I'm at a goddamn loss and haven't even begun to process my new reality yet.

The national anthem begins to play and for the first time in my life while wearing a uniform, I don't remove my hat and put my hand over my heart. I just don't have it in me.

"What team?" His voice sounds as solemn as I feel.

"No clue. Finn's on his way to get answers." I chuckle but it sounds empty.

"Why wasn't Finn in there?" His eyes narrow to match the confusion in his voice.

"Your guess is as good as mine." I walk a few feet and then turn back around to face him. "They traded me, but we have no goddamn clue to what team yet . . . so what does that tell you?"

His brow narrows, and he continues to watch me, his mind running over the same shit mine has on an endless loop. "That Cory didn't expect to initiate a trade."

"Bingo," I shout, smacking my hands together. "So what the fuck is going on, Dad?"

"It's going to be okay, Easton." His sounds less than convinced.

I glare at him with so much to say, but with a mind so messed up I can't find the words to express it.

The crowd roars in my heaven above and echoes down to the

hell I'm currently in. The wall looks so damn tempting to punch.

Even though it's made of cinderblock.

I pace back and forth as the soundtrack to my life plays in the stadium around me. A place I no longer belong.

I've gotta get the fuck out of here before I do something I'll regret.

Fuck this.

"I'm outta here."

CHAPTER THREE

Scout

We need time to consider where your contract falls into play after this unexpected turn of events. Let's reconvene tomorrow morning at eight, after I've conferred with my colleagues."

Numb.

That's all I felt during Cory's hour-long inquisition on why Easton wasn't at one hundred percent. *Lies.* My responses were all lies but they were the only things I could say to support my findings.

Empty.

Throwing up in the bathroom. The nerves finally winning. My struggle to hold on instead of upending the lunch I'd shared with Easton earlier onto the conference table.

Bone-tired.

Rushing through the maze of hallways in the stadium. Somewhere above the mass of concrete a game plays on. Little boys with their dads. Families on an outing together. First dates. Happy times.

The game he was supposed to make his return in.

All I can think about is Easton.

Getting to him.

Talking to him.

Needing his approval that I did the right thing.

I push redial again. His name flashes on the screen but it's his voicemail that answers. Not him.

I thought I was going to turn our lives upside down today but in a totally different way. He'd be traveling with the team on road trips. I'd be here rehabbing the injured guys. The everyday routine we'd gotten used to would be thrown up in the air and turned around. We'd have to figure out a new norm, but at least we'd be in the same place, working for the same team.

Not in a million years did I imagine we'd be doing this from different cities.

I'm startled by the bright sunlight when I emerge from the tunnels out to the gated parking lot for the players and staff. I'm so exhausted, so disoriented emotionally, that it feels like it should be midnight. Just as I reach my car, my phone rings. Desperate to speak with him, I answer without looking. "Easton!" His name is a rush of air.

"What the hell happened in there, Scout?"

He knows.

"Dad." Every part of me sags in defeat. While my dad is the one person I should be worried about the most, I've been furiously dialing Easton instead of calling him to explain what happened.

"I'm hearing rumors. What the hell happened in there?"

My feet and words falter knowing I have to tell him I'm not exactly sure. It feels surreal to me.

"It's a long story," I begin as I climb into my car and continue to tell him the short version of it, knowing how damn ridiculous it sounds even to my own ears.

When I finish, the line falls into an oppressive silence that weighs as heavy on me as the Austin heat beating through the windshield of my car.

"I'm disappointed." His deep baritone rumbles through the line followed by the frail wheeze of his breath.

Strength covering the devastating weakness beneath.

Kind of like how I feel.

"I did what I thought was right." My voice is barely a whisper when I speak, and tears threaten after hearing those two words every child hates hearing their parent say, *I'm disappointed.*

"*What* was right, though?" he asks. "Right for you *or* right for Easton?"

"Dad—"

"People—*men especially*—will come and go in your life but family will always be there. You need to take care of what's yours first. Always."

The sting of his words is brutal and right now I hate him for them. I hate him for making me question what I did. For questioning my loyalty to both men in my life.

My stomach heaves, but I don't say a word.

"Lying is one of the quickest ways to ruin a relationship," he says and has no clue how much those words squeeze my heart since I fear I just ruined two relationships. Easton's and mine with the Aces.

"It's not what—"

"I asked you for one thing, Scout. Don't call me back until you tell me you've done it."

"*What*?" I screech as the panic sets in. "Wait! Don't hang up. How? I mean—what am I sup—?"

"You go back in there tomorrow and you get the damn contract. You fight for what's ours and you don't let them push you around," he says with conviction before being overcome by a violent coughing fit.

"Are you ok—?"

"You mixed business with pleasure, Scout. You risked the contract by letting your emotions get in the way. Fix this and secure next year's contract. Don't call me until you have."

The line goes silent and I'm left sitting in my car with my phone to my ear, tears streaming down my face, and doubt owning my soul. I have no clue how to process the last two hours.

Did I really just jeopardize fulfilling my dad's last wish by putting Easton before him?

"What did I do?" I whisper as I squeeze my eyes closed and drop my head back on the headrest to try and shut everything out for a few minutes. It's futile. The look on Easton's face when he barged into the conference room and the echo of my dad's words in my ears are etched in my mind.

And if rumors are already flying, I need to get to Easton and explain to him the what and the why before the wrong information gets to him. The adrenaline of the moment has worn off. It's given way to the fear that I royally screwed everything up and no one's going to forgive me.

Get it together, Scout.

A knock on my driver's side window scares the shit out of me. I snap my head up and stare at the man standing there—crisp white shirt and tie, mouth set in a straight line, serious brown eyes that demand answers—bent over at the waist telling me with hand motions to roll the window down.

"Who are you?" I shout through the glass as I halfheartedly shove the tears off my cheeks.

"Open the damn window. You better start explaining what the hell happened in there," he says through gritted teeth.

"Excuse me?" There's no way I'm opening the window to this jerk.

He steps back from the window, hands up as if he's just realized how threatening he appears, and he shoves them in his pockets. "Security guard is right there," he says with a lift of his chin to where Arnie is watching us from the guard's booth. I glance to make sure he's there and then back to the man demanding answers and slowly open my car door, because I know it has to do with Easton.

It seems that everything does these days.

11

The hairs on my neck stand on end—my guard up, a steel gate of unknown—as I exit my car to meet him glare for glare. My synapses misfire as I try to connect thoughts and place him.

"You're no Dalton." He shakes his head. "You told Easton he was good, and then I get a call that he's been traded? *Are you fucking kidding me?* Doc always protected his players at any cost. You sure as hell don't. What kind of game are you playing?"

The *fuck you* on the tip of my tongue dies with the punch of his insult to my solar plexus. "Finn?" Easton's agent glares as he nods. "Why weren't you there?"

It's a simple question but the man I wished for an hour ago to help me make sense of the papers I'd seen is now in front of me. I *don't* trust him. He should have been there. He should have never allowed Easton to sign what I saw. A good agent protects their client by any means necessary.

"That's a good question."

I take a step back. "And what does that mean?"

He didn't answer me.

"Why don't you tell me what happened in there, Scout?"

Was he a part of this?

"There were papers . . ." I begin but stop. My pulse pounds in my ears.

Did he know?

"What papers?" he urges.

Paranoia takes over. Tears burn the back of my eyes as I question my own sanity. Why don't I trust the one person I should be able to when it comes to Easton?

But he wasn't there.

"I need to talk to Easton." It's the only thing I have left to say. I stare at him for a beat—more time wasted that needs to be spent finding Easton.

"There's no time. I need answers now. I'm his agent, Scout. You can trust me."

I think of the papers. The scrawled signature that agreed to such ludicrous terms. Any agent who tells their client to sign something like that shouldn't be trusted.

"Trust you?" I laugh with a shake of my head.

He glares, fists clenched, and muscle pulsing in his jaw. "What happened in that room, Dalton?" he demands and takes a step closer, frustration evident and posture threatening.

"If you had been here, you'd already know and then maybe we wouldn't be in this position, would we?" I grit out before turning and getting into my car. My hands are trembling so violently I'm glad I have the steering wheel to hold on to.

He's still staring at me as I pull out of the gated lot on my way to Easton's. I weave through the stadium parking lot filled with tail-gaters finishing up their cocktails before heading in to watch the game already several innings over.

The tears stain my cheeks as I drive. I've nothing more than a pocketful of hope that I can make this right with Easton, but the doubt I feel is as devastating as the look that was on Easton's face. It owns my soul.

CHAPTER FOUR

Easton

Scout told them you weren't one hundred percent.

Finn's words ring in my ears. So does the laugh I gave him that faded off when I realized he was serious.

I swing the bat. Wood meets leather and red seams. My grunt echoes off the concrete walls and the vibration from hitting the ball travels up my arms.

That's why she had that look on her face when I barged into the conference room. Shocked. Fucking. Guilt.

My cell rings. It hasn't stopped. The reporters are relentless. But I don't have it in me to walk the twenty feet to turn it off.

Or smash it to pieces.

Easton. The way her voice said my name echoes in my head. It drowns out the way she moaned it yesterday morning. Talk about adding insult to injury.

I swing again. Connect again. But I feel nothing but anger. I know nothing but rage. I'm nothing but hurt.

It's all such bullshit.

Useless fucking bullshit.

None of it makes sense except for her expression when I went in to confront Tillman. *Now that?* The shocked guilt and wide eyes. They make perfect sense now.

Swing and miss.

The TV drones on. The announcers discuss Drew's bat speed. I tune it out but can't turn it off. It's like I need to watch Santiago behind *my* plate to know it's really happening.

It's all too goddamn much.

I step outta the box and reach for the bottle of Jameson I set on the ledge behind me. The sting of the whiskey has nothing on the hole burning its way through my gut.

I look at the bottle. The downside—it's half empty. The upside— at least there's more liquid Novocain to numb me, and God, how I need the pain to be dulled.

How could she?

The machine pitches the ball and it hits the backstop with a thud the same time my cell phone starts ringing again. Or maybe it never stopped. I can't fucking remember because all I keep thinking is *she spooked.*

I told her I was falling for her—asked her to move in with me for fuck's sake when I've never offered that to anyone else before—and she fucking spooked. Instead of having the guts to tell me she couldn't do it, she went the easy route.

She got rid of me a different way.

My chest hurts like a motherfucker. Another swig of the bottle. A twist of the bat in my hands that irritates the broken and raw blisters on my bare palms. I welcome the pain so I do it again as I step back into the box.

The pitch comes. This time I'm so angry, so unfocused, I miss the ball completely. The sound of hitting only air—*whiff*—is deafening, and I welcome the temporary reprieve from the noise in my head.

She sold me out to push me away.

Away from my home.

Away from my team.

Away from my family.

Away from *her*.

I'm sitting here with my ass in the wind, waiting to see where the fuck my new home is going to be when *this* is my home. With my batting cage here and my glass-wall view of the stadium upstairs I thought I'd play in forever. *This is my home*. I can't be upstairs where I'll see what I don't want to see. Where Scout's perfume clings to the T-shirt on my bed and her lipstick stains the pillowcase she kissed the night before last as a joke. Now it's like a damn beacon making me wonder if that was actually her goodbye.

Like she knew.

"Fuck!" I shout the word out with the next swing and then walk away from the plate with the bat braced over my shoulders, the *whiff* of the machine still pitching balls every twenty seconds.

How am I going to take care of my mom now?

I take another swig of Jameson. My hands ache and the ringing phone is a constant reminder that Scout's somewhere on the other end of it. It takes everything I have not to take my bat and obliterate it into a million pieces. Not just so I don't have to listen to it, but so I'm not tempted to pick it up and hear her voice like I desperately want to.

Whiff. Thump.

Right now I need someone who gets me and fuck all, she gets me.

How screwed up does that make me? My laugh bounces off the concrete walls and my own hysteria echoes back to me.

Whiff. Thump.

The ringing starts again, and I do the only thing I know to drown it out. Ignoring the sting of my open blisters, I step in the box and swing with everything I have.

Grunt. Thwack. Ring.

Over and over until my arms feel like rubber and exhausted beyond reason—*but I still feel*—and so I swing again.

"It's not the ball's fault you know."

Whiff.

Fucking Finn. "Leave me alone."

"You ever pick up your phone?"

"If I wanted to talk to you, I would have. But I didn't." I take a piss-poor swing at a pitch and barely connect. "Go away."

"It was either me or your old man getting the building manager to let us in here and so I figured, you'd prefer me."

Whiff. Thump. Ring.

"I told you I didn't want to speak to you until you have answers, so you better start talking or you can get the fuck out." I grunt with my swing this time and am so tired I could collapse right here, but the whiskey is way more fucking tempting than sleep right now.

"I've been in communication with the team."

I drop the bat from my shoulder and turn to grab the bottle. "I've been in communication with the team," I mimic in his formal tone before I take another drink. "This is my life we're talking about, Finn, not some goddamn negotiation. So tell me, do you know where the hell I've been traded to?"

Whiff. Thump. Ring.

"New York? Florida? Minnesota?" My pitch escalates with each city. So does my temper. "Huh, Finn? Have you got answers for me yet?" I turn to face him.

Whiff. Thump. Ring.

"Will you turn all that shit off so I can concentrate?" he shouts.

We glare at each other through the batting cage nets. The memory of making love to Scout against them is like another fucking knife in my back.

So I shift my focus back to Finn. He looks exhausted—hair sticking up, shirt wrinkled and unbuttoned at the collar, eyes weary—when he's typically always the picture of perfection. Good. At least

I'm not the only one who looks like hell.

Whiff. Thump. Ring.

"Why weren't you there today?" I ask him the same question I've asked him three times already, needing to see his face this time when he responds.

"You don't trust me?" His voice is ice cold but to hell with him.

"I'm finding out trust and loyalty don't have a whole lot to do about nothing these days," I say with a *fuck you* shrug to my shoulders.

He takes a step closer, wraps his fingers in the net so his arms hang above his head as he stares at me through the barrier. "I was told the meeting started two hours later than it did. I double-checked all my notes. My voicemails. They said three p.m. You had a game starting at two, so why have the meeting after it started? I should have fucking known something was going on. Tillman's such a shady fucker. I should have questioned why," he says with a shake of his head and runs a hand through his hair. "And Wylder, if you ever insult me again by questioning my loyalty, you can find yourself a new goddamn agent."

The bite to his tone surprises me and tells me exactly what I needed to know: he *is* in my corner

"Yeah, well, something was definitely going on," I say, ignoring his threat, my laugh that follows loaded with sarcasm.

Whiff. Thump. Ring.

"Easton, please turn that shit off so we can talk."

I hold his eyes for a second longer before turning to flip the switch off on the wall behind me. The soft whirl of the machine slowing down fills the space while I walk to silence the ringer on my cell.

The screen is filled with calls as I scroll. Reporters. Teammates. Finn. My dad. For each one of those, there seems to be about five from Scout. Voicemails. Texts. The sight of them makes my chest ache, because one thing still remains, *she sold me out.*

I grab the bottle to ease that ache but leave my cell as I emerge from the batting cage for the first time in over three hours. I head straight for the bathroom without saying a word to Finn. When I come out of the john, he seems to take a closer look at me.

"You look like shit."

"Yeah, well, can you blame me?" I shrug, glancing over to the wall of my Little League jerseys. It's so much easier to look there than at him. "Just trying to make sense of shit that makes no sense so . . . looking like it seems fitting."

"Fucking Tillman."

"That's putting it nicely."

"The prick won't talk to me until tomorrow morning. I have a nine o'clock meeting. Fucking nine o'clock," he shouts. "Like you were some castoff instead of their franchise player."

"That's what I don't get," I say and take a drink. "It's like they don't have anything set up. Like they didn't even expect to trade me."

"That's what I'm having a hard time wrapping my head around. There has to be a catch here that we're missing," he says as he folds his arms and leans his hips against the wall. "In all my years, when a trade is made, you're told right then and there to pack your bags and move on to the next team. All they told me was to have you clean out your locker by ten tomorrow."

"Before the guys get in." I snort. "Such a chicken-shit move. God forbid I'm there when the team comes in to see how disloyal their fucking club is to its players. What about Boseman? Where the hell was he in all of this?" I ask about the team's owner. The man who has been like an uncle to me and is no-fucking-where when I need him most.

"Still on that trip to the Amazon, reinventing himself or some billionaire shit like that. I've left a dozen or so messages when I couldn't get face time with that asshole Tillman until tomorrow."

"Fucking bad juju, man," I say as I yank the bottle out of his reach when he goes to grab it from me.

"In case you didn't know, it's only six o'clock, East," he says, motioning to the windowless room. "You're already a full bottle in tonight. I need you to pace yourself. Slow it down some."

"Ah, so that's why you're here . . . to come and ruin all my fun?" I roll my eyes.

"I need you somewhat sober in the morning."

I stare at his hand held out, and with my eyes on his, I slowly lift the bottle to my lips in rebellion and smirk. "It's not like I've got a job to go to or anything."

"You never know. They could have you hopping on a plane first thing in the morning and headed God knows where—"

"That's the whole fucking point, Finn. *God. Knows. Where.* Do you know?" I shout at him, arms thrown out to my sides, patience—and what feels like my sanity—gone hours ago. "Because I don't know shit. And neither do you for that matter. I mean this is so fucked up in so many ways and—"

"Look, I know you're upset, but we've got to make the best—"

"Upset?" I yell at the top of my lungs. The temptation to throw the bottle is stronger than the will to drink it. "I gave my goddamn heart and soul to the Aces and for what? For what?" It's as if a tornado of anger is ripping through me. "To be given away?"

"I know, man. I know. It makes no sense to me either. I've got your dad on my ass, I've got the press breathing down my neck, and Scout refusing to speak to anyone but you. All the while, the damn organization is taking their sweet time doling out the details of your trade. I've never seen anything like it."

My feet stop when I hear her name. The betrayal is still fresh and confusing, and I don't know what the hell to think about it, so I pace and then sit and then stand again, unable to remain still.

The smile and kiss she gave me as she left my place earlier is burned in my mind. *Why would she lie?*

I change gears, have to, because I can't think about her anymore. "What about my mom? How am I going to take care of her when I'm in—"

"We'll figure something out."

"And find a place to live—"

"Most teams have a neighborhood where the transitional guys stay—"

"And then there's . . ." *And then there's fucking Scout.*

Or rather, was fucking Scout.

I have to move to abate how everything about me revolts knowing that whatever this was between us is over. Finn lets me be until I stop, hang my head, and attempt to come to grips with everything.

His hand is on my shoulder, squeezing in support. "Let's go upstairs. I'll get you some food while you take a shower. Then we can talk some more if you want. Or not."

"Nah. I'm fine." I can't stomach going upstairs for the next few hours. The stadium lights will be on for the cleaning crew. The last thing I need to see is how they brighten up the sky to remind me of the game I missed. The game I was supposed to make my comeback in. Add to that, I'm nowhere near ready to face the many pieces of Scout scattered throughout my place. Shrugging off his hand, I begin to move again.

"Come on, let me order you food. I'll get some sushi from your favorite—"

"No!" More damn memories come to mind. Scout on the couch trying sushi for the first time. Scout sitting between my legs watching a movie. Scout reading fortunes from cookies about as likely to come true as my trade being a bad dream. "I'm not hungry."

"C'mon, let me do something here, East," he pleads.

"Get me answers."

"I'm try—"

"I know, I know. I just don't get why she lied and said I wasn't one hundred percent when last night—Jesus fucking Christ, just this morning," I rant, more to myself, losing track of time in this concrete tomb, "she told me she couldn't wait to see me on the field again."

"You slept with her?" Finn's asks as he starts piecing together the words I said. *Guess I just let the cat out of the bag.* I break in stride for a beat and then ignore his question.

"What if they changed the terms of her agreement?" I deflect as I reach the pitching mound and turn back around. "What if they told her Doc Dalton wasn't going to get the team contract?"

"I thought you were *tolerating* her." He digs in deeper, ignoring my questions. "I thought you were going to put those ear buds in your ears and listen to one of your damn audiobooks to pass the time so you didn't have to deal with her. What the fuck happened to that, Easton?"

He blocks my path and I stride around him but not before he reaches out to grab my bicep. My opposing arm is cocked back in a second—fist ready to fly. My temper is sick of being tested.

He doesn't flinch, even though so much of me *needs* to get a reaction out of him. Instead he just holds my stare for a beat before looking at my fist and then back to my eyes with a lift of his brows. "Please tell me you weren't just royally fucked over by your physical therapist because of some kind of *lover scorned* bullshit."

I lower my arm slowly and scrub my hand over my face, but I don't answer.

"Are you fucking kidding me?" he asks with a disbelieving laugh as I turn my back to him and stare at a photo of my dad and me, both in our Aces jerseys, on the last day we shared the field together before he retired. Finn groans, and I can follow him pacing by the sound of it. "What happened? Did you have your fun and then were done with her while she was hoping for somewhere over the goddamn rainbow with you?"

"Not exactly." The vision of her standing in my bedroom, shoving a curling iron into her bag with those sexy shoes on, and that shy smile on her lips that shocked to an O when I asked her to move in with me, fills my mind.

"Then what? Throw me a goddamn bone, East, so I know what I'm working with here."

"Drop it."

"No. I won't drop it," he says, getting in my face and ripping the bottle from my hand. "This is my job. To get to the bottom of shit so I can figure out the next step while you get on the field wherever the hell they're going to send you. That's how this goes. So what the fuck happened here, Easton, because I need to know where to start."

Jaw clenched, I shake my head, not willing to admit defeat out loud. I can see the wheels of his mind turning, figuring, assuming. He takes another guess.

"She told you she loved you, and you said no fucking way and so this was her way of getting back at you not wanting to commit to anyone?"

My pride wars with the necessity to tell him the truth I'd rather not admit. "Actually, quite the opposite." My voice is a whisper but the widening of his eyes and surprise in his expression tells me he heard me loud and clear.

"Ah shit," he says in sympathy.

"Yeah," I say as I shrug my shoulders and walk away from him. "Lost my team and got fucked over by my girl all in the same day, so let me be and give me my bottle back, will ya?"

"I'm sorry, man. That's fucking rough." He hands me the bottle and falls quiet, thinking so hard I swear I can almost hear it. Then again, that may be the Jameson talking. "It still doesn't make sense though. If you're not one hundred percent and reinstated, then Dalton's Physical Therapy doesn't get the contract . . . so unless those terms changed, she fucked herself too."

"Exactly," I say in a frustrated growl. "That's why I'm at a loss."

"There's one way to find out." He points to where my cell sits.

"I don't want to fucking talk to her right now." I struggle with believing myself.

"Rip the Band-Aid off. It's easier knowing than wondering."

"No." I'm adamant. Or at least my tone is because fuck if I don't want to tear into her and pull her close all at the same time.

That has to be the alcohol talking.

"I'll give you tonight, but we're going to need answers from someone since God knows I won't trust a damn word coming out of Tillman's mouth in the morning."

I grunt in response.

"We can talk tomorrow before I head into the meeting." He takes a few steps. "You gonna be okay?"

"Yeah. I'm gonna go a few more rounds with the machine." And even that doesn't seem like an escape anymore.

"Okay. I'll send over some food in a bit." He looks at his watch and then back to me. "I'll try to time it after the ballpark lights are out."

He knows. Understands. And doesn't think I'm stupid for it.

"Thanks, Finn."

"Get some rest."

I watch the elevator doors close behind him and drain the rest of the bottle. My hands hurt like a motherfucker but I walk to the cage anyway. This kind of pain I can deal with.

I'm used to it.

"It's gotta be the fucking papers." Finn's voice startles me just as I pick up a new bat to check it for splinters. "They have to be the catch."

"What?"

"I knew Tillman was pulling a fast one. I knew it in my gut when I got that addendum you signed. I wanted to go to Boseman and you told me to drop it . . . but, East, I think that's the key."

"What?" *Speak English, please.*

He strides across the space with a purpose that tells me he's figured something out, but there's not much to get excited about even if he has. I'm still traded. Still removed from my life here. "I need you to think hard about this," he says, voice serious, eyes intense, and all I give him in response is a chuckle.

"The bottle's empty." I throw it up and it lands with a thud onto the turf. "You think I can remember shit, right now?"

"I'm fucking serious, E. When you got hurt, you told me you

signed *papers*. The club sent copies to me. It was a two-page doc with your signature in agreement on the second page."

"Not this shit again," I groan. "We've already beat that horse to death, Finn. I fucked up. I signed on the dotted line, and now I'm paying the goddamn consequences for it."

"That's exactly right. You signed on the dotted line. But how many dotted lines were there? You've always called them papers— *plural*—and I just assumed you meant the two papers I received . . . but it just hit me . . . the way Scout said *'the papers'* like they were the be-all and end-all. Do you remember how many times you signed your name?"

My head is spinning—from the Jameson and from what he just asked. I think back and all I remember is pain, blacking out from it, and then coming to in the locker room with papers in front of me, a pen shoved in my hand, and blank spots in my vision. "Fuck, Finn . . ."

"It's important, Easton."

The words on the pages blurred. My need for the OxyContin to dull the pain surpassed the need to understand them.

"Two . . . maybe three . . . but two for sure."

"Goddamnit!" He smacks his hands together and the sound echoes around the room. "Tillman's stink is all over this. He pulled something over on you. I know it. I'll bet your ass Scout saw it."

"And you weren't there." The words are accusatory although he's already explained why. I'm so sick of excuses when my world's been turned upside down by first a dirty play and now what looks like a dirty deal.

"I'll make this right," he says, but I stare at him, knowing he can't. "If you won't talk to Scout, I will."

"Do whatever you want. It's not going to change a thing," I mumble.

"But I'll have ammunition when I go in there tomorrow instead of an empty barrel." He pulls out his phone. "What's her address?"

"Can you just go?"

"Yeah. Sure. I'm on the right track. I can feel it. I'll talk to her, East, and get to the bottom of this." His smile fades like I should be as excited as he is that he figured this out. *But I'm not.*

I'm fucking devastated.

Tears burn the backs of my eyes, and I shove that shit away as fast as I can because it's not worth crying over.

Women come and go.

Teams are teams. I can still play ball anywhere.

But it's not just some woman. It's *Scout.* The one who gets me.

And it's not just a team. It's the Aces. The one whose blood I've bled since before I was born.

What the fuck is happening?

CHAPTER FIVE

Scout

I'm sorry, Scout. He's not accepting any visitors at this time.

It's the same response I got when I rushed over here after leaving the meeting and the same one I've continued to get each and every time I've attempted to gain access to the building.

The look on Easton's face continues to haunt my certainty as I stand across the street and watch Alec, the doorman of Easton's building, man his post. The same man, who just this morning joked with me as I left for the stadium, is now turning people away left and right. Reporters. Teammates. *Me.*

I glance at my cell again just in case Easton has texted me back. I know he hasn't because it's been gripped in my hand, but I look anyway.

It has rung numerous times though. Calls from Finn wanting answers. Calls from reporters trying to get to Easton. A call from Tino asking me what the hell happened. Calls from everybody I don't want and not the one person I do.

So I've resorted to this—sitting in the dark across the street from his building with a nauseated stomach, salt from my tears dried on my cheeks, and hope waning—while I wait for Alec's shift to end and Simon's to begin.

Each second feels like an hour. Every thought is only exacerbated in doubt and dragged through the mud of my feelings as I wait to see Easton. Explain to him. Beg him to forgive me. Because the longer I sit here, the more I question everything: if I saw what I think I saw, if I made the right decision, how I couldn't have realized earlier that I love him.

Because, yes, *I love him.*

His megawatt smile and loudly sweet gestures. The way he has to have coffee in the morning before he's even remotely tolerable and how he hates for his food to touch on his plate. The way he loves his mom and respects his dad despite everything they've put him through. The way he seems to know exactly what I need, when I need it, even when I don't know myself. Our dance in the country bar. Our venture to play with rescue dogs. A picnic on a baseball field.

And of course, with my realization is the choking panic that hits. And not because I'm afraid he'll leave me, but because I just made sure of it . . . when I didn't even know it.

Nothing like a little dose of reality to make things clear.

Desperate for a connection with Easton, I check my phone again. Nothing. But when I look back up, Alec is giving Simon a quick recap at the door before walking down the sidewalk opposite of me, hopping in his car, and driving away.

It's now or never, Scout.

Clear mind.

Open heart.

It's the only way I can fix this.

I step out onto the sidewalk and run smack dab into the sushi delivery guy I've come to know quite well from staying at Easton's. "Riku!"

"Ms. Scout," he says in broken English as he tries to rebalance his delivery load I knocked off kilter.

"I'm so sorry. I didn't mean to—I'm just—are you okay?" I stumble over words while trying to help him steady his packages.

"Yes. So sorry. I wasn't watching. Such a busy night. So many deliveries," he explains.

"It looks like it." I smile tightly, wanting to be cordial but really needing to get to Easton. My brain is so frazzled but . . . "Is this Mr. Wylder's? I'm heading up there right now and can deliver it for you."

"Yes," he says with an eager nod but then his smile fades. "But my father be very mad if I don't make sure—"

"We won't tell him," I say as I pull a twenty out of my wallet and stuff it into his pocket. "There's your tip, just tell me which bag is his."

"You sure you don't mind bring it to him?" He warms up to the idea, and I'm sure the twenty-dollar tip doesn't hurt either.

"Of course not. I was just heading up there anyway so why not help you out."

He eyes me again, the fear of getting in trouble from his father warring against getting his other orders delivered quicker meaning bigger tips. I can see the minute the latter wins. "Thank you so much." He hands me a bag full of stacked Styrofoam containers.

"My pleasure."

With a huge sigh I watch Riku hurry down the sidewalk before jogging across the street to approach Simon.

"Hey, Simon, sushi delivery for Easton." I hold the bag up with the familiar restaurant's name on it.

Reporters call my name as he looks at me wearily, making me wonder if Alec told him not to allow any visitors to Easton's as he should have. "I need to call him and check first," he says, bringing his phone to his ear.

My smile remains while I slowly die inside knowing this isn't going to work.

"Mr. Wylder, this is Simon at the front . . . Sorry to bug you, sir, but I just wanted to make sure you ordered some sushi for delivery . . . okay." Simon eyes a few people across the street with cameras and nods his head. "Yes. I'll make sure . . . You're welcome."

I swallow down the nerves slowly closing up my throat as I wait for him to hang up and tell me to leave the food with him instead of delivering it myself.

"He got screwed," Simon says with a shake of his head as he pushes open the door and lets me enter the building.

"He sure did," I murmur as I rush past him.

If I thought I was nervous before—thinking and overthinking what I would say, how I would say it, what not to forget to say—I'm a wreck now as the elevator slowly ascends floor by floor to Easton's place.

The elevator dings.

The doors open.

The condo is bathed in darkness except for the front light much like it was the first time Easton brought me here. The memories of that night—our first time together—flash through my mind, but this time the butterflies are over so much more than the possibility of first-time sex.

This time they're over possibly losing him.

"Thanks, Riku. Just put it on the table. Your tip's there." His voice is a deep rumble from the darkness, and the grief mixed with alcohol slurring it breaks my heart.

I freeze. Plans and rehearsed speeches go out the window because now I have to face him, and I don't know what to do.

"Riku? Is everyth—" Easton says seconds before he steps into the foyer, the words dying on his lips when he sees me.

He looks like hell. And gorgeous. All at the same time. His hair is a mess, his face is etched in stress, his jaw a shadow of stubble, his chest bare, and he's still in his baseball pants but they're unbuttoned at the waist. But it's his eyes that devastate me. Yes, they're glossed over from drinking, but it's the flash of hurt I catch before it's cleared and replaced with anger.

Unsettled and uncertain what to say, I hold up the bag of food for him to see. He glances to it and then back to me for a brief second before turning on his heel and walking back into the darkness. "I'm not hungry."

"Easton." His name is a desperate plea.

"If I wanted to talk to you, I would have called you back. But I didn't, and I still don't. You know where the door is."

My stomach drops to my feet as he disappears from my sight. Momentarily stunned, I don't move as that ridiculous fantasy I may have been making up in my head—the one where he'd need me so much he'd pull me into him and all would be okay—incinerates with the ice in his tone.

I scramble after him, desperation in my voice and fear of screwing this up in my heart. "They were going to get rid of you."

"Well, you made sure of that. Save your dignity, Scout, and just go. There's nothing left to say . . . your actions, *your lies*, said it all."

"No. *Please*. Listen."

"To what?" He turns around to face me, but he's a silhouette of dark against the night sky with the wall of windows at his back. "You want me to listen to how you fucked me over? My career? My family? How you made for damn fucking sure that you didn't have to be afraid of me leaving so you did it for me? After everything we've worked for? *Really*? Were you so fucking spooked you had me traded?" The anger in his voice has nothing on the distress tingeing its tone. His words cut deep and are devastating.

He thinks I was spooked?

"You really think that? That I'm so selfish, *so spineless*, that I'd purposely get you traded for my own benefit?"

"Nothing surprises me today. Not in the fucking least. Well, except for the '*you've been traded part*' . . . now, that sure as shit shocked the hell out of me."

"Easton, it's not like—"

"Did you lie?" There's grit in his voice as if it pains him to confirm what he already knows. I open my mouth and then close it, the admission so very hard to make now that I'm standing before the person facing the consequences of my actions.

When he steps forward, his face partially in the light, shadows still dominating the rest, and meets my eyes across the space, the words on my lips die an undignified death. "Just tell me one thing, Scout. Did you know you were going to lie when you kissed me goodbye? Was it all planned? Were you hoping the trade would be one of those sudden 'grab your bags, your flight's about to leave to take you to your new team' so you wouldn't have to see me again and face what you did? Take a good look, sweetheart, because this is what it looks like." He takes another step forward so his face is bathed in the light. "This is what getting fucked over by someone you trusted looks like. It ain't pretty, is it? So thanks for your concern, but I know it's only so you can ease your guilt. Don't think I'm going to help you with that because I'm the one left living with what you did."

"I know, and that's why I've been trying to get hold of you so I could explain," I yell as I step forward, but the glare he shoots me warns me to stay where I am. "Finn wasn't there and then—"

"I've never asked someone to move in with me." His voice is soft and pained and the sudden change in it from his shouting seconds before sucks all the air out of the room.

"That's not why I—"

"Then spit it out."

"The papers—"

"I knew you were going to run or push me away and—"

"That's not—"

"And you made damn sure it was push me away so you'd get the goddamn contract."

"No! Just listen to—"

"Get out!"

"*No.*"

"We're done."

"I'm in love with you!"

32

"*No*," he shouts, hand slamming down on the table beside him to match the thunder in his temper. I jump from the sound as it echoes through the room, but it has nothing on the slamming of my heart against my rib cage. "You don't get to say that to try to make this right. Don't you get that your words mean shit to me right now? You told me I was one hundred percent and then you told them I wasn't. You think I'm going to believe you when you say those three words to me? Pretty goddamn convenient, Scout. You can't even handle me asking you to move in, and yet you tell me you love me to try and make things right? Are you out of your—?"

I snap.

"You signed the goddamn papers," I scream at the top of my lungs, finally able to get a word in edgewise. He's cut deep with his words, purposely hurt me, and it's my damn turn to lash out. I've berated myself all damn day over what I did, but in the end this isn't all on me. "You did this. *Not me.* It was either shipping you off to a Triple-A team in Maine or across town to the Wranglers, so I did what I had to do."

The room falls silent as dust particles dance in the sliver of light from the foyer, and I know for the first time since I've stepped foot in here that he hears me. The stumble of his feet backward. The shocked open of his lips. The narrowing of his brows. "What did you just say?" Drunk meets sober. "What the fuck are you talking about?"

"The papers," I say in a hiccupping sob as the emotions catch up with me. Sensing a chance for redemption at my fingertips, I step toward him. "They fell off the desk. It was a mess. The coffee spilled and papers were knocked to the floor and when I tried to help gather them, your signature was on them and I didn't know what to do and—"

"So you decided to take it upon yourself and—"

"One paper was an agreement that if you weren't one hundred percent they could trade you," I stumble. There's too much to explain, too many words to get out at one time, and the pressure of making this right has my head all jumbled.

"I'm well aware of what it said and the trade part." He shrugs with a condescending chuckle. "You sure as shit made sure that happened, didn't you?"

"But the other one . . . why in the hell would you ever agree to it?"

"What other one? Agree to what?" He steps forward, anger and accusation on his face.

"You gave them consent to send you down to Triple-A."

"What the hell are you talking about?" He's on me in a flash—smelling of whiskey and rage—with hands on my biceps, giving me a little shake before realizing what he's doing and jolting back as if he's been burned.

"It said something about you giving the Aces consent to send you down to Triple-A for the period of a year with a cut in salary, upon return from the disabled list, and—"

"That's bullshit," he yells.

"I saw it with my own eyes. You signed it. On the bottom left-hand side."

Easton starts to speak and then stops, his eyes bore into mine, but there's a look that slowly comes over his face. It's one I don't think I'll ever forget, and I don't understand, but it's there and it's *real*. In the intensity of the moment the thought crashes through my mind that an expression like that should never be on that handsome face of his.

And before I can place what it means, it's gone. Wiped clear and replaced with the hardened game face I knew from watching Easton play on TV before I met him. I scramble to explain further.

"There were these papers. The ones you signed. And then ones from Cory's folders. Notes. Scribbles. They were everywhere, and I was trying to stack them and . . . there were formal trade options. Orders for you to be sent to Triple-A. There was correspondence with Dallas over trading you. There was an email to the manager of

The Portland Surge telling them to demote Gonzo to Double-A because you were going to play for them. I only had seconds, Easton. Seconds. To read and decipher and figure out what—"

"Scout." Serious. Worried. Confused.

Petrified of his sudden silence, I add, "It was trade you or demote you and I chose to trade you."

"You chose?" His voice a mixture of fury and disbelief as he steps back from where I stand. He walks back and forth bracing his hands against the back of his neck as his temper physically manifests in his posture. Frozen in place, I watch as he picks up the bottle on the coffee table and throws it as hard as he can. The sound of it hitting the wall is deafening—a glass bottle against a glass wall—followed by the sounds of the shards hitting the floor. It's jarring and takes me a minute to recover from the sudden outburst.

"East—"

"This is my goddamn life," he thunders. Rage vibrates in his voice. "Who gave you the reins to decide for me? I sure as hell didn't? Do you have any idea what you've done?"

The doubt I'd carried around with me all day slowly slips into dread and fills every ounce of my being. When I answer him, it's the first time I sound unsure, and I hate myself for it. "But it was *Dallas*. Your mom is halfway between here and there and—"

"It's *my* goddamn mom. It's *my* fucking choice. Who do you think you are choosing what's best for me? That's a lot of decisions for someone who couldn't even handle me telling them I was falling for them, don'tcha think?"

"It was a split-second. Maine or Dallas." *Please see my side of this.*

"Total bullshit." He throws his hands my way as if he's done with me and while I know I made the choice for him, this *is* on him.

"Why did you sign the papers? Why would Finn ever let you agree to that? Why wasn't he there today?" My voice is the steadiest it has been since I walked in here. I take a step toward him, needing to know the answer since that signature is why I felt it necessary to make a decision in the first place.

"Fuck this," he sneers. "Don't turn this on me. You couldn't handle any of this, could you?"

"No. Yes. I mean, I did what I thought was best—"

"Best? Best? Are you fucking kidding me?"

I can't even comprehend what is happening right now. I mean I can, but I thought once I explained to him . . . I thought he would be . . . not thankful, but at least understanding. It was a choice between the humiliation of being demoted and sent across the country or being traded to a team within a two-hour driving distance of his mom.

My head is spinning. The fight not making sense and at the same time making perfect sense. I try again. "But it's Dallas."

"It's nowhere, Scout, because the trade hasn't even gone through yet."

My heart falls into my stomach at his words. "What do you mean? I don't—"

"You're the first person to even utter the city Dallas . . . so that means my trade is still in talks and hasn't been completed. You may have seen papers, Scout, but there were most likely more. Others covered in notes from talking with teams like the Orioles or Tampa or the Mariners."

Oh my God. What did I do? Panic, disbelief, shock. All three become an eddy of emotion tearing through my system and wreaking more havoc than I ever thought possible.

"Your face says it all. So yeah, thanks for nothing. You win, Scout. I'm gone."

"I didn't win shit, Easton," I yell, grasping for straws as the eddy of emotion turns into a tornado and slams into me. "Do you think this did me any favors? Do you think I got the contract? I don't even know yet. I have to go back in the morning to find out—"

"You and your precious goddamn contract. It's always been about the contract, hasn't it? Not me? Only you." Disgust is what I hear in the bite in his voice.

"No. No." I take a step back to try and calm the situation. His temper. My sobbing. His accusations. My denials. "Please. Just listen to me. The only reason I remotely care about the contract is because of my dad."

"Convenient." He snorts as he turns his back on me and stumbles to the windows leaving me fumbling.

"Don't you see *I'm* the one who could lose everything?"

"*Poor baby.* Forgive me if I'm not feeling much sympathy for you and—"

"No, that's not what I meant by—"

I cut my own words when I can't hold back my sob anymore. It's pointless. This conversation and trying to reason with him while he's drunk. Fighting to explain my actions, my decisions, myself, when he's right. It wasn't my place to make a decision about his life for him regardless of the circumstances or my selfless intentions behind them.

I stare at him—the broad shoulders and proud stance—and think about the first time I saw him like this and what that led to. My heart aches for him. For the road he's traveled, for how hard he fought to get back again, only to be blindsided by Cory.

Much like how he fought for me. Why is it that now when I can admit to myself I'm in love with him, I'm going to lose him? Literally and figuratively.

"Easton . . ."

I made a mistake.

I should have stalled for time.

I should have . . .

I love you.

"Maybe you shouldn't have lied." The derision in his tone only serves to reinforce what I already know.

"You're not listening to me. If you'd actually hear me you'd see that . . ."

"Believe me, I am hearing you, more now than ever. It's your actions not your words that speak fucking volumes."

"I did what I thought was—"

"*Stop*. Stop saying that. It means nothing to me." He strides to the kitchen. Glass rattles before he pulls out another bottle of whiskey from the liquor cabinet, and takes a long swig from it while I silently beg for him to stop. I've never seen him like this—helpless, hopeless, careless—and knowing I contributed to this is killing me. When he finishes his drink, he slams the bottle down for emphasis. "What you did was put yourself in a prime position with that fucker Tillman. I'd be out of the picture—no stress, no distractions, no sleeping with the player to screw up the contract hanging over your head, and no worry for you about a guy who's going to leave you. Thanks for making sure this went nowhere. And thanks for thinking you know what I want out of my career and making a decision you're not qualified to make. Thanks for nothing, Scout. Go to your meeting tomorrow. Take whatever the Aces give you. Be happy with the result. You screwed me to serve your dad. And while I get it, I don't." He flops down into a chair facing the view beyond with his back to me. "We're done, but then again, I guess we never were *started* according to you . . . so, uh . . . see you around, Scout. Or not. You know where the door is."

He makes a show of lifting the bottle in the air and then bringing it to his lips. When he finishes his drink, he slouches down farther into the chair and continues to stare into the darkness.

He doesn't say another word.

There's nothing else left to say.

CHAPTER SIX

Easton

I should pick them up.

The little green shards of glass all over the floor. Reminders of Scout. Of the explanations she gave. The words I hurled. Of everything that is broken.

I should pick them up.

But I don't.

I stay where I've been seated all night. And now I guess morning. Head pounding. Gut turning. Eyes staring.

At the empty stadium. The one I couldn't stand to see lit up last night is vacant now. A mausoleum of memories of my career. I reach down to the new bottle of whiskey, but just run my fingertips around its rim, knowing I don't need any more.

But I take a sip anyway. Tip the bottle to my lips to drown out her voice in my head.

Formal trade options. Correspondence with Dallas over trading you.

To block out the look on her face and the hope that slowly faded from her voice with each and every accusation I threw at her.

Orders for you to be sent down. There was an email to the manager . . . you were going down to play for them.

I can blame her all I want, but I did this. I knew some day it would happen. That my secret would ruin something I loved.

But not like this.

Not with these kinds of consequences.

I only had seconds, Easton. Seconds.

The sky is grey. Moody and gloomy and miserable.

I'm in love with you.

Another drink. Then another.

There's too much noise. In my mind. In my heart.

Why did you sign the papers? Why would Finn ever let you agree to that? Why wasn't he there today?

There's no sun to light up the sky like normal. The pinks and oranges that filled it yesterday as we made slow, sweet love are gone.

I scrub a hand over my face. Try to wipe the memory away because it hurts like a bitch. The soft sighs. The throaty moans. The smell of her skin. The feel of her lips.

I'm in love with you.

"Fucking hell, Wylder," I say to no one, knowing I should be thinking about the game. About where I'm headed. About what it's going to feel like cleaning out my locker. About what I'm going to say to my mom when I drive out there to see her later today and prepare her for my departure.

But I'm sitting here thinking about *Scout*. About the position I put her in. About the decision she made. About how I blamed her because it was so much easier than telling her the truth.

The bottle feels heavy in my hand. It's so tempting but I opt to drink it rather than throw it like I did the other.

The fight in me is gone.

It left when Scout walked out.

When I pushed her out.

When I forced her to take the blame.

I'm in love with you.

Did she mean it?

What does it even matter now?

She still betrayed me. She didn't fight for me.

So why should I fight for her?

Get up, Easton. Take a shower. Clean yourself up. Start packing.

Stop hurting.

My cell rings again. It's the third time in an hour.

I give in. Relent. Give up.

"Finn."

"I just got the paperwork. What she told you last night was right. It's Dallas. The reporters are rabid for an explanation, so Tillman's holding a press conference at eight thirty to announce the trade. I'll be there, and then I'm going to hound the fuck out of him in our meeting and demand to see all the documentation. I want to see what that slimebag had you sign and . . ."

He keeps rambling but all I hear is Dallas. I should feel relief. I should be able to breathe a bit easier knowing the where. *She was right.* It's close enough that I can still take care of my mom. It's close enough that I can come home. It's the next-best scenario to being in Austin . . . and yet I won't be an Ace anymore.

The one certainty in my life is no longer there.

". . . and I'm going to let him know when Boseman returns, I'll have him looking into the shady shit he pulled. I want Tillman's balls nailed to a wall for—"

"Cancel the meeting, Finn."

"What?"

"There's no need to fight it. When and where do I need to report to the Wranglers?"

"I don't understand. What's going on?"

The same thing I've done my whole life. Dodge. Avoid. Distract.

"I'm done. It's over. Accept the terms. Book me a flight. Or I'll drive there. What-the-fuck-ever. Just tell me when I need to report, and I'll be there."

"But Cory needs to be—"

"No meeting, Finn," I say firmly as my fingers tighten on the neck of the bottle and my fingers on my other hand end the call.

The sky's still grey.

I have a feeling it's going to be that way for a while.

But this is on me.

Not Cory.

Not Finn.

Not Scout.

All me.

The guilt's worse than the fear.

But there's no need to argue anymore.

I can handle this.

I brought it on myself, after all.

CHAPTER SEVEN

Scout

It took everything I had not to stop by Easton's on the way into the ballpark. To go there and hope he would be somewhat sober and tell him he's an asshole for saying what he said to me, *and* admit I'm a jerk for assuming to know what he'd want in the decision I made. We could scream and fight and get it all out and then I could sit there with him while he waited to hear about his trade. I'd help him bide his time to try and get us back on an even keel, and then when the word came through, reassure him it was going to be all right.

But I didn't stop.

Because hung over might be just as bad as drunk. And because he made it clear I'm the last person he wants to see.

I'll let him have that.

I'll give him some time.

But if he thinks I'm going to let him be done with me that easily, he's crazy.

He fought for me. To gain my trust. To make me want *more* with him. To make me see not everyone leaves. To ensure I fell in love with him.

And now it's my turn to earn that back from him.

I'm just not quite sure how to do that when we might be living in two different cities.

Easton's worth it. I need to figure out how to make it work, but every single ounce of effort is what I'll give.

God, yes, I was hurt last night and still am by some of the things he said. But after replaying our fight in my head over and over while I stared at the ceiling in a bed less familiar to me than Easton's, I realized there was a missing piece to the puzzle. It was the look on his face that kept flashing in my mind. He's not telling me something and I can't figure out what that something is.

I'm petrified I won't be able to fix this. Fix us. My stomach is in knots over where to start.

Then there's my dad and his damn contract. He's the reason I'm sitting in this waiting room obligated to meet the man responsible for this turmoil and one who I don't trust in the least.

A daughter's duty versus a woman's wants.

"It's going to be a few more minutes yet, Ms. Dalton," the receptionist says motioning to the closed conference room door with the Aces logo on it.

"Thank you. I'm going to use the restroom then."

The bathroom mirror only serves to reflect what a shitty night of sleep I had and how poorly I did covering it up with makeup. And the sad fact is I hate myself for being here. For picking the contract over trying to make things right.

Family first.

And while I'm choosing the contract now, opting to do something for my dad, I make a promise to myself to take care of me next.

With a deep breath and a resolve I barely feel, I head out of the bathroom and come face to face with Cal. We both freeze.

"I hope you were successful at whatever it was you were trying to accomplish, Ms. Dalton, considering you did it at the expense of my son's future." Disdain drips from his voice. "Your little lie had some serious consequences."

"It cost me more than you can imagine," I say softly, voice breaking, as I try to keep my composure.

"Really?" he sneers as he steps into me. "You don't have a clue what this cost Easton. You tell me to protect him, praise him, and then you screw him over? It's my son whose life has been turned around. He took less money for years to stay right here and have a life instead of the constant moving around most players do. To be loyal . . . But then again, it seems you know nothing about loyalty, do you? Your true colors burned bright, Dalton."

"There's more to the story than—"

"Ms. Dalton, Cory will see you now," the receptionist interrupts from the doorway, and I wonder how much she heard.

"Thank you," I murmur with a tight smile.

"*Asshole*," Cal mutters under his breath. I snap my head his way, hoping for one more second to explain what I can to him, but he's already walking the other way.

The only thing he's left unspoken is whether he was referring to Cory or me.

". . . and that is why I still believe Dalton's Physical Therapy would benefit the Aces organization successfully with a team contract," I say, completing my spiel with conviction all the while looking at the man across the table from me and wondering how I got myself into this position. Why I'm fighting for a contract with a team where I can't trust—or stand, for that matter—the man who would be my boss.

"And yet you couldn't get Easton Wylder rehabbed and back on the active roster in the time frame allotted," he rebuts.

"Correct." Every part of my body revolts at the lie. "As I expressed when I was brought on, I disagreed with giving him a time frame. Every body recovers differently from injuries."

"But I believe your other words were, 'I can have him ready by mid-August.'"

Asshole. "Yes, that is correct."

"Hmm," he murmurs as he sits back in his chair and levels me with an unrelenting stare as if he's trying to intimidate me. I meet his stare and don't back down. "And what should I do about the matter that you breached the parameters of your contract?"

"In concern to?"

"Having a relationship with the player you were charged to rehab."

Is that what this is all about? Did Cory want to call me in here just to pull his chest-thumping bullshit and remind me he's in control? Use this as his leverage and to justify why he traded Easton?

But even then, it doesn't explain why Easton's signature was on those damn agreements. *Or why Finn let him.*

"If I recall correctly, Ms. Dalton, I'm referring to your violation of section D, part five of your contract."

Every part of me clings to my attempt at civility when all I want to do is tell him where he can shove said contract.

"Well, seeing as how my personal life is none of your business—"

"It is my business when you're contracted with the team."

"Noted," I say with as much courtesy as possible as I attempt to regain some of my footing. "But seeing as how being in a 'relationship' with Mr. Wylder didn't influence my opinions regarding his recovery, then our 'relationship' shouldn't be taken into consideration. You'd think I'd give him preferential treatment. That I would be swayed to deem him one hundred percent, so he could return to the active roster. And somehow or other, because I didn't show such favoritism, he's been traded, which leads me to feel partially responsible for the situation." It's my turn to stare at him with eyebrows arched in an exclamation point to my comment.

"Mr. Wylder's trade has nothing to do with you. There were agreements in place before you came on board."

"Agreements? Like heal in a set time frame or be traded? I've worked in a lot of clubhouses, but I've never seen those stipulations made on a player's rehabilitation." I'm pushing the envelope, I know I am, and yet I can't help it. All I can think of is the devastation on Easton's face last night.

"It's a standard practice I implement for the teams I work with."

"Standard practice? Trimming costs is one thing, but making a body heal on a clock . . . I can't imagine why an owner would allow that policy."

He sighs as if he's bored with this conversation already. "There were terms agreed upon by Mr. Wylder. Just like the terms you agreed to and broke in your contract."

"I did." I draw the words out intentionally, not oblivious to his sudden change of subject.

"My concern, Ms. Dalton, is how do I know that if I were to give you the team contract, this *situation* wouldn't happen again?"

"Tell me something, Mr. Tillman," I say shifting in my seat and leaning forward with hands clasped on the table in front of me. "Is this *no relationship clause* a standard part of your contract or was it only amended for me? If that's the case, I'd hate to *one*, think of the organization as being sexist, and *two*, that they'd be narrow-minded enough to not think men can't have relationships with other men too."

He furrows his brow, and for a split second I fear I've gone too far. Maybe he's one of those men who can't handle being challenged by a female. In my line of work, I learned early on that assertive women often scare men.

He chews the inside of his cheek for a moment, and I swear I see a hint of amusement in his eyes despite the silence suffocating the room. "Dually noted . . . but that still doesn't give me an answer."

"To which question?"

"How do I know it won't happen again?"

It's a loaded question, and one I know I need to heed carefully. "Considering you're in the midst of trading my *boyfriend*, then it's a moot point. I'll be here, and he'll be wherever you send him so . . ."

"I can see why the guys on the team like you," he muses, leaving me to wonder momentarily if that's a compliment or a slight. He stands from the table and walks to the window of the conference room to look to the empty ballpark beyond. When he doesn't finish his thought right away I opt to remain silent and wait him out.

"I came in here today with half a mind to let you go. There are rules. You broke them. There were terms of your contract, and I'm a stickler for following contracts to the letter. More importantly, you did not satisfy our agreement. But between your company's reputation and your ability to handle whatever is thrown at you, you've given me pause in doing that." He turns to look my way, and I meet him head-on.

"You're over halfway through the season, Mr. Tillman. Your current physical therapist's last day is next week and most other therapists qualified to handle a club and its rigorous expectations are already employed."

He shakes his head and chuckles at my sales pitch. "Very true, so that's why I'd like to give you till the end of the season to show me what you've got. A probationary period, if you will. You can use the staff we have already or bring in your own, but you've got the next fifty, hopefully seventy-ish days if we make the playoffs, to prove you can handle the needs of this team."

I swallow over the nerves that suddenly hit me and allow relief to flood my system. I may *not* have let my dad down yet.

I hope he can hang on long enough to see it. Seventy-ish days when you're grateful for the next minute, the next breath, can seem like forever.

"I'll get the contract drawn up now."

CHAPTER EIGHT

Easton

"**E**aston, how does it feel to be changing teams for the first time in your career?"

Cameras flash and add to the percussion pounding in my head as reporters surround me.

"How's your shoulder? Are you ready to play for Dallas?"

A camera hits against my shoulder. Questions are shouted. Hands on my back trying to steer me. Microphones shoved in my face.

"Easton, at the press conference this morning, Cory Tillman stated you are parting with the team on good terms. We'd love to hear your opinion about that statement."

I glance up and am blinded by another flurry of flashes as I try to push my way through the throng of reporters. All questions I don't want to answer. Another dash of salt in my open wound.

"Easton, do you have anything to say to the fans of Austin who have followed you since you started?"

That question stops me and is something I can't ignore. I pause, my eyes down, hidden beneath the brim of my cap while I figure out what to say.

There's a slap on my back that I shrug away from. "Need some help?"

I look over to my dad, surprised as hell to see him here. Relief fills me as the sound of the cameras clicking assaults my ears, everyone desperate to capture the photo opportunity. Father and son. The end of a legacy. No more Wylders on the roster.

"Go 'head," he encourages with another squeeze of my shoulder and nod of his head.

I clear my throat and address the reporters. "Austin will always be my home regardless of where I play. The people, the city, and the atmosphere is in my blood, and I've been one of the fortunate few to have had the chance to stay as long as I have with one team. I'll miss my teammates. I'll miss the incredible fans here. But more than anything, I'll miss being an Ace. I wore the jersey as a little boy wanting to be just like my father . . ." My words fade as I look to my left and notice Santiago standing nearby, hands shoved in his pockets, and shoulder leaning against a wall, watching me. Our eyes meet for the briefest of moments and I hate that he's here, listening to what feels like an intimate moment with the city I swore I'd never leave.

"East . . ." my dad prompts, forcing me to turn my attention to the slew of reporters around me, waiting for me to finish.

". . . and I was one of the fortunate ones who got to grow up and be exactly what I wanted to be. So yes, I'll miss Austin. The fans. The team. Even you nosy reporters snapping my every move." I earn the laugh I was working for and nod my head. This time when I try to walk away, they let me while my dad remains and answers questions.

Glancing back, I watch him in his element—with the attention on him, answering how he feels, knowing I've been traded by the team he's been loyal to his whole life. I can't help but wonder if his sudden appearance was a sincere show of support *for me* as my father or as an Aces representative wanting to ensure I gave the proper company line.

Fucking doubt.

It's like a cancer you can't erase until it grows and grows and eats at every part of you. I glance over to where Santiago stood and then back to my father, still chatting amiably with the reporters, before heading into the clubhouse, *one last time.*

"So Dallas, huh?"

I should have known he'd be here. Just like he's always been throughout my life. There is no Manny-man or Easy-E exchange like we've done over the years. This time it's different, and I know he feels the same.

"Can you believe that shit?" I murmur to try and lighten the mood. I shake my head but my eyes don't leave my nameplate adorning my locker. That would be his doing. Leaving it there for me instead of removing it the minute the trade has been made like is typical protocol. "I've lived my whole life thinking the designated hitter is cheating and now I'm headed for a team who plays with one."

"Traitor."

"Let's save that term for Tillman."

"Agreed." His chuckle makes me smile even though I'm at odds with everything about being here. "You okay?"

I sigh and shake my head as I look at the scratched hash marks in the rear corner of my locker. The tally I kept my rookie year of how many homeruns I'd hit, and even despite a clubhouse renovation, he kept those there for me.

When I don't answer, he goes in for the laugh, in pure Manny style. "I mean we both know you look like shit and smell like eau de whiskey, but"—he places a hand on my shoulder and squeezes—"*you okay?*"

"What can I do, Man? Isn't this part of the game?" I turn to look at him for a second, meet his eyes from beneath the lowered bill of my cap, before looking back at my boxful of shit I've kept over the years. Good-luck charms and tokens from fans who'd touched me. A St. Christopher's medal given to me by Dex, the little boy from Make-A-Wish who spent an incredible day with me, and then whose funeral I attended three months later. The tattered note my mom gave me the first time I ever dressed in an Aces' uniform to take the field.

So many memories. So much history.

"For most it's part of the game, yes, but not for you. This team is all you've known."

I want to tell him thanks for stating the obvious but don't even have the effort to muster the sarcasm. Besides, he doesn't deserve my shitty mood being taken out on him. He's on my side.

"It doesn't make any sense, Manny. None of it does. So I'm just trying my best to wrap my head around it and the fact that tomorrow I might be in a Wrangler's uniform."

"Might be?"

"Yeah. Finn organized for me to be evaluated by their lead PT. I'll do the song and dance and if I get approved, I'll get to play."

"You'll get approved," he says with absolute certainty.

"*I will?* You never know, every PT has his own opinion," I say perpetuating Scout's lie.

"How far is it from Dallas to Temple?" he asks, knowing that my outrage lies with more than just changing teams. He knows about my mom.

I stare at him for a beat before letting it go. "Driving? It's a little under two hours." I nod, thinking of how this complicates matters. "It's a straight shot down I-35 but two hours is two hours, you know?"

"Yeah . . . but it's better than across the country," he muses as he takes a seat beside me, facing the opposite way. He doesn't say anything else when I know he wants to. And as the silence settles, he makes his point with minimal words like usual.

It could be a lot worse. That's what he's implying. And while he may be right, everything about this situation still stings like a son-of-a-bitch.

"True," I finally say but don't quite feel.

"You'll do great there. Fuentes is something else. He'll be a fun pitcher for you to catch. And a challenge. His curveball is wicked. Then there's McAvoy. He's got some high heat—"

"I appreciate it, Manny. You trying to make me feel better so I say this with no disrespect . . . don't waste your breath."

"I figured as much," he says with a soft nod. "Does it make you feel any better if I say you were shafted?"

My laugh this time is real, and it sets off the pounding in my head. "That's the least of what I got. What are the guys saying?" I ask, curious how Tillman's playing this.

"They're pissed. Confused. Rumor is Scout threw you under the bus. Saved herself somehow by screwing you."

"Are you asking me?"

"Only if you think I am." And there he goes again with his leading statements. I knew he'd get back to his point sooner or later.

The locker room falls silent. I rub the St. Christopher's medal between my fingers while he gives me the time I need to figure out what to say. I could throw her to the wolves. Distract. Diverge. Stop people from asking the questions I don't want asked. Make her the villain to blame. And yet, even I'm not that much of an asshole.

"She didn't do me any favors, that's for sure," I finally say.

He whistles softly. "Screwed by your girl and your team. That's rough. Sorry, son."

"Yeah, well, I guess one clean break is better than a few little ones." But hell if those breaks aren't hitting me where it hurts.

"Just remember not everything is what it seems to be," he says, standing to his feet.

"What's that supposed to mean?" I ask, looking up to meet his eyes.

"It means she was fighting for you. And then, if rumors are true, she wasn't."

"How the hell do you know that? What are you talking about? Were you there?"

"Only when there was complete chaos. Coffee spilled on everything. Papers everywhere. Tillman's clothes were splattered with it. People scrambling, trying to save the documents and clean up the mess."

"What does this have to do with anything, Manny?" I ask as he heads to his office and holds up one finger before disappearing for a few seconds and then returning with something in his hand.

"I helped clean up the coffee," he says as he stops a few feet from me. "I was there when Tillman's assistant tore out of the conference room needing paper towels and so me being me, I helped. I didn't even realize Scout was in there until I walked out and heard her voice. I assume she was under the desk picking up the papers that were all over the floor . . . but I didn't think much about it. I mean, I knew what the meeting was about, and yet I didn't worry because it was you. *And it was her.* I was more concerned with getting back downstairs to wish you luck and to let you know I'd be in the stands. But then the call came through and you stormed out of here. When I found out what had happened, I was beside myself, East."

"You and me both."

"It's total bullshit. I was so flustered by it all, it took me the better part of the game to remember where I put my keys. After searching everywhere, I found them on the credenza in the copy room. Just as I was about to leave, I noticed a sheet of paper on the floor sticking out from beneath it. I thought nothing of it other than to put it back on the table for whoever dropped it . . . but when I picked it up, it was this. It's so very different than the rumors, so I didn't want to leave it and get her in trouble."

"What the hell is it, Manny?" All this build-up and he's still holding on to it.

"You've got a hot-headed temper sometimes. I can only imagine how long you stood in that batting cage last night, breaking bats and smashing balls, to try and calm it some." I chuckle and open my palms face-up so he can see how right he is. The blisters are cracked and swollen. "I know you better than you think, Wylder."

"True." And it makes me sad how well he does, and how much I'll miss seeing his ugly mug every day. "But what's on the paper?"

"Maybe you shouldn't be so tough on her, huh?"

"How do you know I was tough on her?"

It's his turn to chuckle then raise his eyebrows at me. His expression saying, *I know you better than you think.* I roll my eyes as he glances toward the closed door of the locker room before holding up the paper and clearing his throat. "Thank you, gentlemen, for your time. I'd like to give you a rundown of Mr. Wylder's progress to date . . ." Manny continues reading Scout's prepared speech for Cory and with each word, each sentence, the horrible things I said to her last night come trickling back. Yes, I was drunk. Yes, I was angry. But was I really that stupid to think if I pushed her away she wouldn't look too closely and find the truth?

Hell no. It's Scout. She's gotten to me. *Like head-over-heels gotten to me.*

". . . And so it is my professional opinion that Mr. Wylder is more than ready to return to the active roster. Not only do I think he's over the fear of reinjuring it, but his dedication to his physical wellness is unrivaled by any other player I've rehabilitated thus far in my career." Manny looks up from the paper and meets my eyes. He doesn't say anything else, just hands it to me and nods before patting my shoulder.

I glance down to the paper written in Scout's penmanship. The all-capital style I've gotten used to seeing on her notes.

"It'll be the first time in my career I don't have a 'Wylder' on one of these," he says with a sadness I feel in every bone in my body. He slides the nameplate out above my locker and hands it to me. "It's going to be strange."

No shit.

And without another word, he walks out of the locker room and leaves me alone. I study the nameplate, turn it over in my hand a few times, and then look at the letter in my other hand.

I stare at the words on the page until they blur together and my eyes burn.

What the hell have I done?

CHAPTER NINE

Scout

I *made a deal with the devil.*

It's the only thing that repeats in my head. Over and over. Each step on the sidewalk pounds it into my brain. I compromised my morals, gave up a piece of myself, and signed a probationary contract with the Austin Aces and Cory Tillman.

A man I don't trust as far as I can throw him and with a team who just screwed over Easton.

All for my father. To fulfill *his* desire to end his career with a contract in every major league clubhouse.

But what about me?

At what point do I do something for me? When do I face the harsh reality that I'm the one who's going to be left here all by myself, and family loyalty or not, I still have to live. *And he still dies.*

With each step, each thought, I feel more and more alone. My emotions whirl in a kaleidoscope of frenzied thoughts. I feel weak. Cheated. Complicit. And there's nothing I hate more than a woman who doesn't stand up for herself . . . and yet I've done just that. I've sold my soul to the devil, and my heart's not in it to make it work, even when I know I have to. *Family first*.

Add to that, I have no clue how to fix things with Easton. I don't have a mother or girlfriends to ask for advice, and everything I know about relationships I've learned from the male perspective. Unfortunately that doesn't give me any more insight beyond ignore the person, go drink a beer, and shove the blame onto somebody else. It's kind of hard to fight for someone when they're locked in their guarded tower and leaving town soon.

But he slayed dragons for you.

And that thought alone has the tears I'm fighting back burning hot by the time I unlock my front door.

Adding insult to injury, when I enter, everything in my apartment reminds me of Easton. More to the point, the layer of dust and the empty fridge is a stark reminder of how much I've been living with him even though neither of us have officially acknowledged it.

I toss my purse on the couch and wonder how I'm possibly going to accept the outcome of the past twenty-four hours. Can't I just rewind them? Do them over? I'd gladly welcome the panic I felt when Easton asked me to move in with him instead of this frantic feeling of everything being out of control.

The ringing of my cell breaks my train of thought. I have a ridiculous glimmer of hope it might be Easton, that he's calling to tell me he wants to see me before he leaves, but the thought dies quickly as I recall the things he said to me last night.

But it's the caller's name on the phone that freaks me out and has me answering as quickly as possible.

"Dad?" I'm breathless and chills race over my skin, as the bone deep fear that something has happened to him hits me.

"So?" It's all he says and the sudden rush of panic I had turns into a tickle of irritation at the back of my neck.

"So?" I mimic with a healthy dose of disdain. Why is he calling me? Was yesterday all an act? The *don't talk to me until you get the contract* and all that?

"Did you get the contract?"

"A probationary one until—"

"That's not a contract."

Seriously? That's all he has to say? I grit my teeth and bite back the smartass remark on the tip of my tongue.

"I'll be in charge of the Aces' PT until the end of the season, and then the organization will determine if they want to give me next year's contract. I'm sorry if that's not good enough for you." There's an unexpected bite to my tone but it's been a rough few days, and he's being an ass trying to make me feel like I didn't fulfill my responsibilities.

He makes a noncommittal sound on the other end of the line and it only serves to fan the flames of the anger I harbored on my walk home.

"What's that sound supposed to mean?"

"Just disappointed is all."

There's that word again.

"So what? You're going to hang up on me now? Not talk to me until late October to see if I get the contract?" Sarcasm laces my tone but everything else is one hundred percent anger. *And hurt.* I'm so sick of the mind games. So over feeling guilty. So tired of always not feeling good enough.

"You didn't fight hard enough."

My temper snaps.

"Fight hard enough?" I screech. "I just made a deal with the devil, Dad. You'll get your wish. No worries there. You'll get your contract, but when you're gone, I'm the one who will have to live with it. Not you. I'm the one who'll have to work for a total prick who seems to dirty every decision. So you may win, but I'm the one getting screwed."

"Ahh, so this does come back to the player after all."

"You're damn right it does. And his name is *Easton*, not *the player*. How is it he got screwed over twice in the same situation?"

"He's a big boy, Scout. He can take care of himself. Besides, trades are a part of baseball."

"*A part of baseball?*" I shout, throwing my free hand in the air as if he could see it. "That's the line you're going to take when it interferes with your damn contract? Because this isn't the baseball I know. Trading franchise players because they didn't recover in time isn't right. It's shady. And that isn't the game you taught me. It's nasty and unfair. It's—"

"You know what they say about life and it being fair." His chuckle rumbles over the line but all I hear is condescension. All I feel is his mockery.

"This is a person we're talking about. Someone's life. It's not some game."

"But it is a game. Clear mind. Hard heart, Scouty-girl."

And there's something about the mantra I've heard my whole life—the one repeated to toughen me up, the little girl without a mom in a world full of boys—that doesn't sit well with me for the first time in as long as I can remember.

"What if I don't want a hard heart, Dad? What if I want a *full one*?" I let my question hang on the line with the rattle of his breathing the only sound. "That may have worked for you. And it may have worked for me growing up to help deal with not having a mom and then again when Ford died, but now . . . now, *I want to feel*. I want to love. So you can have your hard heart. You can shove your daughter away so you don't have to see her upset over the fact that you're dying and you're all she has left, but that's crap. You're denying us both time and moments and memories and laughter. It's complete bullshit. It's so selfish on your part that I can't keep my mouth shut about it any longer." My voice breaks as I try to catch my breath.

"That's not what I'm—"

"No. You don't get to disagree with me," I shout over him like I never have before. My hands tremble and I walk from one side of the room to the other, asking myself what the hell I'm doing, but the hurt is real and raw and I can't hold it back anymore. "You're the one robbing me of more so that you don't have to feel. So that you don't feel guilty. Screw that. I won't accept that from you anymore. Death is selfish. And you're being selfish too. I love you with all my heart. Everything I have is because of you. Everything I am, I owe to you . . . but you know what? *Screw you.*"

"Scout." It's a guarded warning I don't heed.

What's he going to do? Hang up on me? Probably. So I fight the urge to rein it in and leave the damage where it is. It's too much, too fast, too out of control, and so when I suck in a deep breath and tell myself to apologize and leave well enough alone, I do the exact opposite.

"I don't understand what is going on with you. You've never had a selfish bone in your body, and yet now when I need you the most, you're being selfish. So who do you want to be, Dad? The guy I remember or the one I resent because you were too busy caring about your empire and damn legacy that you didn't once stop to think that *I am* your legacy. *Me.* Your blood. I'm the goddamn one who matters. So maybe you should think about that before you tell me what I did wasn't good enough or that I didn't put my family first. I'm only one person, and I'm so damn exhausted trying to make everyone happy. I need to step back and think about what will make me happy for once. Me! The only one who will be left."

I end the call and throw my phone onto the kitchen counter without a second thought. I'm so angry, so hurt, so overwhelmed that before I know it, the tears sliding down my cheeks turn into huge, heaving sobs I can't control. It's as if everything I've been holding in has been let go and the floodgates have opened.

The worst part? I feel guilty for saying what I said but won't take any of it back because it's true. And doesn't that make me selfish just like I accused him of being? For needing to get that all out so I can make myself feel better?

I want Easton. The admission makes me cry even harder because

I've never needed anyone, and now that I do, I don't know how to get it back. *Get* him *back*. What if I can't make us right again?

So I cry harder and let all the suppressed emotion slowly slip out with each and every tear. Time passes. The tears slow but don't stop.

"Open up, Scout!"

Easton's voice rumbles through the closed door and even though every part of me jolts to life at the sound of his voice, it only manages to make the sobs resurface.

He pounds harder, and I hesitantly make my way to the door. I don't want him to see me like this and at the same time all I want to do is see him.

When I swing the door open and see him standing there, I all but break. He looks so weary, so worn out, and the sheer sadness I see in his eyes probably rivals mine.

"Ea-Ea-ston, I'm-so-sorry," I hiccup out in an attempt to make this better. *I know I can't*, the die has already been cast.

"No," he says. I don't understand why, but I don't have to because within a heartbeat, he has his arms wrapped around me and is pulling me against him. "No. No. No," he continues to murmur as the tears come harder.

I can't stop them. I try, I really do. I snuggle deeper into him. Memorize the feel of his arms, the rumble of his voice through his chest, the heat of his breath on the top of my head, the sound of his heartbeat beneath my ear, and the scent of his soap. And knowing I somehow had a hand in pushing those everyday things I've become used to further away just keeps the anguish coming.

"I'm so sorry." I repeat it over and over as he just holds me tighter and keeps telling me no.

When the heaving sobs have finally subsided some, Easton steps back and frames my face with his hands. Shaking his head ever so subtly, he looks at me with deeply saddened eyes and rubs his thumbs back and forth on my cheeks. The muscle pulses in his jaw. His lips part and then shut as if he's trying to figure out how to say what he needs to say. Instead of saying anything at all, he leans forward and presses his lips to mine.

He kisses me with a passion I've never felt before. It's soft and sweet but there's so much more to it.

It's a hello.

It's a goodbye.

It's an apology.

It's a declaration.

And I do the only thing I've ever been able to do when it comes to Easton. I acquiesce. I give him everything I have. Every piece of me. Every part of my heart.

But this time there's no panic. There's no fear he'll go away because we both know he will, but I'm beginning to feel secure that he'll come back.

It's like in this sudden madness, I've found calm.

I've found him.

I kiss him back as tears slide steadily down my cheeks, the reasons behind them slowly transitioning from sadness over everything with my dad to acceptance and want for more with Easton.

Our hands slide over each other's bodies as our tongues dance. The pads of my fingers over his skin reassure. The brush of his thumb along my jawline comforts. The heat of his body against mine calms. The taste of his kiss soothes. It's like every kiss we've ever shared before and nothing like it simultaneously.

And as if we're not close enough, Easton wraps his good arm around my waist and tries to lift me so I'm the same height as him without breaking our kiss. I slide my legs around his hips and revel in the feeling of this. Of him. Of the moment where we're pouring everything we've been through over the past few days into this kiss instead of words that can hurt and scar and wound.

When the kiss ends, he rests his forehead against mine and we stay like this—connected but silent—with my legs around him and my exhale his next breath.

"East—"

"No. Shh." He shakes his head, his forehead moving ever so slightly against mine. "No apologies. No talking. I need you, Scout. Right now, I just need you."

I answer the only way I can, by leaning forward and pressing my lips to his. And I'm not sure why I expected there to be urgency between us, but there isn't. Not when he walks me to my bed and lays me down. Not when we lazily remove our clothes while the sweet seduction of our lips on each other's continues without pause. Not when he parts my thighs and slips into me.

The room fills with soft moans and sweet praise as our bodies join and our hearts connect. My hands slide down the hard lines of his torso so I can feel the muscles in his backside as he moves in and out of me.

No. There is no urgency. I let him take what he needs from me. Pleasure. Satisfaction. A claim. A tether to his life here to reassure himself he has a place to come back to. A home. Something of permanence.

So we ride that crest, where pleasure burns into ecstasy and lust gives way to love. And with one arm braced on the side of me, Easton leans back and looks me in the eyes for the second time since I opened the door.

"I need to watch you," he murmurs and then grinds into me in a way that feels so good my gasp turns into a moan. His eyes, hazy with lust darken even further. "Come for me, Scout." Another drive of his hips. Another swell of pleasure. "I need to see what I do to you." On this thrust he pushes as deep as he can go and pulses so the head of his cock rubs right where I need it the most.

My hand on his ass digs into the flesh while my other grips tight on his forearm. My orgasm builds slowly, softly, teasing and taunting until there's no way I can hold it off. So with his eyes on mine, and my body surrendered to his, I come in waves. One after another until all that's left is the ripple effect of tingling to my fingers and toes.

When he follows soon after, there is no wild groan I've become accustomed to. There is no crazy jerking of his hips. He keeps his eyes on mine as long as he can until he can't fight it. His eyes close. His face pulls tight. My name is a shuddered moan on his lips.

And as his orgasm subsides and he rolls onto his back pulling me and gathering me into him, all I can think of is while he may be taking what he needs from me, he has no idea that he's just given me more than he could ever imagine. *I needed this.*

Him.

Security.

Love.

The prospect of having a future with someone.

We lie there, our heartbeats slowing down, while I try to figure out how to address the elephant in the room that the sex didn't erase.

"I saw your comments to the reporters," I finally say to ease us into the conversation we need to have but don't want to.

"And . . ."

"I think it was smart. You set the tone and even though Cory held his press conference, it is your words that will be heard the loudest. You'll negate any rumors by coming off as a complete professional who is in love with the city he's always called home."

He chuckles. "Well, I'm glad you think I had that much forethought, but I was only reacting to the question. This city means a lot to me, and it's going to be weird not wearing an Aces uniform anymore."

And of course there's that silent dagger to my heart. "I can't say I'm sorry enough, Easton. I shouldn't have—"

"Don't apologize. You did what you thought was best."

He doesn't say anything more but my attention hangs on those words because he never says *he* thought it was the *best* decision. "Yeah, but you're still traded."

He scrubs his hands over his face, the chafing against his stubble filling the room. "Apologizing isn't something I'm good at, but when

I mess up, I say it. I said some mean shit to you last night. Stuff you didn't deserve regardless of whether you were put in a position to make a decision or not . . . so I'm sorry, Scout. For blaming you. For accusing you. For being a dick."

"Thank you," I murmur as his hand pulls me in closer to him even though we're already skin to skin. "I don't understand though . . . how did this happen? How could Finn advise you to sign that agreement?"

"There's so much more to it than that. I can't . . ." His voice fades off but his distress is more than evident. "I signed it after I was injured and . . . after ten years together, I sign wherever he says to sign."

"How can you trust him with anything else, Easton? New contracts? Negotiations? Anything? I mean he singlehandedly—"

"I'm handling it," he says curtly followed by a heavy sigh that oppresses everything in the atmosphere. "Christ . . . just . . . I'm already addressing it, okay?"

"Mm-hmm," I murmur still unsatisfied with the answer, but drop the subject because I know he has a lot on his plate.

"My flight leaves in the morning."

Those words make my chest constrict. "I assumed." I lift his hand and press a kiss to the center of his palm as tears threaten but for a completely different reason.

Don't go.

Stay here.

With me.

I don't say anything to him though. I can't make him feel guilty for leaving when I was the catalyst behind it, so I clear my throat and try to suck it up. Clear mind. Full heart.

"There's so much I need to do and not enough time to do it in." His voice is quiet, resigned, and all I want to do is fix it, fix this.

"What can I do to help you?"

"If I had my way, I'd stay right here. With you. Like this." He presses a kiss to the top of my head between words, and as ridiculous as it sounds, it causes butterflies to flitter about in my stomach. *He doesn't hate me.* I didn't realize how much I feared that until this very moment. "But I have to go see my mom."

As much as I'd love to be selfish and keep him all to myself, I know I can't. I'd never interfere with his need to take care of his mother just as I know he'd never do the same when it comes to my father.

"Would you like me to go with you?"

CHAPTER TEN

Scout

"**I** should warn you that sometimes when I show up, she's . . ." he starts as he slides out of the driver's side of the truck, pulling my curiosity from the gravel lot and mobile homes around us.

"No need to," I say quietly as I meet his eyes, noting he hasn't moved. His hand's still on the driver's side door as if he can't decide whether he wants to shut it or climb back in and drive away. He's uncomfortable. Uncertain. Now that we're here, he's not sure if it was a good idea to introduce me to this side of his life. It's in the way he chews the inside of his cheek and the hesitancy in his actions when he is usually so sure of himself.

So I do it for him.

Instead of waiting for him to open the door for me as he typically does, I open it, climb out, and meet him where he's moved to the front of the truck.

He glances to the front door and then back to me. "I just need to see her before I leave," he says, resignation in his tone, and I can't tell if it's because he doesn't want me here or doesn't know what he's going to walk into.

"I'm looking forward to meeting her." I reach out and link my fingers with his in silent reassurance. He's already prepared me for his mom and her illness and this connection is my reminder to him that I'm not here to judge her or how he handles her.

Besides, I want to soak up every minute I have left with him. He's crazy if he thought he was going to leave me behind.

He presses a kiss to my temple, his lips lingering a few moments longer than normal before sighing and walking down the path to the front of the house. Hanging plants adorn the front area by the railing with colorful garden knickknacks adding character that makes me smile.

And even funnier as we climb the three steps to one of the better-kept homes in the park, is that I'm suddenly a tad nervous. *I'm meeting his mom.* And I actually want her to like me because I know how much she means to him.

Easton knocks on the door and squeezes my hand as a woman's voice calls out, "Coming." When the door opens, the woman on the other side emits the sweetest gasp. "Easton!" She's over the threshold and in his arms in seconds, clinging tightly to him and him to her. "You came to see me." Her voice is muffled from being pressed against his chest, but the love overflowing from it is undeniable.

"Hi, Momma." The affection in his is just as endearing.

"Look at you." She leans back and looks up at him, her smile wide, her hands reaching up to touch the sides of his cheeks, and her eyes only for him. "So handsome. Are you okay? I was so angry when I saw the press conference this morning. I was down at the bar and—"

"At eight thirty in the morning?"

"Don't give me that. I was only stopping in to have a Bloody Mary or two and say hi to everyone is all." She pats his cheek as I quietly watch him grit his teeth and hold back his chastisement. "But what if I need you when you're gone? What if—"

"I brought someone I want you to meet."

She startles back, her hands immediately going to pat at her hair in true feminine fashion. "But I'm not made up . . . " Her voice fades off when she notices me standing there, no doubt looking worse for wear with eyes rimmed red from my crying jag.

She turns my way and for the first time I get a full view of Easton's mother. The resemblance between the two is uncanny: dark eyes in the same almond shape, same cheekbone structure, same smile with the little bit of crooked to it. Her eyes look tired, the lines etched in her face tell a story all of their own, but her smile is kind and welcoming.

"Hello, Mrs. Wylder. It's so nice to meet you." I hold out my hand and she grabs it immediately to shake it warmly.

"It's so nice to meet you too." Her smile widens as she glances to Easton, my hand still in hers. "She's so pretty."

I blush immediately as Easton chuckles. "Yes, she is. Momma, this is Scout Dalton. Scout, this is my mom, Meg." He looks toward me and for the first time I can see the apprehension fade.

Meg stares at me a beat longer than normal, eyes narrowing as she gives me a quick and unabashed study. "Oh, I'm so sorry, where are my manners? Please, come in."

In an instant she becomes a ball of energy with nervous hands as she turns to go inside, hitting her hip against the doorjamb, apologizing, and then doing it again as she enters. Easton's hand is back in mine again and for the briefest of seconds he pulls me against him, presses the softest of kisses to my temple and murmurs, "Thank you," before ushering me through the door.

The inside is clean but definitely lived in. The couch cushions have been worn bare in some spots, the far room is stacked with boxes of products and gadgets that seem to never have been opened, and the television is on, a baseball game playing on its screen.

It's an Aces game, that much is obvious, but I'm a little startled when I see Easton, his number 44 visible when he turns and walks back to the plate from the pitcher's mound. I meet Easton's gaze briefly, and he just shakes his head as if this is normal. That she lives in the past and watches replays of his old games.

"Easton's never brought home a girl before," she murmurs as she straightens magazines. "Do you want a drink? Let's have a drink," she says despite my polite refusal.

I hear Easton sigh softly as his gaze follows Meg when she flits to the kitchen. The sound of bottles clinking fills the small space followed by her muttered self-chastisement. There's more clinking. Easton clenches his jaw and shakes his head before looking back to me. "Excuse me for a sec, okay?"

"Of course." I try to catch his eye to tell him *it's okay*, that she's just nervous, but I'm sure he's made the same excuses for her illness more times than he can count. Besides, he's already three strides to the kitchen, his voice a soothing murmur before the glass bottles clink once again. Letting them have their privacy, I gravitate to the farthest part of the room to study the picture frames that clutter every inch of the wall.

And every single one of them is of Easton.

Much like Easton's jerseys in his private field, these pictures tell the story of his life and in much more detail. A toddler sitting on his mother's lap as she looks adoringly at her husband. A little boy standing beside his father with a fishing pole in hand and a bass flopping on its hook. A slightly older Easton, in a cowboy hat way too big for his head, standing between his mom and dad—both stunning in their own rights. Snapshots of a childhood he doesn't talk much about.

And then the photos begin to change. Cal becomes absent while many of them are of Easton in various baseball uniforms. The transition from boy to man is visible in each one. There are a few others, and I assume they're from his prom, graduation, and family functions.

I could stare at them forever, but the quiet murmuring across the room pulls my attention. Easton is hunched down so he's eye level with his mom, their profiles mirror images, and he's talking softly to her, trying to calm her. He takes a glass off the counter that's full of amber liquid and hands it to her, his hands cupping hers before she lifts it to her lips and takes a sip.

Both of their eyes close as she drinks—hers as she gets the fix she needs from the drug that provides it and his from knowing his love for her is not enough to break the cycle. And when he looks my way, the defeat is in his eyes but so is the love for her. He hates her addiction—that much is obvious—so, he does the only thing he can: love her. It's heartbreaking to know how hard this is for him and to see it firsthand.

"What are you thinking about?" His fingers twirl a lock of my hair as the fireflies flit all around us and the crickets and frogs add to the night's soundtrack.

"A lot of things," I murmur against the heat of his bare chest.

"Like?"

"Like why we both have perfectly nice beds and yet we always find ourselves having sex elsewhere."

His laugh rumbles through his chest. "Are you saying you don't like the atmosphere?"

I lift my head to where the moon's light reflects off the lake water, hear the trees rustle in the breeze around us, and know there's nowhere else I'd rather be than right here, right now.

"It's no fuss, no frills."

"Exactly. You're a no-fuss, no-frills girl." He plants a kiss on the top of my head. "And this is romantic. You can say it's not, but I know you're a secret romantic at heart."

"Looks to me like someone might have listened to a romance

book or two."

"Oh, please." He pats my bare bottom with his free hand. "I knew there would be no distractions out here and I needed that. With you."

"Agreed. Besides, who could say no to a sudden stop on the way home for some skinny-dipping and a little lovemaking in the moonlight?" I return the kiss to the middle of his chest and love the way his fingers tighten on my hair momentarily. A subtle acknowledgement that I affect him.

"Not this guy." He falls silent for a bit more and then says, "You said you were thinking about a lot of things. What else?"

"Let's see," I say as I rest my chin on his chest and look up to him. "I was thinking how cool it must be to have two parents who love you so much they'd do anything for you. I've never had that."

"I'm lucky." His sigh fills the night around us. "Even with everything with my mom and how demanding my dad is, I know I'm lucky."

"You're good with her, you know."

The laugh he emits is self-deprecating. "I feel like I'm just feeding her addiction sometimes, but at the same time, I know I've done everything I can to help her, so what else am I supposed to do? Push her away? Keep her under lock and key? She won't leave the damn trailer park. I've tried to buy her a house, move her closer . . . she won't do it. As you could see with the recorded baseball game, she's stuck in the past. She says the love of her life will come back for her someday and God only knows who that is. Sometimes I think it's no one at all, just a figment of her imagination the alcohol encourages most days. Other times I think it's a real person."

"Maybe it's your dad." The words are out without thought and he shrugs at them.

"Now you're appealing to the ten-year-old boy in me who used to pray for my parents to get back together so I could have a normal life. I gave up that hope a long time ago."

"It must have been hard."

"No harder than what you had to deal with," he says. I love he can say it so casually and I don't get my defenses up. After letting the comment settle, I turn the topic back to him.

"You're good with her. You're sweet and loving and most of all patient. A lot of people would have pushed her away, but not you. You're her whole world and it shows."

"Yeah, well, let's hope she's okay over the next few months while I'm gone. Then in off-season I can figure a long-term plan on how to take care of her."

"She seemed good with it. Like knowing you were going to be gone was a temporary thing."

"She hid it well, but I could tell she was freaking out."

"Like I told you, when we left, if she needs help, I could come out here when I'm in town."

"I can't ask that of you, Scout. It's always a crapshoot with her. I never know what I'm going to walk into when I show up. Today was good. She knew I was coming, so she wasn't occupying her resident booth at the bar. Other days, I'm left to clean up what the alcohol has left me with."

"You're a good son, Easton. And the offer still stands."

"Thanks." His finger traces a line up and down the length of my spine and chills me despite the warm night air. "Do you want to talk about what you were so upset about when I showed up earlier? I can think it was over me, but I'm not that much of an arrogant jerk to make that assumption."

"I had a one-sided argument with my dad," I finally admit and then fall silent, not wanting to ruin this time I have left with him.

"You didn't get the contract then?"

The harsh words I said to my dad come flooding back. "That's the problem, I did get one. Cory granted me a probationary agreement until the end of the season. At that time, he'll decide if they want to sign me for next season."

"You don't sound happy."

"Why are you surprised by that? I feel like I'm betraying you by taking it. Having to work for Cory, for the team, just to fulfill my dad's wishes . . . it makes my skin crawl."

"We all do things for our parents sometimes that don't always feel good," he muses with a tone that tells me he's talking about himself as well. His mom. His dad.

"I told my dad as much. I said some things I probably shouldn't have but . . . I couldn't help it. Between what you said to me last night and then having to deal with Cory and feel like I was compromising my morals, I couldn't hold it back anymore."

He pulls me tighter against him and holds me there for a moment. I appreciate him not trying to give advice or fix anything and just let me get it out.

"I understand why it's important to him—the contract—but is it really that important? Shouldn't spending the time he has left with those he loves be more important?"

"And I assume that's what you told him?"

I chuckle. "In terms a lot less polite."

"Yeah, well," he says, "there's always that time when you have to stand up to them. It's not easy, but you always regret the things left unsaid more."

"Let's hope I don't regret the things I did say." *Let alone what I didn't say.*

Our conversation falls quiet to the sounds of crickets and frogs and the occasional jake brake on the highway a few miles east. And the longer we lie here and enjoy each other, the more I think about the past twenty-four hours. The things I said to Easton. The things I didn't say. The fact that I told him I loved him and he didn't accept it. That he thought it was a desperate plea to ask for forgiveness when it was probably the truest thing I said in that whole argument.

I need to say it again.

"Easton, there's something I want to clarify about last night. There was something I said that—"

"No," he says as he shifts on his elbow, my body moving until we're face to face. He puts a finger under my chin and tilts my chin up. "I don't want to talk about last night. Or our argument. Or baseball at all." He leans forward, brushing his lips to mine, his tongue a teasing touch. "I want to lie here in the long grass with you." Another brush of his lips. "Hear your laugh." This time the kiss lasts a little longer. "Taste your skin." An open-mouthed kiss on the underside of my jaw. "And make love to you until we watch the sun rise." If he'll accept a sigh as an answer then he just got it, and when he leans back to look in my eyes, I can see he already knows it. "I want to drown in you tonight, Scout. I want to forget the world, forget what's going to happen tomorrow, and drown in everything about you, starting now."

With my heart in his hands, his lips on mine, Easton lays me down and does just what he promises.

There is no further conversation needed. There is no need to mention the obvious about what will happen tomorrow morning. There is no scramble to reassure each other that we can survive this . . . because for some reason, we just will.

I know it.

And that's the weirdest feeling of all.

CHAPTER ELEVEN

Easton

"**H**ey." I press a kiss to her temple.

"Mmm."

"I've gotta go," I whisper when all I want to do is climb back in bed beside her warm and way too tempting body and pretend like I don't have to leave.

Her body jerks as she wakes and realizes that even though my room is still dark, it's time for me to go. My duffel on the kitchen counter and my dad waiting in the car to drive me to the airport confirm that.

"East." Her voice is a sleep-drugged rasp and her hair is a wild mess that I'm sure still has leaves in it from last night. Both call to every part of me to stay. And when awareness hits her, she sits up in bed, eyes alert but movements still sluggish. "Let me brush my teeth. Get up. I need to walk you out. I just—"

"Shhh," I say as I lower myself to the bed. "Don't get up. Stay in bed and get some sleep."

I pull her into me and just hold on. Breathe her in. Her perfume.

Her shampoo. Our sex still on her skin.

"I'm gonna miss you," she murmurs against my chest and fuck if I don't feel her chin quiver as she fights back tears.

"Me too, but we'll see each other soon. We'll talk every day. We'll make this work, Scout. I haven't fought this hard to lose you."

She clings to me, and I can feel her shoulders shudder. I fucking hate that I'm doing this to her—leaving—when I promised I wouldn't. "I meant what I said," she finally says.

"What was that?" I ask, hand smoothing down her hair.

"*I love you.*"

And right there—three simple fucking words and I'm a dead man. A total goner to this woman who is a mess of contradictions and who unexpectedly stole my heart along the way.

Yeah, she said it the other night. She hurled it at me in a fucking argument, but I'm no stranger to a woman desperate enough to declare her love for me to try and keep me on the line. So I let it go. I didn't bring it up. And I figured if she meant it, she'd say it again.

And she just did.

So this, right here, right now, is real. She means it. And fuck me, it feels damn good.

"It took you long enough." I chuckle into the crown of her head and pull her in a little closer as she struggles to get away from me.

"You're an arrogant ass," she says as she swats playfully at my chest.

"Yeah, well, this arrogant ass is in love with you, too." I bring my hands to the side of her cheeks so I can look at her eyes through the dim light. I want her to see I mean it.

"Oh." Her smile is unsteady and her eyes glisten with tears.

"Yeah. *Oh.* But it's true," I murmur before brushing my lips against hers, morning breath and all, because I'm not going to pass up one last chance to kiss her.

And when I walk out of my house to this new unknown, I feel like maybe all of this can work out.

I never let her broach *how* we're going to manage this.

I never let her have a chance to get spooked.

I just told her how it was going to be. Me going to work. Her going to work. And us making this thing between us work.

Besides, she loves me.

Me.

Just when I felt like everything was falling apart, I'm beginning to wonder if maybe they were finally falling into place.

CHAPTER TWELVE

Scout

He told me he loved me.

Of course I was naked, half asleep, and he was leaving, but he told me he loved me. *Was in love with me.*

How perfect was that since we're so far from perfect anyway?

He told me he loved me and I didn't spook.

For a girl who's shied away from those emotions her whole life, to hear those three words and feel like I'm walking on air instead of wanting to run, is a pretty crazy about face.

But I'm in his bed, surrounded by his scent, and I know it's going to take everything I have to leave it, knowing I won't see him again for a while. I roll over and am met with my cell phone next to me. *Odd.* I know there's no way I left it there. When I reach for it, there is a Post-It note on its screen. All it says is "Listen to me."

I scramble to sit up, eager to hear the message like a ridiculous schoolgirl waiting for her crush to call.

"Good morning," Easton's voice comes through the speaker in that rough grit of his that has me closing my eyes and missing him already, although it has only been a few hours since he left. "Grab my shirt. Put it on. And then listen to your next message."

With a smile on my lips, I frantically look around the room for his shirt only to notice it's actually on the pillow beside my head. I laugh to the empty room as I pick it up, bring it to my nose and breathe him in before putting it on.

"First things first, Kitty. I left something for you on my favorite spot in the kitchen."

I'm out of the bed, racing down the hallway to the kitchen island, my mind thinking back to last week when he was making us grilled-cheese sandwiches for dinner. How I hopped up on the counter to watch and before I knew it, my thighs were parted, his tongue was working me into a frenzy, and the sandwiches ended up burned to a crisp.

Best grilled cheese I've ever not *eaten.*

When I reach the kitchen, there's a calendar on top of the counter. It takes me a minute to figure out what I am looking at. In his scrawled chicken scratch, Easton has marked the days of the month through to the end of the season with a D for Wrangler's games and an A for Aces games.

"See the orange circles," he says in the message. "Those are the days we get to see each other, whether we're in passing cities or we have a day or two off. I'm staking a claim so you don't decide to hang out with your other boyfriends on those dates." I know he's joking, but my head is shaking back and forth like he's crazy. "Next clue: The first time you ever came to my apartment, how was it I finally got you to come here?"

I stand with my hands on my hips for a second as I look toward the glass wall of windows and then realize what he's referring to. *The bathroom.* I jog to the guest bathroom in the foyer and laugh at what I see there. On the counter is a CD case. It's an audiobook. Stephen King's *The Last Gunslinger.*

"If I'm stuck listening to whatever romance book this is that you uploaded to my iPod, then you have to listen to my kind of book too.

Besides, those plane flights to and from cities can be boring and the last thing you want to do is talk to Tino and Drew. I plead the fifth to anything they say about me . . . so listen to this book instead. I'll be giving you a test, and you're going to want the reward for getting all the answers right." My smile couldn't grow any wider if I tried. I pick up the set of CDs and listen to the rest of the message. "What's the one place you couldn't wait to see? I believe I had to fight to kiss you because you wouldn't shut up about it."

Right now, I'm going to kiss you senseless, Scout, and I want to fucking enjoy it. So, for the love of God, woman, use those lips of yours on me and not on words.

I'm on the elevator in a flash, the car descending to the private field down below. When the doors open, I'm hesitant to step off it. It feels strange being here without Easton. This is his place. His solace. And yet curiosity gets the best of me.

I flick on the lights and begin to walk around, looking for the next item. It takes me a second to see the Mason jar on home plate. When I pick it up, all I can do is shake my head at the dozens of Wint O Green Life Savers inside it.

"There's one Life Saver for every day left until the season ends. Our own little countdown of sorts. Plus I threw a few extra in there in case one of our teams makes it to the playoffs. When you suck on it, think of me." His chuckle is deep and suggestive. "And finally, where is the one place I stood, looked at you with the stadium lights in your hair and knew there was no turning back when it came to you?" I make a face at the phone. "Don't roll your eyes, Kitty. Think about when you stood there and got me like no one else ever had."

Excited, I get on the elevator to head to the wall of windows where Easton and I first realized there might be more between us than passing lust. When I get there, I'm not sure what I'm looking for. I stare at the empty stadium below, mesmerized for a moment as I recall that first night: the linking of our pinkies; the darkened apartment and stadium-lit sky; the feeling of being understood.

It takes me a moment to see a key ring with a key on it sitting at the base of the window. Uncertain how this makes me feel, I stare at it for a moment as I try to comprehend what he's giving me. What he's saying to me. Because yes, he offered it the other day . . . but that was before everything, and now there it is—a new and shiny and silver key to his house attached to an Austin Aces keychain.

I pick up the phone and laugh at myself and my trembling fingers as I dial up the next voicemail. "I know right now you're probably standing there wondering if you should be spooked or not. Thinking you might have said the words but this makes things real— it makes us real—and that part freaks you out. I didn't go to bed last night, Scout. I sat and watched you sleep and wondered how this was going to work out. How with two crazy schedules and being in different cities was going to work for us . . . But it's going to. So take this key. Use it. Don't use it. But know it's there for you. The closet is half-empty for you. The drawers. The everything. And while you're hyperventilating, know this . . . I've never met anyone like you, Scout. You challenge me. You make me laugh. You encourage me. But more than anything *you get me*. My need for this game that I love as much as I hate. How I love my parents even when I feel like the strings I still have tied to them are strangling me. How a picnic on a hill watching a Little League game where we root for strangers is what I need sometimes. So when you get scared, when you wonder how any of this is going to work, remember that I left you a key because I plan on coming home to you. Did you hear that? I plan on coming home . . ."

Every part of my body is covered in chills when the message ends. I just stand there looking at the key on the silly keychain with tears blurring my eyes and push replay again.

And again.

CHAPTER THIRTEEN

Scout

"**H**ey."

His voice. It's exactly what I need to hear. After my dad being stubborn and refusing to speak to me. After dealing with Cory and his bullshit.

This unexpected phone call from Easton is what I need to center me.

"Hey, Hot Shot." I try to play it cool and not feel silly that it's only been hours since he left and I'm already a mess of female hormones I don't want to lay claim to.

"What are you doing?"

"Making my eyes cross working on plans, schedules, and staff for the team. Sam's last day is Wednesday, so I'm trying to figure what personnel I should keep, who I should bring in, all that kind of stuff." I look at my desk covered in papers and then out the window to the locker room beyond and half expect to see Easton there, calling me and pretending not to be talking to me as he'd done before.

"Sounds thrilling."

I laugh, the gravel in his voice sexy as sin. "It is. For me, anyway.

I take it the team made it there okay? How's Chicago?"

"It's muggy as hell. But good."

"It's a great city. I worked there last year for a while, but with the Cubs, not the Sox. How are the other players treating you so far?"

"Good. Like one of the guys. They're all a little shocked about the trade and being supportive. Some of them heard through the grapevine that this isn't the first time Cory has screwed over a player so they're asking a lot of questions. For all I know, they're rumors and so I'm not really commenting. . . it's just different, you know?" There's a trace of sadness there that he clears from his throat. "But guess what?"

"Tell me."

"I'm cleared to play tonight." The excitement in his voice matches the sudden surge of it I feel.

"Really?"

"Mathers couldn't believe the Aces hadn't cleared me."

"Mathers is a competent therapist. I figured he'd see through my lie and reinstate you," I add, wondering what Mathers must be thinking about my own competency considering I deemed Easton not fit to play. "I'm happy for you, but then again, I already knew it." My voice wavers on the last word as I try to keep my emotions at bay.

"You'll watch?"

I laugh and draw the attention of some of the guys wandering in and out after their workouts. "I wouldn't miss it for the world."

"'Kay. Thanks. I've gotta go but I wanted to call, tell you . . . hear your voice."

And that softening heart of mine continues to melt.

"Hey, Wylder?"

"Yeah?"

"Have a game."

He laughs. "Is this like have a day?"

"Yep. *Have a game* . . . but make it a kickass one because I'm keeping points."

"Points? Are those like the brownie points I cashed in before?" he asks playfully.

Damn, that was fun.

"Something like that." I laugh as his name is called in the background.

"Call you later?"

"Have a game, Easton."

The call ends.

I love you.

I test saying it in my head, those ridiculous female hormones taking over again, but when you're not used to saying the words, you don't know how often is too often? Because it's almost as if now that I've acknowledged it, I realize I've felt it all along.

I would have never let him in otherwise.

CHAPTER FOURTEEN

Easton

"**Y**ou look pretty damn good in blue, Wylder."

I chuckle as I glance over to Stidwell and bump fists with him. "Thanks, man."

"We're glad to have you but fuck, man, you got a raw deal."

"Well . . ." I lift my eyebrows and laugh. The sting is still there but my brand new blue catching gear on the bench beside me dulls it a bit.

"I get it. You can't talk about it," he says. "For what it's worth, everyone's talking about Tillman. About the shady shit he pulled with you, and now because of your high profile, people are listening to Reagan's complaints about what he did to him in Baltimore last year. How he pulled the same crap there. Cutting costs at any price isn't the way to win a pennant . . ."

"True," I say but shrug it all off. Right now I have a game to play—my first one back—and hell if I'm not amped up to cross the line and dirty up my cleats. I look up and a few more of the guys have gathered around. Some I know in passing. Some I've never met.

Some I've played with before when they were Aces. Well aware anything I say can be quoted, I play it safe. "Karma's a bitch."

"It is," he says as he hands me my hat. "Like I said, we're glad to have you."

"Thanks, guys."

And when I tip my hat onto my head, a shower of blue glitter rains down on me. Hair, face, clothes, floor. Every-fucking-where.

The guys are doubled over in laughter while Stidwell tries to keep a straight face. "Tino said we needed to welcome you properly to the team. Besides, he said blue's your color."

Motherfucker.

I can't help but laugh, the damn glitter falling in my mouth when I do, because my boys—*the anti-Santiago brigade*—knew the perfect way to get me to relax before I take the field for the first time in what feels like forever.

They made it feel just like home.

CHAPTER FIFTEEN

Scout

"Oh come on. You can tough this out," I encourage as I press Dillinger's leg from where his calf rests on my shoulder. He grimaces and hisses out a long low-sounding breath as I stretch the tightened tendons he overextended last week.

I hear the comments made under the breaths of some of the guys. I'd be deaf if I didn't. I'm more than aware of what my body position with Dillinger looks like to them—like I'm trying to mount him—and yet I can't care. This is my job. To get him feeling okay before he pitches tonight. Every win counts with the Aces one game out of first place, and the season slowly coming to an end.

"Can I be next?" I glance over to where Santiago stands and then return my attention to Dillinger as I ease the pressure off and lower his leg back down.

Moving from my position between his thighs, I look back to Santiago. "I wasn't aware you were injured."

"I'm not but if you're handing out free therapy like that, count me in." He smirks and everything about it makes my skin crawl.

"There's a long and distinguished line in front of you, Santiago.

Guys who really need me. So I suggest you get in the back of the line. If I have the time, we'll see about working on your problems, but I'm pretty sure fixing your issues is above my pay grade." I lift my eyebrows and just stare at him to let him know I'm not taking his shit.

Dillinger whistles low and soft as Santiago narrows his eyes and then turns and walks away.

"Not all of us are assholes," he says garnering my attention, "but it seems a lot of them are acting like it lately."

"It goes with the territory," I say with a nod, trying to keep my professional, tough-girl façade in place. At the same time though, I'm relieved to know I'm not seeing things that aren't there. The over-abundance of towels accidentally being dropped when I enter the locker room. The suggestive, snide comments here and there. The offers to go out on a date despite my continued refusals. Things that never happened when Easton was here, his claim staked even though we thought we were on the down-low. "You good and stretched? Ready to strike 'em all out tonight?"

To have a game. I smile and think of Easton.

"Always." He offers me a big grin before heading out to the main part of the locker room.

"You okay?" Drew asks the same time he knocks on the doorframe.

"Yep," I say as I blow out a breath, but the look on his face says he's not buying it.

"You sure?"

"Yes. Thanks. Can I help you with anything?" I ask, this little visit out of the ordinary for him.

"Easton's looking good. Strong. Only that lucky fucker would return to a new team after such a long stint on the DL, hit three homers, and throw out every person who attempted to steal on him in his first week back. It's like he's superhuman or something." He laughs with a shake of his head.

"Don't tell him that or we'll never get his ego to fit through the door."

"Ain't that the truth. You catching his games at all?"

"Of course." I offer a sly smile. "You guys play out there, and I sit in here and watch him on my phone."

"Traitor." This time his laugh is loud and draws more attention from the guys.

"The same can be said for the management of this team and what they did to him."

"Yeah. It's still not sitting well with the guys. Everyone's on edge. If the front office can do that to Easton—Mr. Ace himself—then they can and will do it to anyone. It doesn't make for good team morale."

"How could it?"

"There are rumors that Cory's on the bubble. I guess Finn finally got hold of Boseman, and he's pissed about what Cory did with East. That he never approved the trade. The goddamn left hand doesn't know what the right hand is doing and still someone got jacked off."

"So eloquent," I say with a roll of my eyes, but I'm more intrigued than ever. Is Finn trying to cover his ass? By advising Easton to sign that addendum, he's the one who's ultimately responsible for letting the club have a decision to make in the first place. And the fact that he still represents Easton makes my stomach hurt.

But that's not why Drew is here to talk to me. I can tell there's more and am curious what it's about so I make small talk until he gets to it.

"I know it's been tough for you. The guys are being dicks, giving you constant bullshit, and strutting around naked."

"It's nothing I can't handle," I say. "I'll make a few quips about how small their dicks are and before you know it, the towels will stay on and it will all stop."

"Yeah, but you shouldn't have to handle it at all. You're being professional and they're acting like sexist pigs."

At least he's accurate in his description. "Let's hope those sexist pigs don't ever find themselves injured because I won't be as gentle with them as I would with you."

But I need to get a handle on it. And soon. Or else Cory's going to think I'm incapable of running the program.

"I like the way you think." He stares at me and chews his bottom lip for a moment before getting to his point. "They knew you were sleeping with East so they've just assumed you have a thing for baseball players. I guess they're thinking they might get a chance with you too."

I snort at how ludicrous that is but then realize he's not joking. "There's no chance there. I'm still with Easton."

"Hmm." It's all he says. The damn sound makes my stomach drop to my toes and allows doubt to fester when it hasn't been there once since he left.

Sure, I miss him. Sure I hate knowing he might be out in a bar with his new teammates and a woman might be hitting on him . . . but that could happen here too. That little hum in Drew's throat tickles at the base of my neck and tugs on insecurities lying dormant.

"Is there something you're not telling me?" I hate that I even ask, well aware it undermines my professionalism, and yet I hang on to the silence and wait for his answer.

"Nah. He's a good guy. It's just I've never seen him like this over a woman."

"So . . . what? You wanted to feel around and see if I'd take any of the guys up on their offer? Make sure I'm true to Easton? I appreciate your loyalty to your friend, but we've got things between us handled just fine."

The ringing of my phone interrupts the conversation. I don't mean to do anything more than to silence the ring and send it to voicemail but when I see Sally's number on the phone, fear has me answering as quickly as possible.

CHAPTER SIXTEEN

Scout

The clinical white walls feel like they're sapping every ounce of my courage as I rush down the hallway.

"His fingernails were blue. I should have known." Sally wrings her hands as she keeps up beside me toward wherever we're going in this maze of hell.

"How could you have known?" I ask but don't really pay attention to what I'm saying because being here has transported me back to three years ago. Back to when the doctor told me my brother, Ford, had died. How after hearing those words, I felt like every ounce of blood had been drained from my body and all of the oxygen had been sucked from the room. The sadness that was nothing short of crippling. The emptiness inside that felt like it went on without end.

Snap out of it, Scout. This is Dad. Not Ford. And he's going to hang on longer. He *has* to hang on longer than this.

"I found tissues with blood on them. He said it was because he cut himself but . . . I should have known he'd coughed it up." A tear slides down her cheek and I know she cares about my dad. The next-door neighbor turned best friend turned to we-never-discussed-their-relationship. Deep down I know love is involved and at this point and time, I wonder why I never pressed to ask more.

The things you choose to think about when you don't want to think about the now.

"You couldn't have known, Sally. This isn't your fault."

STAT codes are called over the PA system and shoes squeak on the floor as nurses and doctors rush to save another person, another life.

And yet I know my dad's can't be saved.

"The fluid built up in his lungs. They call it a pulmonary—"

"Edema," I finish for her. I've researched this disease every which way from Sunday since he was diagnosed and know the signs, the symptoms, the ladder of demise.

"The cardiologist changed up his blood pressure medication to help clear the fluid out. She said once it lessens, he'll be able to head home."

A wail of "*No, please no,*" floats out of a room across the hallway and every part of my body twists in despair. I *know* what that helplessness feels like.

"I shouldn't have called you in such a state of panic. But the ambulance came and I was afraid that it was—"

"Don't ever apologize for calling me, Sally." I pull her into me and we cling to each other in the middle of the hallway, trying to find comfort in one another even when we know the man we both love is losing his fight.

Day by day.

Hour by hour.

Bit by bit.

And when we release each other, both with eyes filled with tears, I turn to find we're where we need to be, room 412. Fear, hope, desperation, guilt—all four run a tyrannical rant inside me as I prepare myself to see him. To apologize in person for the angry words I said to him last week.

When I gather the courage, I enter the room with Sally's hand on my shoulder in support, and my heart lodged in my throat. My dad's lying in the bed, leads are attached all over his chest and he looks like he's hooked up to an army of machines. His face is pale and eyes are closed. I notice how scraggly his hair looks—longer, unkempt—and I'm immediately brought back to when I was younger and he would wear his hair longer as was the style.

When he was healthy. Invincible.

Not wanting to disturb him, I walk forward and sit in the chair beside him as Sally steps out and gives me some privacy. I lay my hand over his, study the still slightly blue nail beds, and revel in the fact his skin is still warm, not cold like the last time I held Ford's hand. I stare at him then, memorize the new lines etched in his face and wonder if this is how it will end for him. In a hospital with unfamiliar surroundings. Or will it be at home in his sleep overlooking the field he loves full of the memories we made together?

The tears come at the thought. Of the sadness wrapped in bittersweet.

His hand moves beneath mine, and I whip my eyes up to meet his weary ones.

"Hi."

He nods his head ever so slightly and closes his eyes for a very slow blink before opening them and looking back at me. "No crying," he demands in a quiet rasp.

Unbelievable. "Don't tell me what to do."

"You're going to have to leave if you cry."

I chuckle, astounded when I shouldn't be. He'll never change, even when he's like this. "You're in no state to tell me what to do so you need to just lie there and rest, while I sit here and worry. *Or cry.* That's how it's going to be, Dad, whether you like it or not. Got it?"

He stares at me for a moment, eyes hardened steel, but he doesn't have enough strength to keep them that way for long. They begin to soften as the disease saps his strength and causes him to relent.

He nods softly and closes his eyes. "Thank you for coming, Scouty-girl."

And with those words, I know we're okay. He's forgiven me for the things I said to him.

I squeeze his hand gently. "I'll always be here, Dad. Get some rest."

CHAPTER SEVENTEEN

Scout

"You okay? I haven't been able to reach you all day." I want to sink into the sound of his voice and pretend it's his arms wrapping around me. And knowing he's there has the tears that have been burning all day threaten to return.

"Yeah." It's all I can manage to nod my head without giving away how much I need him right now.

His brown eyes narrow and fill with concern across the FaceTime connection. "Scout?"

"Just a rough day all around." I muster a smile and clear my throat. "My dad was taken to the hospital so I spent the better part of the day there just sitting with him and watching him while he slept . . ." I go on to explain everything.

"I'm sorry I can't be there with you." His smile is soft and sincere and I miss everything about those lips. "But he's going to be okay? I mean . . . for now."

"Yeah. He'll get to go home in a day or two. Once his lungs clear a little . . . but the doctor says it will most likely happen again. And then again. Each time it will be worse until . . ."

He just nods to let me know he understands. "I'm sorry."

"It's okay. It's just been a day."

He stares at me across the silence of the connection, looking as tired as I feel but unknowingly giving me everything I need right now. Him. Only him. That's all I seem to need these days.

"Oh my God," I say with a shake of my head as I snap out of my funk. "You hit another homerun tonight. You're on such an incredible roll."

"Shh," he says quickly like a little kid, eyes flashing a warning that makes me laugh more than I should.

I hold my hands up in surrender. "My apologies. How could I forget baseball superstitions? If you talk about it, you jinx it."

"Something like that." His grin is infectious.

I miss the feel of it against my lips.

I miss the chafe of his stubble against my skin.

I miss him.

"You watched the game?"

"Of course. I've watched every game. This one I watched with my dad though. Against nurse's orders, I climbed in beside him in his bed, and we watched it. He critiqued everything about you, you know."

"Of course he did." He laughs. "How did I fare on the Dalton barometer?"

"He thinks you look good. The rotation of your arm. The strength in your throws. Everything. I mean, how can he not when you threw out Jenkins trying to steal—"

"Come visit me this weekend." The way he says it stops all train of thought.

"But I thought the plan was—"

"Plans change. And I miss you." *Be still, my beating heart.* "I'll be in New York. The Aces have a two-day break and their next stop is New York, so you'll just come early. Spend the weekend with me. I need to see you."

My heart soars and my reply is automatic.

"Yes."

His chuckle is sleep-drugged. "Better bring those brownie points with you."

I laugh for what feels like the first time all day. "You've earned so many, Wylder, you might need to start calling me Betty Crocker."

Better yet, Betty *Cocker*.

CHAPTER EIGHTEEN

Easton

Damn.

Is it fucking pathetic that the minute she walks into the lobby of the hotel every part of me stirs to life? My heart. My dick. My fucking breath.

The skirt and cowboy boots she's wearing only encourage every fantasy I've ever had of her. The ones that have been on repeat in my spank bank since I left home.

It's been ten long days. Ones filled with the high of returning to this game in peak form and the lows of sleeping in an empty bed every night.

Looking around, she adjusts her carry-on bag on her shoulder. A man walks by and turns his head to get a second look.

Move along, prick. She's mine.

I pick up my phone and type: **Hey Betty Crocker, turn to your right. I'm in the back booth.**

She smiles when the text hits her cell before making her way toward the swanky bar. It takes a second for her eyes to adjust to the darkened atmosphere but the moment she spots me, her lips curl up in that shy smile of hers before heading my direction.

I watch her hips sway. The shape of her legs. The bounce of her tits. And every part of me demands I get up and waste no time taking advantage of all those and more, but hell if I don't want to savor her too.

"Is this seat taken?" she asks, eyes devouring me despite the coy smile on her lips.

So that's how she wants to play this? Bring it, Kitty.

"It depends. *Is it*?" My eyes run up and down the length of her body and my dick hardens at the knowledge of just how addictive everything is underneath.

She angles her head to the side and stares at me for a beat. Grey eyes telling me so much more than her lips are saying. "That depends on what you have in mind."

My laugh is rich but strained. "Oh, I've got a lot of things in mind, sweetheart, but I'm a man of action. I prefer to do things instead of simply talk about them."

"And what type of things do you . . . *like to do*?" Her voice is breathless. Her nipples hardened against the fabric of her shirt.

"Why don't you take a seat and find out?"

She looks at where I pat on the seat beside me and then back to me. "My daddy taught me to never talk to strangers."

I chuckle as I lift my brandy to my lips, eyes locked on hers over the rim of the glass. "And mine always told me how important it was to make new friends."

She breaks character for a moment—smile widening, head shaking—before she holds out her hand and carries on the charade. "Kitty. Nice to meet you."

"Easton. Believe me, Kitty, the pleasure is *all* mine."

She slides into the booth next to me and we stare at each other for a few seconds, eyes saying what our bodies are begging for.

"Hi," she finally says.

"Hi."

"What brings you to town?"

"I play baseball."

"Like big bats and balls, type of baseball?" She feigns innocence and fuck if she's not adorable.

"Something like that." I chew the side of my cheek enjoying this game.

"Do you always drink before you have a game?" She nods to my tumbler.

"Only when I'm celebrating."

"And what exactly are you celebrating, Easton?"

I swear to God, the breathless tone to her voice is like fingernails scratching ever so slightly over my balls. It's so damn sexy. "We'll get to that in a moment," I murmur propping my elbow on the back of the booth. I run my finger over my bottom lip. I need something to occupy my hands since all they want to do is touch her. "What about you? What brings you to town?"

"I'm a baker."

My laugh is loud but she keeps character. "What is it you bake, *Kitty*?"

"Brownies."

"Brownies?"

"Uh-huh."

"Did you know I happen to love brownies?" I say as I give in to the temptation and touch her. My hand to her thigh, and hell if touching her doesn't make me want to speed this game up despite the promise to myself to take it slow.

"You do? What is it exactly that you love about them?" I stare at her lips as she speaks and imagine them wrapped around my cock. The red lipstick leaving its ring as a mark.

"I like the batter," I say and glance around the restaurant to make sure we're out of sight range, because I can't hold back anymore. She's here, beside me, playing this coy little vixen and damn if I'm not going to act on it.

What man wouldn't?

"The batter?" She shifts a little, much like she does in the cab of my truck with her knee bent on the seat and her body angled my way.

And of course I look down. Have to. Tanned, toned thighs greet me. My mouth waters. My dick hardens. My control tested.

"Mm-hmm," I murmur as I place my hand right where I want to run my tongue—up the inside of her thigh—and slide it up, her skirt bunching with it as I go.

Her body tenses, and I love that she wants me as badly as I want her. Skype sex is fun. Getting off watching her get off is hot. But it's not the same. It's not *this*. The touch. The scent. The reaction. Not in the least.

"I like to dip my finger in it." *Fuck. Me.* My fingertips rub ever so softly over the seam of her pussy and all I feel is the heat of her skin. She's not wearing any panties. Her breath catches. Her fingers tighten on the tablecloth. Her legs part a little wider. "Then work it around the edges of the bowl so it's covered in the batter." I slide my finger between her lips and groan when I find her wet. Her mouth parts. Her thighs tighten as I dip my finger into her. "And then I like to put it in my mouth. Suck it all off." I run my finger up again so it hits her clit. Her hands fist now. Her hips lift ever so slightly so her thighs hit the underside of the table and beg for more as I do exactly what I said. Pull my hand away and put my finger in my mouth.

Fucking hell.

Her taste. It's enough to drive a sane man crazy. Add to that the look on her face—pure sex—and I know our charade is over.

I lean forward and press my lips to hers. A teasing taunt of a kiss that gives me a hint of what I've been missing and reaffirms that I need the rest. Right now.

"I do believe I want more of that batter, pretty Kitty," I murmur against her lips.

"Being as you're a man of action, I suggest you take what you want."

"Not here," I say, loving how her eyelashes flash open. "This place is too respectable for the things I plan on doing to you."

"*Oh.*"

"You asked what I was celebrating, now it's time for me to show you."

I throw some bills on the table, grab her carry-on from the seat, and with her hand in mine, *attempt* to walk as inconspicuously as possible with a hard-on the size of Texas.

We step into an elevator and the minute the doors close, I'm on her. Lips and tongue and hands and body. We're a mass of want and need and desire and greed. Pressed up against the wall, it's like I can't get close enough to her. My hand is under her skirt. My tongue is between her lips. Her hand is cupping my cock.

The elevator slows at my floor. The car dings. We shock apart as if we're about to get caught. Luckily when the doors open there is no one there. With her hand in mine, we make our way to my room. We don't speak. Routine movements seem difficult when I'm high on the goddamn taste of her.

I think in actions. One at a time.

One foot in front of the other.

Key card. Green light.

Door handle. Twist it.

And the minute the door clicks behind us, we continue what we started. We're a frenzy of clothes coming off and lips trying to meet in between.

We're a litany of broken phrases. *My God.* I've missed you. *Hurry.* I can't wait any longer. *That feels good.* Oh God. *Now.* Right now.

Fuck this slow shit.

I'm taking no prisoners.

My fingers are in her pussy. Her nails are digging into my shoulders.

Her orgasm is my end game.

My tongue sliding over her. Teasing her clit. Working her hub of nerves. Then sliding into her. The taste of her my own fix.

The scratch marks on my back the only trophy I need.

My dick sliding between her tits. Then her lips wrapped around it. Sucking it. Working it. Her nails teasing my balls.

A free-for-all.

Pushing her thighs back. Burying my dick into her. Working her over until her muscles tense. Her pussy pulses. Her moan fills the room.

A race to the finish.

The rush of pleasure. The surge from my balls to my dick. My vision goes spotted. My head grows dizzy.

Her name on my lips.

And then when we recover, we'll start all over again. Maybe then I can go slow. Maybe then I won't feel so out of control. Maybe then I'll get my fill of her.

Then again, maybe not.

It's Scout, after all.

CHAPTER NINETEEN

Scout

"We're having all kinds of firsts today," I tease as we walk, hand in hand, through the bowels of Yankee stadium.

"We are." He laughs. "Hotel sex for one."

I swat at him. "That's not what I meant, you pervert."

"It's true though."

"It is, but I was referring more to this." I squeeze his hand and stop in my tracks forcing him to do the same, our hands extended between us. "Me getting to see you off before a game and wish you good luck."

His smile is shy and inviting, and I wonder if there will ever come a time when he looks at me like this and butterflies don't tickle every single part of me. He tugs on my hand and pulls me so I land against him. "That is a very good first," he says, brushing a lock of hair off my forehead and tucking it behind my ear. But it's the way he looks at me—like he can see into my soul—that unnerves me and invigorates me in ways I never knew possible. "I can think of another first."

"What's that?"

He leans down and kisses me. A brief touch of tongues. A quick loss of breath from the punch of emotion he packs into that tender kiss. When he leans back and I lower from my tiptoes his smile is into megawatt territory. "I get to kiss you. In public. Without worrying about who's going to see or what contract clause we're going to violate—"

"Rule breaker," I tease, but realizing he's right, I kiss him this time.

"Only when it comes to you." We stare at each other for a beat with giddy smiles on our faces that look ridiculous but can't be helped. "You gonna be okay?" he asks, referring to sitting in the stands by myself to watch the game.

"Who me?" I laugh putting my hands out to my sides. "Stadiums are my second home."

"My bad. How could I forget?"

I take a few steps back, teeth sunk in my bottom lip as we stare at each other before he nods and turns to head down the hall to the locker room.

"Hey, Hot Shot." He turns. Looks at me. "Have a game, will ya?"

That grin returns full force. "Always."

The chords fade from the national anthem and somehow, across the crowd, Easton finds me in the seat he was able to get me just to the visitor's side of home plate. *The closest you can possibly get to me without being on the field*, he'd said. And when I'd laughed, his response was that *You're mine for only forty-eight hours, and I'm not going to waste a single minute of it being apart from you.* For a man who doesn't read romance novels, he sure knows how to make me feel swoony.

Our eyes meet, he tips his hat and nods, a slight smile on his lips before jogging off the field to the dugout.

"He's a different person with you, you know."

Startled, I turn to my left to find Finn sitting there. My back is up immediately, my displeasure and lack of trust in him front and center at the mere sight of him. "No one asked you."

He chuckles and it scrapes over every nerve I have. "I can tell you're thrilled I'm here."

"It's none of my business if you're here or not." I turn to face the game. The first pitch is thrown. A strike low and questionable, and Johnson, the Wrangler at bat, feels the same way by the way he looks back to the home plate umpire.

"Good seats, huh?"

Crap. That means he got them for Easton in lieu of making me sit in the family section that typically has *okay* seats. I swallow back my vitriol and replace it with manners. "Thank you. Yes, they are."

The crowd cheers as Johnson strikes out and jogs back to the dugout. I keep my eyes there, study Easton sitting on the bench with his leg guards on, as he laughs about something one of his teammates says. It's warming to see him in his element and kicking ass at that.

The next two outs happen quickly and the inning switches from the top to the bottom. Easton jogs out to the plate, all business, and I have to say it's sexy as hell to watch a man do what he does best.

Especially when he squats down and gives me a view of his very fine ass.

"May I ask what it is about me that pisses you off so much?" Finn finally asks after being on the receiving end of my cold shoulder.

"Only if you want me to be honest."

"It's not an act, is it? You really don't like me."

I turn to look at him and shake my head. He doesn't waver from my gaze, just holds it without flinching. "I don't trust you. Any agent who tells their client to sign an agreement like you did Easton, isn't out for their client but rather out for themselves. The question is what exactly is in it for you? You get your fifteen percent commission regardless of where Easton plays, so why give him bad advice unless you and Tillman have something going together on the side?"

He lifts his eyebrows and takes a slow sip of his beer, then looks back to the game unfolding before us. He watches Easton throw down to first base and almost pick off the runner taking too generous of a lead off the bag. "I see." It's all he says, but his expression says so much more that I can't decipher.

"Are you trying to tell me something different happened?"

This time when he turns to face me, his eyes are harder, and there's a grit to his voice. "Just so we're clear, Tillman's a fucker, and I hope he gets what I think is coming to him. As far as Easton is concerned, he's like a brother to me. I would never do anything to intentionally hurt him or his career. You don't have to like me. You don't have to trust me. All that matters is that Easton does. So long as both of us are rooting for the same thing for him—success, health, a long career, happiness—that's all that should matter." The emotion in his voice surprises me, and there is really nothing more I can say to refute what he says.

Because it's true.

I don't have to like him to love Easton.

My knee jogs up and down. My hands are clasped. Finn is sitting forward on the edge of his seat. Tension fills the stands.

The score is tied with only one out and the Wrangler's pitcher bungled up the beginning of the inning. His pitches wouldn't hit the spots they needed to hit and now two batters later there are runners on first and third base. That means the runner on first is going to steal.

With less than two outs, no catcher risks throwing down to

second base to get the runner out because that means the runner on third may try to score. It's too risky.

No catcher but Easton Wylder that is.

Finn knows it too.

This is what sets him apart from the good catchers and makes him great. His cockiness. His justified belief in his abilities. His confidence in his body.

I study Easton. His stance behind the plate with one hand tucked behind his back, fingers twitching in anticipation, waiting for the ball to be pitched so he can do what he does best.

The pitcher checks both runners on first and third to try and stop them from getting too far from the bag. He winds up. He pitches.

With lightning-fast reflexes, Easton has thrown the ball with laser precision to second base. The tag is made. The runner's out. And before the umpire even finishes throwing his thumb back in the "you're out" signal, the shortstop is throwing back to home plate where the runner from third base is barreling down the line toward Easton.

He catches the ball split seconds before the runner slams into him full force. Easton is knocked to the ground with the runner on top of him but with the ball held tight.

The umpire signals out, and I jump out of my seat cheering like a maniac in a stadium full of people rooting for the Yankees. I high-five Finn. He whistles in celebration.

But it's when I look back toward the plate, that my heart drops. Easton is still sitting there. His chest protector is being taken off him. His face a mask of pain I've seen before.

"*No. No. No.*" I'm out of my seat flying up the aisle needing to get to him when I have no clue where to go. All I know is I need to get there now. "Finn, where? Tell me where? Get me to him."

He jogs ahead of me, weaving in and out of fans, as every part of me rejects what I just saw.

It feels like forever, but it's only minutes before we're out of breath and descending in an elevator. When it opens a security guard stands there.

"I'm Easton Wylder's agent. She's his personal PT. We need to get to him now."

He eyes us as my hands shake, trying to get the pass Easton handed me earlier from my purse.

This can't be happening.

"Here," I all but shout when I find and hold it up. Before he has a chance to respond, I'm running down the hall following Finn toward the locker room.

His shoulder was good. Strong. It can't be happening again.

Please let it not be happening again.

I can hear him before I see him. His cry of pain. His groaned *"Fuck."* And when I clear the doorway, my heart drops to my feet. He's on a table, his face distorted in agony as the team doctor evaluates his shoulder.

"Easton." It's the only thing I say as I rush to his side.

"When I threw . . . I felt it tear," he says, a grown man reduced to tears.

But these tears aren't from pain.

They're from a valiant man terrified he's going to lose the only thing he's ever known.

CHAPTER TWENTY

Easton

The pain.

It's fucking brutal.

I pop an Oxy.

It dulls it temporarily.

The surgery was a success.

Dr. Kimble's voice rings in my ears. The look of hope on Scout's face fresh in my mind. But it's been a week and the pain is still so goddamn vicious.

The cheers from the stadium outside my condo are a fucking slap in the face every time I hear them. The opening notes of *Welcome to The Jungle* echoing up to where I sit. The fireworks from the left field wall at the end of a win. All are reminders of what I'm missing. What I might be losing.

"You sure you're okay?"

I glare at my dad who's acting like my frickin' babysitter. Like that's not humiliating. But Scout's at work—with the Aces—and I'm here.

Broken.

Injured.

Completely fucked and feeling sorry for myself.

"I have some news that might cheer you up," he says, trying to sound upbeat.

"Nothing's going to cheer me up unless you tell me that Santiago was hit by a bus. He's the reason for all this. He started the chain reaction. The cocksucker." His head jostles from my honesty, and I don't really fucking care.

I'm in a bad place. I've fallen down the goddamn rabbit hole and if I keep popping these Oxy, I might want to stay there.

"That's not how I raised you." The warning is given and it takes all my restraint to say you didn't raise me at all, Mom did. But I'm lucid enough to know that's dick-ish, so I bite my tongue and resist taking out my misery on him.

When I don't say anything else, he continues. "I think Boseman is going to fire Tillman."

I should be happy over this announcement, feel vindicated, but all I feel is spite. "Little too late for me. Not like that's going to help me any. Besides, he's another person who needs to get hit by a bus," I say without remorse, the pills beginning to take effect, starting to relax me, even though all I feel is rage.

"Son."

"Don't *son* me. Don't fucking anything me. You hear me? Your head was so far up his ass that I'm surprised you're not looking through his belly button. You have no right to chastise me."

"I'm going to give you that one. Just this once," he sneers. "And chalk it up to the drugs and the pain. But you need to remember who you're talking to, whether you're a grown man or not."

We glare at each other—him in that calm, passive expression that is anything but the argument I'm aiming for. "Sorry I can't be as perfect as you."

His laugh is tinged with a sarcasm I don't understand. "I'm

anything but perfect, Easton. The older I get, the more apparent that becomes."

A muted roar of cheers filters through the window from the stadium. I clench my teeth and squeeze my eyes shut for a moment as I try to find civility.

It's not an easy task these days.

"Dad, I'm good. Scout will be back in a bit. You can go."

"I don't think that's—"

"All I'm going to do is sleep. Please." *Everyone needs to leave me the fuck alone.*

"You sure?"

"Yep."

He shuffles about a bit, tries to stall, but finally, the elevator doors shut.

Silence. At last.

I pop another Oxy. I close my eyes and wait for that calm to hit me.

The upside, I'm back in Austin. I'm with Scout. I get to sleep in my own bed.

The downside, I can't even hold her. I watch her go to work every day for the fucker who screwed me over. And I don't get to play the game I love until next season.

Frustrated. Moody. Pissed. I shift to the chair by the window and watch what I can't have.

The only good news of the day is Karma's raised her head.

Let's hope she meets Tillman full force.

And maybe she'll take a little detour and settle the score with Santiago while she's at it.

CHAPTER TWENTY-ONE

Scout

He's sitting in the same spot I left him.

In the same clothes as yesterday.

I've got to do something to snap him out of this funk. It's been two weeks, and every day he seems to become more and more depressed.

"Hey." I throw my keys on the counter and pick up the bottle of Oxy, quietly counting how many are still in the bottle to make sure he's not overmedicating.

"Hey." No emotion. No anything.

Three pills are missing. I can handle that number. Just one less thing to worry about when it comes to him.

"What did you do today?"

"Same shit. Different day," he replies, sarcasm tingeing its tone.

I approach where he sits in his chair facing the window and run a hand through his hair, my fingers scratching gently at his scalp.

"How about we get dressed and go get something to eat?" I suggest, just like I did two days ago.

"I'm not hungry," he grunts.

"How about we watch a movie?"

"I'm sick of watching TV."

I walk in front of him, hands on my hips, and look down at him. He doesn't lift his head. He doesn't meet my eyes. It's as if I'm not even present.

Frustrated, worried about him, and needing to feel close to him somehow, I try the only thing left I can think of.

"I've got an idea," I say, the smile playing on my lips and suggestion lacing my tone. Placing my hands on both arm rests of his chair, I dip down to give him a kiss.

"No." His hand on his good arm flies up and pushes me away.

I stumble back a few steps. Embarrassment stains my cheeks, as tears burn hot in my eyes. My chin quivers as I fight back the humiliation and struggle with remembering that he's not himself and doesn't mean it.

But it still hurts.

"I know you're struggling with this, Easton. I know you're pissed off at the world and your body . . . but I'm here. I have no idea what to do anymore to help you." He finally lifts his eyes to meet mine. They're flat and lacking all emotion. "Your body I can help heal"—his laugh is loud and condescending—"but your mind? I can't help you there without you telling me what you need from me."

"I don't need anything from you." And those words only serve to cut me deeper.

"You refuse to go anywhere near the windows when I'm home. You say you don't want to be reminded of what you're missing, and yet every time I come home, you're sitting there, staring at exactly that. You won't go out. You won't talk to me. You won't do anything. It's been two weeks since the surgery and I'm still sleeping in the guest room." I'm whining. I know I am, but it's only because I'm worried, and I miss him desperately, but feel completely helpless.

"You don't understand," he finally says, gaze still fixed on the view beyond.

"You're right," I say, dropping to my knees in front of him. "I don't. So help me understand. Please, Easton. Just let me in."

"I told you I don't need anything and I meant it."

His words sting regardless of how many times he says them.

"I think you should talk to Finn and consider the offer," I say, trying to get him to focus on something other than what he's lost.

"You also think taking a walk outside will make everything better. Why don't you just kiss my boo-boo while you're at it? I'm sure that will work miracles and heal me. Right?"

"Don't be a dick."

"Then don't act like my mother." His eyes meet mine. They're hard and angry and unrelenting.

"I think I'm going to sleep at my place tonight." I choke back the sob threatening to come out.

"Good idea," he sneers and then looks back toward the window, effectively dismissing me.

I stand there for a beat, hoping against hope that he'll apologize for being a prick, that he'll ask me to stay, but he does neither so I leave.

When I exit the building, I stop in indecision but ultimately decide to walk the several blocks home to clear my head and dull the hurt. While I know he's having a difficult time adjusting to the fact that he busted his ass to get back to the game to have it ripped back away just as he was making a killer comeback, I don't know how to show him the bright side of things.

I need to get him out of his funk.

With each step, I realize I might have an idea how to help him. I dial my cell. "Scout?"

"Hey, Drew."

"How's the asshole?"

I laugh because he has no clue how right he is. "If you want to know the truth, right now he's been upgraded to *fucking asshole* status."

"Ohh. That bad, huh?"

"Yeah," I say, knowing I sound like I'm playing around. The hurt is still real, though. "I think he needs some testosterone intervention."

"We tried. I called him yesterday to get him to come out with us after the game. I even offered my chauffeuring service to him but he declined."

"That's cuz you drive like a maniac." I laugh.

"Every man's got to have one wild streak."

"Oh please." I glance around as I approach the backside of the stadium, the halfway mark between both of our places. "What if you take the party to him? He won't leave the house. I'm not sure if he doesn't want people to see him with his sling or if he truly is pissed at the world . . . but he keeps pushing me away and . . ." My words fade off as I try to fight back my tears. I'm certain he can hear them in the waver of my voice, though.

"You okay, Scout?" Concern floods his voice.

"Yeah. I will be. We had a fight, and I just need a break for the night."

"You sure?"

"Yeah." I clear my throat. "Yes. I'm fine."

"Go home. Go out with friends. Do something and leave the fucker to us. I'll call Tino and JP and round up a few others. We'll head over. He won't be able to refuse a pack of us. Besides, we have a long plane ride tomorrow to sleep it off."

I'm distracted by something to my left through the narrow opening of the exterior wall. For an instant I think I see Cal and Santiago talking in the stadium's parking lot.

"Thanks, Drew," I say, distracted as I step back to look again.

But when I look again, it's just Cal, hands on his hips, and an expression I can't make out from the distance.

I jolt awake. I'm disoriented. I'm on the couch. *My couch.* Not Easton's. My pulse races as I try to figure out what I was dreaming about.

And just as my heart starts to calm, there's a clink on my window. It scares the shit out of me, but also makes me wonder if I didn't have a nightmare at all and that's what woke me up. I glance at the clock—it's three a.m.—and grab my cell on the coffee table beside me, ready to dial 9-1-1. *Am I'm overreacting?* Leave it to me to call the cops when there's a branch hitting the window or something benign like that.

Just as I have myself talked into that theory, the noise happens again—*tink*—but this time it's several at once, almost as if . . . what the hell?

I get up from the couch, crouch down, and creep over to the window. I probably look ridiculous, but no more ridiculous than thinking there is someone throwing pebbles at my window in the early morning hours. As I pull back the curtains to look out, the noise hits again. I'm startled by it, and surprised when I look out to see Easton standing in my front yard.

I have the window open in a beat. "Easton. What are you—it's three in the morning."

His laugh floats up to where I am and as mad as I am at him, the sound of it so very welcome.

"Do you know how pathetic I am?" he asks, but finishes the question with more laughter as he stumbles and affirms my assumption that he's more than a little drunk. "I can't even be a decent Romeo. You're on the first story and I can't even throw rocks that high because I have to do it left-handed. As you can see, my left-handed aim is for shit."

I'm on the second story, but I guess he had a good enough time with the guys tonight to forget how to count properly. I fight the smile tugging at the corner of my lips just like him being here tugs on the strings of my heart.

"Guess what?" he asks, lowering his voice to a whisper like he has a secret.

"What?"

"I'm drunk as fuck." His chuckle echoes up to me. "But I needed to come here. To see you. Do you know you live a long-ass way from me? Too far. *Way too far.* That's why you need to give up your lease because it's way too far to walk when you're drunk. And I'm drunk. Wait, where was I?" He scratches his head with his good arm and looks like a little kid who just woke up from a hard sleep—hair's a mess, clothes are rumpled, and a sheepish grin is on his lips. "Oh. Yeah. Explaining. I needed to come here to apologize. *Apologize?* Is that the right word? Yes. I believe it is."

I can't help but laugh. He looks adorable, and I swear he's actually smiling for the first time since he was injured in New York. "And so you decided to walk here. You could have called, you know?"

"Nope. Not good enough." He shakes his head a little too hard and then basically giggles when the world around him spins from the alcohol. "I wanted to try and be like one of your romance books, so I decided to come and stare at you up on your balcony."

"But I don't have a balcony." This is too much fun, he's too much fun, to not give him a hard time.

"Where is your imagination? Pretend, will you?"

"Okay. What am I supposed to pretend other than I'm on a balcony right now?"

"That I look like Fabio." He flips his pretend long hair with his hand.

"Eeeewwww." I giggle.

"You're ruining the scene I'm setting here," he scolds.

"Yes. Sorry." I try to keep a straight face, but it's incredibly hard to do when he's so endearing. "Continue. Please."

"As I was saying, I thought I should come across town, and say, *Scout, I was a dick.* A big and fat and hairy one. Not a manscaped one. The kind that's so gross you get pubes in your teeth and can't get them out."

Oh. My. God. I double over with laughter. Tears well in my eyes from laughing so hard and trying to take in what he just said. It's a train wreck and hilarious and all I keep thinking is I hope my neighbors are not hearing any of this.

When I stop laughing and can keep a straight face, he's standing there with his hands on his hips and his eyebrows raised silently asking if I'm done yet.

"I'm sorry. I didn't mean to laugh at you." I snicker. "But how exactly do you know about a man's pubes in your teeth?"

"Oh. God. No." And then his eyes grow wide as he realized how what he said sounded like. "I was just talking. Not from knowledge. That's just . . . I'm doing something here. I'm apologizing, right?"

He's so damn adorable.

"There's only one problem with your apology, Hot Shot."

"What's that?"

"Romeo and Juliet both kill themselves in the end."

"Oh." His face is a picture of shock, and regardless of how hard he tries to hold back his own laughter, the giggles hit him again. "I guess that shows you I can't read for shit."

"We'll just say that details aren't your strong suit."

He shrugs. "Hey, Scout." His voice is more serious now and pulls my attention.

"Hey, Easton."

"I love you."

And there he goes stealing my heart again.

"You're forgiven."

"Good," he says animatedly as he part-jogs, part-stumbles up the stairs to my front door. "Because when this alcohol burns off, my arm's gonna hurt like a motherfucker, and I'm gonna need your nursing skills."

"Oh really?"

"Yep." He looks back up to me. "Preferably the kind in a tight white uniform dress thingy with a zippered front and lots of cleavage. Oh, and garters. Garters turn me on."

I leave the window as he rambles and rush downstairs. When I open the door, he's staring at me—three sheets to the wind—but he's still the best thing I've seen all day.

CHAPTER TWENTY-TWO

Scout

"**J**ust checking in to see how you're doing?"

"I'm fine, Scouty-girl. Just fine."

"Liar."

"Perhaps." His chuckle is interrupted by a coughing fit. "How's the program coming along?"

I look to the charts and dry erase boards I have lining my office walls and smile. "Good." *I think.* "I have Ramos traveling with the team so I can stay back and work with Dillinger and Wiseman." *And to be home just in case you need me.*

"The knee and the elbow."

"Yes." I shake my head at our shorthand. "I want to be the one to nurse them out of surgery."

"And I'm sure you sending Ramos on the road trip had absolutely nothing to do with Easton still being in town."

I smile. Sigh. And then lie. "Not at all."

"I'll start believing that about the same time you start believing I'm doing just fine."

CHAPTER TWENTY-THREE

"Be sure to let us know when you need another break from East," Tino calls from the locker room as I make my way out.

"We had a great time." JP snickers.

"I don't want to know," I say, hands up in mock surrender. I've been in enough clubhouses not to be shocked by whatever it was they were talking about. Besides, ignorance is bliss.

And yet as I push through the door, I can't help the automatic smile remembering how that night ended. With Easton in bed with me for the first time in two weeks. Sure he was propped up on all kinds of pillows to alleviate any strain on his muscles and the healing tendons, but he was still in bed beside me, fingers linked with mine.

"Privilege doesn't guarantee you can handle the sport." I hear Cal's voice before I see him. And when I clear the corner, I'm startled to see Santiago opposite him. Both men startle back when they see me standing there, but there is no erasing the tension snapping in the air between them.

"Everything okay?" I ask when I know damn well their

conversation is none of my business.

"Yes. Fine," Cal says, taking a step toward me. "Just discussing a team matter."

"Oh." My eyes flit from Cal to Santiago and then back to Cal, uncertain if I believe what he's said. "Okay."

What the hell was that all about?

The exchange is still on my mind as I head home but I'm probably making more of it than there really was. Maybe Cal was defending Easton. Maybe he was telling Santiago he'll never be able to fill his son's shoes. And maybe pigs can fly.

I chuckle at the thought as I wait politely for sorority girl to exit the elevator, nodding to her in a brief hello, before getting on, turning my key in the panel to give me access to the penthouse.

It's not until I enter the condo that I realize how exhausted I am. When I find Easton reading some papers on the couch, I drop my purse on the counter and move toward him. He tosses his papers on the table the minute he sees me and smiles.

"Hi."

"Hi." He looks so damn inviting that I sit down and curl up next to him as best as I can without hurting his shoulder.

"Watcha reading?" I ask.

"It's, uh . . . nothing. I'm just looking over some of the examples and new pamphlets for the upcoming projects for the Literacy Project." He presses a kiss to the top of my head. "I figure I might as well do something while I'm injured."

"That's very honorable of you, Mr. Wylder. *And very sexy.*"

He chuckles. "Sexy, huh?"

"Incredibly."

"How sexy?"

"Brownie points kind of sexy."

"I'll have to keep that in mind and use it to my advantage in the future." He chuckles and pulls me in tighter against him, and as the comfortable silence settles around us, all I can think of is that he smells like home. It sounds strange but after traveling so much in my life, never having anything of permanence, it's a welcome thought. "I talked to Finn today."

Proceed with caution. That's my first thought considering the last few times he's talked to Finn about the offer to be a guest commentator for a game on Fox Sports has ended in a fight.

"You did?" I ask innocently enough.

"Yeah." He falls silent as he fidgets with a lock of my hair. "I still haven't decided what to do. I kinda feel like it'll look like I'm giving up. Public perception is always harsh . . . one minute they're gossiping I took the gig because I'm washed-up and the next thing you know, the Wranglers believe it and let me go . . . And then I am washed-up."

"You're being absurd," I huff, knowing how fragile a man's ego is, but also thinking these kid gloves need to come off so he can face reality. "People will think just the opposite. You're not washed-up and never coming back. Instead they'll think you're smart for hooking a second gig while you're recovering for next season."

"I think you're underestimating how vicious the press can be."

"Who cares what the press thinks? You sure as hell never have, so why start now?"

"It's not that easy, Scout. You look at the world through these rose-colored glasses."

"And what of it? Maybe I like pink." I shrug, not offended in the least of my positive outlook. "And it is easy. You've talked baseball your whole life. You go on camera, talk about the one thing you know inside and out. Give some color commentary and insight during the game and that's it. I've watched you do it numerous times with the local Aces broadcaster, and you're a natural."

"That's not the only thing I know inside and out," he chuckles, voice full of suggestion, as his hand finds the curve of my ass and squeezes.

"True," I murmur, those warm fluttery feelings returning with a vengeance because he definitely does know me inside and out. "But there will be no cameras or color commentary in our bedroom."

"You're such a spoilsport," he says playfully.

"And you're changing the subject."

"You noticed?"

I roll my eyes. "You're afraid it's going to make you look like a has-been . . . how about you look at it from the glass half-full perspective? It's visibility. It's keeping your name relevant in the game when you can't be on the field. Who knows? Maybe it will lead to something you can do off the field when baseball is over some day."

"After baseball is death."

"Stop being so dramatic. You know that's not true. There will come a day when you can't play anymore. Why not start trying to figure out a way to stay in the game, but not be the game?"

He falls silent and I know I've piqued his interest. "Baseball is all I've ever known." His anxiety is palpable and for the life of me, I don't know how he can't see what I'm trying to say to him.

"That's my whole point. If it's what you know, then try to capitalize on it and plan for the future."

"It's scary to think about *then*. About what happens when my arm gives out for good or my knees can't take the abuse anymore. About when this game is over, you know?" His voice is raw with a vulnerability I never expected.

"I know," I say and press a kiss to the center of his chest before shifting so I can see his face. There are lines there, concern marring his handsome features that I wish I could take away. "Easton, there is no other sport on the planet where you play one hundred and eighty-six games in a season. None. That's a lot of wear and tear on your body. At some point in the distant future, it won't be worth it anymore. You have to realize there is life after baseball. The question is, whether you want that life to be free and clear so you're not reminded of what you're missing daily, or if you want to be a part of it somehow because it'll always be in your blood."

I hate to see the tears glisten in his eyes. I hate knowing he's this upset by the mere mention of when he can no longer play. Then again, he's been living in this state for the past year with a cruel glimpse of his greatness between injuries . . . so maybe he knows all too well the hurt leaving the game will cause him. The void that will remain.

"You think I can do it?" I hate that for a man always so confident in himself he sounds like a little boy right now.

"I know you can."

CHAPTER TWENTY-FOUR

Scout

"**H**e's sleeping right now. Do you want me to wake him?"
Yes.

"No. It's okay, Sally. How's he doing?"

I hate that she pauses when she answers. "He's sleeping more and more each day. I hate it but at the same time know it's the only time he really gets any real peace. The doctor said that's pretty much what we can expect; the hours of sleep to increase more and more as his heart weakens and tires."

Squeezing my eyes shut, I take a deep breath to try and hold back the tears. I know the truth regardless of how hard I cling to hope. *I don't want him to die.*

"How are you doing, Sally? Are you sure you don't need me to hire a nurse to give you a break? You do have a life of your own."

"I already told you I'm fine. Besides you know how stubborn he is. It's a miracle he even lets me be here to help him," she says.

"I appreciate it. I really do. If there was a way to get this contract for him and take care of him, I would do it all myself."

"I love him too, Scout. You don't need to thank me."

And there's something about the way she says the words that makes the first tear slip over. It's stupid to not think of them as a couple, but I find solace in knowing my dad was able to experience love again after devoting his whole life to loving Ford and me.

"I'm glad he has you." My voice is barely a whisper when I finally find the words to speak.

"How about you? How are you doing? I know you must be under a lot of pressure to win that contract for your dad. Just know he loves you regardless."

I nod my head as I look to where Easton is shaving at the bathroom sink and know what she says is true, but I still wish I could hear it from my dad.

"Can . . . can you just tell him I called? It's nothing important. I just wanted to hear his voice."

"Tell you what. How about I go and put the phone in there with him? I know it sounds silly, but sometimes when I need to know he's okay, I'll go sit next to him and listen to his breathing. Maybe if you hear it too, it'll put whatever is on your mind at ease for a bit."

She's right. It does sound silly and yet I find myself saying, "Thank you. I'd like that."

"That's what I thought. Just hang up whenever you feel better."

There is noise on the phone as she walks to him, some rustling as she lays the phone down.

Then there is the sound of him breathing. It's even and the rattle is a little louder than last time we talked, but it's still there. *I needed this.* To know he's still with me. To know his heart still beats.

And just like when I was a little girl scared of the monsters under the bed, I snuggle deeper under the covers and listen to his breathing to soothe my fears away.

I may not be snuggled up against him with his big hand holding mine like he did back then, but it still feels the same.

Knowing he's still there soothes me.

He saves me yet again from the things I don't want to face.

CHAPTER TWENTY-FIVE

Scout

"Hey, Scout."

My back's up immediately at the sound of his voice. "What can I do for you, Santiago?" I ask as I turn to face him, not one to ever leave my back to him for more than a beat.

"I hear it's a big night for that boyfriend of yours. He's gonna try and make himself useful."

In my periphery I see some of the other guys stop what they're doing at their lockers and turn our way.

"So you need nothing, then?" I ask, face a picture of innocence. I'm not giving the prick what he wants—to get under my skin.

"I bet Daddy set this up for him. Don't you? With all those connections of his, I bet he set up his wonder-boy-son nice and pretty just to keep that precious Wylder name in the spotlight."

"You have a good night then." I give him a sickeningly sweet smile as I turn on my heel and head toward my office. By the time I round my desk and sit down, Tino is standing in the doorway.

"You okay?"

"For the life of me, I don't know how you handle sharing the same uniform with him every night, let alone the same damn field," I say.

"It's a job." He shrugs. "There will always be coworkers you hate and you just have to deal. There's nothing else you can do."

"Talk about team morale. Go Aces!" With sarcasm lacing my tone, I pump my fist in mock support

"Believe me, most of us feel the same way. Our only hope is that Boseman ousts Tillman and then pushes Santiago out after him."

"Fingers crossed he does because it sure as hell would make my job that much easier."

He looks over his shoulder when one of the guys laughs out loud before looking back to me. "How's he doing?" he asks, voice lowered.

"He won't admit it, but I think he's nervous."

"Why? He's done it a hundred times before with the local channel here."

"I know." I think back to the murmured words of encouragement I gave him when he kissed me goodbye on the way to his flight this morning. "But he is."

"A bunch of us are heading down to Slugger's to watch the broadcast and drink a few in silent support for him before we fly out tonight. You're welcome to come if you want."

My smile is automatic. "Thanks, but I've got some work to do here and then I'll probably catch it at home."

"Can't handle all this testosterone, huh?" he teases.

"Some days, no."

My knee jogs up and down as the familiar notes of the Fox Sports jingle plays. It's not often I actually watch a game on television for the hell of it. I'm typically studying a player I'm rehabbing to see how they are faring and what I need to work on with them. I've never

purposely tuned in just to watch the broadcasters.

But today is different.

Today Easton is taking a huge step out of his comfort zone, and like the text I sent him an hour ago said, I am so very proud of him for doing so.

The camera pans across the field—the green grass, stark white lines, and players milling about—before the lead broadcaster begins to speak.

"Welcome to another summer night of baseball here on Fox, ladies and gentlemen. The sky is clear, the popcorn is popping, and the bats are swinging here in Amco Park for America's favorite national past time," he says as the camera switches to them sitting in the broadcast booth. I squeal like a schoolgirl when I see Easton. I know I'm biased but he's so handsome with his headset on and a smile that only those closest to him can tell hints at his nervousness. "Thank you for tuning in. I'm Bud Richman and tonight we have special guest, Easton Wylder, of the Austin Aces and more recently the Dallas Wranglers to talk with us during the pregame show. Thanks for joining us. How's the shoulder coming along?"

"Good. Healing," he says eyes flicking back and forth from the camera to Bud.

"Are you ready for a good battle of the bats tonight?"

Easton smiles. "That's definitely what one would expect of tonight's match-up."

"Tell us, Easton, as a player, how would you size up either team if you were to play them?"

Easton talks for a few minutes about the pitching and the fielding, and I can see him physically start to relax. There's easy camaraderie between him and Bud that's likeable and not over the top. Easton comes off as personable and knowledgeable and I'm sure his insight is attractive to the male viewers while his looks are more than pleasing for the female viewers.

"We're minutes away from the first pitch, ladies and gentlemen, so without further ado, I'll let Easton have the honor of announcing the starting line-ups."

The camera pans from Bud to Easton and there's total *silence* as Easton's face looks like he's a deer in the headlights. His eyes widen and then become panicked as he says "uh" a couple times before looking over to Bud for help.

It's only seconds but my heart jumps into my throat from the look on Easton's face.

"Oops, sorry about that, Easton. It seems we forgot to show the newbie how to work the switches up here in the booth. I hate it when we do that." He laughs like a seasoned professional while I'm screaming at the TV over how they could throw Easton into the press box and not show him the damn controls. "In the meantime, starting for the Colorado Rockies tonight, batting first and playing center field . . ."

Bud drones on going through both sets of line-ups as I pace the living room. I'm sure Easton is livid and embarrassed and all I want to do is fix it for him. That's a huge screw-up on Fox's part and I'm sure Finn will give them his two cents if he's not on the phone already.

The station goes to a commercial break without the camera panning back to Easton, and it takes everything I have not to pick up the phone and call him, reassure him, and give him support.

When the commercial break is over, the camera spends most of the time on the field before finally focusing on the booth. Easton's there next to Bud, his posture a little stiffer than before, his features a bit more stoic. Bud continues to talk and this time when Easton responds, his responses lack the energy they had before. It's almost as if he's holding back or scared to elaborate. And his discomfort comes across loud and clear to the viewer.

They talk about the pitchers and what to expect from each team for the night and then Bud wraps up the segment. "When we come back, baseball fans, we're heading for the first pitch with the two teams that might end up being a preview of your National League playoffs. Easton, why don't you take us to break and tell the nice folks at home all about our sponsors."

And when the attention shifts back to Easton, he's frozen again. Almost as if once the camera focuses on him, he can't speak. Bud looks his way and chuckles softly. "Sorry there, Easton. It seems the booth doesn't want to function for you today. I'm giving Easton instructions here to read the teleprompter and it's not working. We'll take this break, and I'll make sure to plug our sponsors when we return. Stay tuned for an exciting night of baseball, folks."

And when they cut to commercial, I force myself to breathe.

This is not good.

Not at all.

I wait with bated breath for them to come back from commercial break and when they do, the game starts.

Bud calls the game. He talks nonstop and any additional commentary from Easton is only added when Bud asks him. His personality is void. His engagement is forced.

It's a train wreck.

As the ninth inning comes to a close and the bleeding stops, all I keep thinking is, *I pushed him to do this.*

Should I have backed off? Should I not have talked him into it when he wasn't comfortable in the first place?

"Hey," I say cautiously when he answers the phone.

"Not now, Scout. I don't want to talk right now." His voice is nothing short of frustrated devastation.

"Can you tell me if you're okay?"

"I'll see you tomorrow when I get home."

And the line goes dead.

CHAPTER TWENTY-SIX

Easton

"**C**an I get you another?"

"A double, please." I pull my hat lower and welcome the dim lighting in this hole-in-the-wall bar on the outskirts of Austin.

He slides the amber liquid across the scarred bar top. "Thanks."

"Heading anywhere special?" he asks, trying to make conversation I don't want him to make.

"Home."

"That doesn't sound like it's a good thing." He chuckles.

"Not tonight it's not," I murmur as I take a long swallow and let the burn run its course.

"You piss off your old lady?"

"Something like that."

I glance down at my cell as another text comes through from Scout, and after staring at it for a bit and wondering how I'm going to face her, I power down the phone.

I'm not ready to talk to her yet.

To disappoint her again.

To let her know this man she loves is not who she thinks he is.

"Easton? You okay, son?"

The question of the fucking day and I don't even have the effort to answer it anymore. Only twenty-four hours since my broadcasting shitshow, and I'm still hiding. But Manny just waits before quietly taking a seat a row behind me while I keep staring at the empty seats around me. The pristine grass in front of me. The dirt groomed to perfection.

"Thanks for letting me in here."

"Of course. Any time. This place is still your home. You'll always be an Ace in my book."

I mull over his words. They might be true, but right now I don't feel like I belong anywhere.

"I miss the magic," I finally say. My confession surprises me, but I've never spoken truer words.

"You've had a rough go of it this year," he says softly.

"I used to sit here as a kid. Before the seats filled up for the game and the guys took the field for batting practice, I used to sit here and feel the magic in the air. It was like I knew something special was going to happen that night."

"I remember well. Finding you out here. I used to always wonder what you were thinking about."

"What if I can't ever get it back, Manny?" I itch for another drink. Anything to numb the fear robbing my courage that led me here instead of home . . . where I should be. It's easier to keep running—*hiding*—than to face the truth that has finally caught up with me.

"Sometimes things happen in life that at the time seem one way, but in reality it's the magic recharging so you can find it again."

"Not this time."

He makes a noncommittal sound but doesn't say anything. We sit in silence in the magic kingdom of my childhood as I try to figure out how to take the next steps I need to take.

"Scout's looking for you, you know. She called here worried."

"Yeah."

"She's a good one."

"She sure is," I sigh.

It's a fucking shame I'm not.

CHAPTER TWENTY-SEVEN

Scout

"**W**here have you been? It's been four hours since your flight landed, and I've been worried sick."

I rush out to the foyer just in time for him to brush past me without meeting my eyes or saying a word. There's relief in seeing him safe and sound, but that slams head first into anger when I smell the stale scent of alcohol. I've been worrying myself sick while he was in a bar somewhere drinking?

"Easton?" I follow him to the bedroom where he drops his bag on the floor and then walks right past me again on the way out without speaking.

This is bad.

He has to have seen the commentary online. The twitter storm of jerks using shitty hashtags #EastonEatsIt #DumbJockEaston, the memes already circling his wide-eyed stare into the camera. The pundits have had their say from behind their keyboards and harsh is putting it nicely.

I scurry after him despite his obvious desire to be left alone, because that's what you do when you love someone. You try to help them.

"Please. Talk to me," I say as he stops at the wall of windows and stares blankly at the view beyond. I reach my hand out, wanting to offer comfort, but hesitate.

"Don't." It's a warning. A threat. A reflection of his mindset.

He wants a fight. It's in the set of his shoulders. The clench of his fists. The aggression in his posture.

The silence stretches, his anger and malcontent sucking up the air around us until it begins to eat at me too. For being worried when he couldn't bother to be considerate and let me know he was okay. Because he's shutting down, shutting me out instead of turning to me like one is meant to do in a relationship.

"Do you know what it's like to live your whole life as a lie?" When he speaks, the words are barely audible, but the resignation mixed with spite is what rings the loudest.

"What's that supposed to mean?"

"Tell me, *oh Scout who wears the rose-colored glasses*, how exactly would you rate my performance last night?" The question is so loaded there's no way I can answer it and satisfy whatever it is he's looking for.

"That's not fair to—"

"That bad, huh?" His chuckle is self-deprecating at best. "So bad you can't even lie to me and tell me it wasn't horrible and that I'm not the laughingstock of baseball right now? The dumb jock who can't manage to put two sentences together?"

"But you did," I say trying to figure out my phrasing so I don't light a match to ignite his temper broiling just beneath the surface. "You started out strong. You did an incredible job giving insight and feedback. You were a natural. And then the teleprompter didn't work and Bud didn't teach you the controls—"

"Do you know what it's like being compared to Cal Wylder my whole life?"

"No one's comparing you to him in this situation." I'm desperately trying to follow his sudden shifting thoughts. "You're not your dad, Easton."

"You're goddamn right I'm not," he thunders, every syllable a combative verbal assault. "I could never be like him. The perfect fucking man who does nothing wrong and turns everything he touches to gold like Midas."

The doorbell chimes, alerting us that someone is coming up the elevator.

"Ah, would you look at that? I'm sure that's good 'ol Cal right now coming to pat me on the back and thank me for being the fucked-up son tarnishing his perfect goddamn reputation."

"Easton." It's a plea for him to think before he opens the door and unloads his temper on his father.

He pushes the button to open the doors and says, "Welcome to Easton's fucked-up party!"

But it's not Cal standing there.

It's sorority-letters girl.

Her face softens when she sees Easton, while every part of me tries to make sense of why the girl from the lobby has access to the penthouse.

Access that only Easton can grant.

"Easton." Her voice is soft, sympathetic. "I wanted to make sure you were okay and didn't need me . . ." Her words fade off when she notices me standing there.

"Not now, Helen," he says with a kindness he hasn't afforded me since he walked through the doors. He glances over his shoulder at me—eyes wide with panic—and then back to her. "I can't . . . just . . . not now." His hands fist and he gently hits the side of the wall with one as if he's not sure what else to say.

"I'm sorry. I didn't mean to . . ." She says something else he responds to—quiet murmurs I can't hear from where I stand—which give the appearance they know and are comfortable with each other. She steps back into the elevator, glancing quickly my way with concern in her eyes before averting her gaze as the doors shut.

I stand in silence, stunned and confused over how they know each other when I've basically lived here for the past three months and a "Helen" has not been mentioned once. But I sure as hell have passed her downstairs more times than I can count. In my scattered emotional state I jump to the worst conclusion and even though I know it can't be true—that Easton is cheating on me with the sweet co-ed from the lobby—my stomach revolts.

"Who was that?" Accusation is loaded in those three words.

"Let it go, Scout." He shakes his head and continues to stare at his fist still resting on the wall.

"No. I'm not going to just *let it go*. Who the hell was that?" I become more insistent as the seconds pass. My heart races and that bone-deep mixture of disbelief and fear start to reverberate within me. Am I right? Has he fooled me all along?

Is the player really *a player*?

"Scout." It's a warning I don't heed at all.

"Don't *Scout* me. I love you, Easton. I love you when I never thought I could love someone, but I don't deserve to get the shit end of the stick from you just because I'm the one here. I'm so confused right now. You had a rough go yesterday. I get it. You want to be pissed and go have a drink *or ten* before you come home. Fine, but next time remember there's someone here waiting for you. Worrying about you. And that means you have to think of them even when you're at your goddamn worst. You have to pick up a phone and tell them you need time and space—be considerate—so they don't work themselves into a frenzy worried sick you're not lying in a ditch somewhere dead when you're MIA for four hours. That's what you do when you're in a relationship, Easton. Unless this is your way of telling me we're not in one." I choke over the words, the thought suddenly sinking in. "If that's the case, Helen's *visit* makes a lot more sense to me."

"You're delusional," he barks and just stands there, blinking his eyes a few times as if he's struggling with what I said. Then for the first time since he's walked in the door, he *finally* meets my eyes. I see defeat in them. I see sadness. But most of all right now I see fear and *that* exacerbates the panic I feel. "You actually think she is . . . that I am . . . *fuck*!"

"What?" I plead. "Just tell me."

"Goddammit!" he says throwing his hands up as he paces back and forth, agitated and needing to move. "She was coming because of last night."

"Last night?" My head spins to understand how she's connected to his broadcast last night, and his inability to explain freaks me out. "What about last night? You won't even talk to me about last night but you've talked to her? Who the hell is *she*?"

He emits a frustrated growl like nothing I've ever heard from him before. It sounds like a man on the verge of breaking, and I don't understand it and I'm scared by it.

"The teleprompter wasn't broken. They didn't forget to teach me shit."

"Okay." I stretch the word out as I try to make the correlation between that and *her* and whatever is going on here. "Easton, I don't understand what—"

"You want the truth?" he shouts as he turns to face me. *I always have.*

"I thought you were telling me the truth."

The little laugh he emits does anything but reassure me. "Ah fuck it . . . I can't do this anymore."

My heart tumbles to my feet and I feel like I can't breathe. "*Do what anymore?*" I whisper, afraid of the answer.

Us.

This.

What?

He paces again. I can see his agitation. Can sense his hesitancy. Every step he takes freaks me out further. *Have I lost him?* I silently wait for him to say it. To tell me he can't do this with me anymore. That we're over. *I feel sick.*

After a minute he stops a few feet in front of me, his face a picture of despair. "I fucked up last night."

Tears well. My pulse pounds. My mind spins. "You slept with Helen?" I can barely get the words out and when I do I'm met with his laugh. Loud. Hysterical. Disbelieving. And every part of me revolts at being mocked. I'm in his face within two seconds, my anger getting the better of every single part of me. "You asshole!"

He catches my hand before my slap connects with his cheek. I struggle to get away from him as my emotions tumble out of control and into a vicious eddy whipping through me.

"No, Scout. You don't get it," he finally grits out as if it pains *him.* I swear to God he better start explaining, because his words are implying one thing and his actions are saying another. "I'm not cheating on you."

"Then what is it? What is so damn secretive that you can't talk to me about it?" I pace from one side of the room to the other, my adrenaline amped and emotions frayed on all edges. "You tried to be a sportscaster. It didn't go well. Big fucking deal. You move on. You find something else. You let it go. How fucking hard is that?"

"It's not that easy," he says, expression softening and brows narrowing.

"Yes, actually it is."

"Not when you've lived a lie, it isn't."

That feeling of dread returns but for completely different reasons. The man standing before me now looks completely defeated and that's ten times more unnerving to me than his temper.

"Easton? What is it?"

"Helen's my tutor."

His explanation is so unexpected I can't help the laugh that falls from my lips, but it dies a short death when his face remains deadly serious. "Tutor?"

"I can't read, Scout. Is that what you want to know? That my brain can't read any better than an eight-year-old? That the words on the page shift and change when I stare at them and so I've skated by my whole goddamn life keeping this secret from everyone?" His voice escalates as his fear manifests with each word he speaks. My heart shatters into little pieces for him as he stands here in the middle of his foyer with the tears welling in his eyes. "So that's my secret. Are you happy now?"

"No." It's a whispered answer reflecting how stunned I am while he stares at me, a man broken by the cloak of shame he's wrapped himself in his whole life.

And it's only a split second of time, but I see the minute he feels the weight of what he's just confessed. He gasps and staggers backward a few steps before turning, pushing the button for the elevator, and getting on it.

I call to him as the doors begin to move but he doesn't stop them from closing. He just lowers his head and lets them shut.

And I'm left staring at them in shock, with whiplash so violent my brain hasn't quite caught up to grasp the magnitude of what he's clearly struggled with for years.

I should run after him.

I should prevent him from leaving by telling him it's going to be all right.

But I think we both need a bit of time to wrap our heads around what he just bared.

I am stunned.

Completely, utterly stunned.

CHAPTER TWENTY-EIGHT

Scout

"H e's not here," Manny calls out and startles me as I jog through the clubhouse. "He was here about two hours ago but then he was headed home." He steps into view, concern written all over his face. He must know how upset Easton was about the broadcast.

"He did come home, but then he left again. I just really need to find him."

"He finally told you, didn't he?"

My feet falter at his words and I stare at him wondering if he's talking about the same thing I'm worried about. And yet he can't be. But the look on his face, the concern and empathy he's emitting, tells me he does.

"Don't worry," he says after we stare at each other for a few minutes. "You don't have to say anything to me and betray his confidence. I liked you before, but I like you better now because of that . . . but know that *I know*. Easton doesn't know I do, but I do. When he was little, I was the one who sat and helped Easton with his homework. His dad's rule was it had to be finished before he was allowed to go sit in the dugout and watch the game. I was the only one around to help him when he struggled to complete it."

My eyes well with tears as I think of the frustrated little boy hiding his trouble from the world. "Manny, I don't know what to say."

"You don't have to say anything, Scout. I knew he couldn't keep it a secret forever, and yet it was never my place to say anything to him. It's his business. But he's like a son to me, and my heart broke for him last night when I watched the broadcast. He was so incredible, and then he wasn't. I knew why, and I hated myself for not reaching out to him and trying to help him somehow."

"It's not your fault," I say, but his expression says he doesn't believe that's true. I think he's as upset over watching Easton's humiliation as I am.

"Just know that I don't think he's ever told anyone. For a man to have to admit his shortcomings to the woman he loves and think she'll look at him as less once he does is a damn hard pill to swallow."

"I'd never think less of him. In fact I think more of him for finally admitting it."

He sniffs back the moisture pooling in the corner of his eyes despite his muted smile. "I knew you would. And for the record, I don't know nothing about nothing." He nods. "I've got to get back to work, and you need to get out of here since it's your day off." But I don't move, I remain in place as I contemplate my next move. "Try the Little League field," he advises before turning and walking down the hall.

Of course. The place he goes to clear his head.

With each step I take on my way to the park, I replay the facts and figures I'd researched once Easton left. The ones that kept me from chasing him down and denying him the time he most likely needed to come to terms with knowing that someone else knows his secret.

After a lifetime of protecting it, it's probably hard to process.

Every part of me sighs in relief and sags with despair when I reach the park and see the figure dressed in black sitting alone on the outfield slope.

Easton.

I make my way over to where he's sitting and take a seat beside him without saying a word. Our silence stretches as I pull out pieces of grass and split them apart.

I wait patiently, knowing Easton needs to take the first step in this conversation. I sought him out to show him I wasn't running away, but I can't force what happens next. Letting him lead wherever this conversation goes might help him feel in control of something when everything else in his world seems so out of control.

While I wait for him to figure out how much he does or doesn't want to talk about this, I think about my Google search after he left. Article after article about blue-chip college athletes who couldn't read or write with more than a fourth grade ability and yet they were given degrees because they were the cornerstone of whatever team they played for. I looked up dyslexia, trying to figure out if that's what Easton meant about how the words shift and change. I gorged on the information, reading as quickly as possible to try and understand more, and to occupy my time to prevent me from chasing after him.

And I looked for signs I've missed in our time together, but there really aren't many. He's become a master at disguise.

He has a literacy charity. I thought he was trying to help kids out—be a good guy. To draw the conclusion that he, himself, suffered from it would have been asinine. I think of the papers he was looking over and threw on the table. He told me they were lessons for the kids. Looking back, I wonder if they were Helen's lessons for him.

He loved audiobooks. *Big deal.* A lot of people love audiobooks. That doesn't mean they can't read.

I try to think of any one time that stands out where he was more than obvious and I can't. He's so practiced in hiding it that even the woman he lives with didn't realize it.

And then it hits me. The contract. The signatures agreeing to being traded or demoted to Triple-A.

And as if he's reading my mind, he finally speaks. "It wasn't Finn's fault, you know?"

"I realize that now," I say softly.

"He wasn't even there. I signed the papers. It all happened so quickly. Tillman shoved the papers in front of me, and I didn't have the time to work out what they said. I couldn't make them make sense."

"You were in pain."

"That's no excuse." His laugh is self-deprecating. "I let you assume it was Finn, blame him, and that's pretty shitty of me to allow you to think ill of a guy who has done nothing but protect me my whole career. I'm the reason I was traded to the Wranglers. Fuck, *that's* hard to say out loud." He pauses and lies back on the grass, looking at the sky that's turning orange from the approaching sunset. "I'm the one who caused all this. I'm the one who put myself in the position no one would have ever agreed to and all because I can't read."

The words clog in his throat, almost as if they are physically hard for him to say aloud, and I get it. They must be. I nod, uncertain what to say. I want to keep him talking like I did the last time I sat next to him on the grassy slope in the outfield. This time though, there is no game going on to run distraction. It's just him. And me. And everything left unspoken.

The field before us is empty. The bases have been removed. The chalk lines erased by little feet that have run over them. Proof that everything can be made to look perfect if need be.

Just like Easton has had to do.

"I've always been able to outrun it. Slide by. High school was easy—I became the master at cheating. Notes written on my palm. Papers scooted to the edge of the table of the girl sitting beside me. A little flirting goes a long way at that age. College was tougher, but when I found out I could pay people to write my papers or I was conveniently sick for exams, I was given more leeway—take-home tests others did for me . . . you name it, and blue-chip athletes like me get it. The administration doesn't care if you can't pass a class—they'll fix it for you—so long as you win the college World Series and bring more money into their school. Advertising dollars and team memorabilia can fund an awful lot of salaries. And when I couldn't get around reading a book, I'd get the e-textbooks. They were particularly helpful when I could listen to them on the voice app thing a Kindle has."

"Like Whispersync?"

"At times, yeah." I glance back to him and hate that he won't look me in the eyes. He shouldn't fear what I'm thinking of him. "Then when I was drafted my sophomore year, it was the biggest relief to not have to be constantly stressed over managing it all. I figured I'd beaten the system and came out no worse for wear. I was a major league baseball player. *Why did I need to fix the problem now?* I had Finn, who I trusted, and if I really needed to read something, I'd make an excuse so I could take it home and take the time to figure it out."

"Your parents didn't know? Finn doesn't know?" I ask, thinking back to how easy Manny picked up on it, but know that's not my secret to tell.

He shoves up off the grass and walks back and forth a few feet, the nervous energy eating him up. "I always thought they knew—I mean, how could they not? But with my dad traveling all the time and me pulling in passing grades, they thought I had somehow gotten a handle on the reading that had troubled me in first and second grade . . ."

"That must have been so hard for you though."

"Hard?" He laughs. "That's an understatement. I've become the master at distraction when I have to read something. I mean, give me enough time, and I can figure the words out. I can make out which ones are faced the wrong way and then sound the word out—my God, I feel like such a loser saying this to you. I'm an adult and I have to study a paragraph for an hour like a third grader so I can understand it."

He stops moving, closes his eyes, and pinches the bridge of his nose as he attempts to control the anger and shame before turning his back to me. His shoulders are strong and proud and I can't imagine what this is doing to him having to explain something that most would find fault with him over.

But not me.

"Easton . . . you don't have to explain anything," I murmur softly.

He laughs in response and draws in a deep breath but remains facing away. "I know I don't . . . but at the same time I do. You probably already think less of me for it, so I need to get it all out now."

"No. I don't. I think you're brave, East—"

"Brave?" He turns back around, arms out at his sides and face a mask of confusion. "How can you think someone who's basically spent their whole life tricking people into thinking he's smart, is brave?"

"Is that what you think you were doing? Tricking people? I call it surviving, Easton. Sure it wasn't life or death, but it was your battle. Your struggle." I rise to my feet so I can match him word for word. "And no one is allowed to tell you it isn't important or you're any less of a man because of it. So I don't want to hear you say it again. I don't think it. I'm here. I'm not going anywhere. So you need to figure out how to handle the fact that I know and don't think any less of you at all. You got that?"

He just stares at me as if he wants to believe me but is afraid to. I hate every bit of self-doubt I see plaguing him.

There's a shout on the field at his back and he turns to see what it is. A man and two middle school-aged boys jog onto the field. We watch as they begin to set up what appears to be batting practice: a bucket of balls on the mound with the dad, one kid putting on a helmet at the plate, the other grabbing his glove and running to left field. The dad eyes us for a moment, strangers on the hill, before tipping his hat to let us know he sees us and then turning to instruct his son at the plate.

We watch this as-old-as-time-dance between fathers and sons. The dad pitches, the son hits, and the dad instructs before starting the process all over again. The one boy in the outfield near us glances our way every once in a while when he has to shag a ball that has bounced near us. He has the same dark features as Easton and for a few brief moments, I picture Easton as a father doing the same thing with his sons someday.

The thought brings a smile to my lips.

"Kid's got a good swing," he says after a while, falling back on the easy topic of conversation.

"You would know," I nod, quick with the praise. "Tell me about Helen. That must have been a huge step for you." Just saying her name reminds me of that fleeting fear I had that he'd cheated on me.

I hate that he's still hesitating but I need him to know he can talk to me about this. The more he does, the less he'll feel isolated in what must have been a pretty paranoid and lonely world.

"After I signed the addendum and Finn saw it, I knew I'd screwed up. Ironically I didn't even know how bad considering Cory only forwarded the trade agreement and not the Triple-A one." He shakes his head.

"Asshole."

He chuckles and nods. "True. Finn became unglued when he found out what Tillman had done. Having me sign them without representation. From there on out, he started questioning every move Cory made when it came to me and tried to alert Boseman of them."

I nod, so very glad I was wrong about Finn.

"But the more Finn pushed, the more scared I grew that he'd figure out the truth. So I tried to play it off with him. I told him to drop his complaint to Boseman about Cory making me sign the addendum under duress. I assured him it didn't matter anyway because I'd be rehabbed and healthy and would get reinstated. Little did I know what else Cory was going to pull." He shakes his head. "It was my fault, Scout. I let you blame Finn, but it was one hundred percent on me. Christ, it was the first time my inability to read had a monumental effect on my life."

"You were in severe pain. You can't know if you would have done anything differently."

"I made the same excuse to myself at first. Believe me, I was the king of spinning the truth to make me feel better . . . but, there were serious repercussions this time around. I knew I needed to do something, and then coincidently, I had a meeting with the volunteers at the Literacy Project. Helen was working there to get hours in for one of her classes—she's studying for her teaching certificate at University of Texas. She's great with the kids, patient, knowledgeable. I knew she was struggling with studying and working two jobs to pay for school . . . so I made her an offer: I'd pay for her tuition, if she'd tutor someone for me. After realizing I wasn't joking, she was thrilled at the prospect. I had my lawyer draw up agreements binding her seven ways from Sunday from disclosing who she was tutoring. Once she signed everything, I let her know it was me."

I imagine how surprised she must have been as we watch the two boys switch spots. They stop for a moment to talk as they pass each other, both looking our way briefly before settling into their new positions.

"We've made some progress. I've become quicker at tricking my eyes to make the letters go the right way and reposition them, but I still have a long way to go."

"But at least you're on your way."

"Being on my way doesn't fix what happened last night. God, it was *horrible*." He sighs the word out and scrubs his hands over his face as he relives the evening. "I didn't know I was going to have to read anything, Scout. I would have never agreed to it had I known. I thought it was the same as when I've been in the booth here. You just talk, shoot the shit about baseball, and that's it. Now I'm the universal hashtag and poster boy for dumb jocks everywhere."

"It wasn't that bad—" I start, but he holds up his hand.

"Don't. I don't need to be coddled. I saw everything from the posts on social media to listening to Jim Rome bash me on the radio. I know how bad the comments are, and you know what? They're right. When the teleprompter started scrolling, it was moving so fast I couldn't use the strategies Helen is teaching me to trick my brain and make sense of the letters. I froze. Plain and simple. I was caught so flatfooted that trying to cover it up would have only made it worse. It was bad. I know it. And the critics and anonymous keyboard warriors sure as shit know it."

"For all they know, it's just what Bud said. The teleprompter was broken and they didn't teach you the controls of the soundboard."

"In a perfect world, yes. But this world is far from perfect. Bud was there. The camera crew and sound engineers were there. They know there was nothing wrong . . . and all it takes is one of them to have a beer with a friend, make a comment in passing, and next thing you know, Easton Wylder is exactly what all the kids in school used to call me. *Dumb. Stupid. Slow. Retarded.*"

"And?"

"And what?" He turns to look at me like I'm crazy.

"Anyone who has ever listened to you speak or been around you knows that's not true. And that's a lot of people, Easton. Just because you can't read well doesn't mean you're not intelligent. You've made sure you were educated in other ways . . . so what's the big deal if people find out? No, hear me out," I say as he starts to argue with me. "People don't need to know you can't read. All they'd know is you have dyslexia and the teleprompter was moving too quickly for you."

"Why would I ever do that?" he asks, the words a hushed whisper as if it's incomprehensible why I'd suggest something so *ridiculous*.

"Because dyslexia isn't something to be ashamed about. There are so many others out there like you, Easton. People who are embarrassed because they too have a learning disability and are afraid others will make fun of them. Like the kids in your program, for one. What if they knew the man they idolized was just like them and still successful?" He shakes his head. "There's power in sharing your shortcomings with others. It may open you up, but it could allow others to overcome their own hurdles."

His hand goes up to pull on the back of his neck as he turns to watch the boys and their dad still at it. Pitch. Hit. Instruct. Repeat. Focusing on them is the only way he can escape from the riot of insecurities inside of him.

The kid at the plate cranks a fly ball to left field. The pop off the bat is unmistakable as it soars high in the sky. The dad gives a huge whoop as the other son runs our way. When the ball stops a few feet before us, Easton steps forward and picks it up just as the kid slows to a stop before him.

"I think this belongs to you," he says as he holds out the ball. When the boy looks up from the ball to Easton and realizes who is standing in front of him, his expression is absolutely priceless.

"*Holy shit,*" he says and then startles when he realizes he cussed and puts his hand up to his mouth. "You're—he's—oh my God—don't tell my dad I said shit—*Dad!*"

By this time the kid's father is making his way to us, curious about the stranger talking to his son with his other boy not far behind. Their reaction is just as priceless when they recognize Easton. All three of them are slack-jawed with shock.

Once the dad collects himself, he reaches his hand out. "Leo Tompkins. And this is Ollie and Archie. We're all huge fans. How's the shoulder healing? And a *Wrangler*? Really? How are you—sorry, I'm rambling. I'll stop now."

Easton chuckles and the sound is so very welcome after the despondency I've heard in his voice today. "Easton Wylder. It's a pleasure and the shoulder's slow going, but it's healing." They shake hands. "And this is Scout Dalton." Introductions are made and then Easton turns to Ollie and Archie. "You've both got great swings. Keep practicing with your dad, and you'll be hitting it out of the park like it's nothing."

Both boys look star-struck from his praise—eyes wide and full of disbelief—and I wish Easton could see that *this* is what people see. Not his shortcomings or what he deems as flaws. *But this.* The whole package. The personable hero that little boys and girls all over Austin and beyond wish to grow up and be like someday.

"Thank you," Ollie says. "I want to play just like you when I grow up."

"Can you autograph a baseball for us?" Archie asks.

"Sure, but I don't have a pen," Easton says as both the kids and the dad look deflated when they realize that not one of us have one. "How about this? How about you head over to the stadium tomorrow before the game. You ask for Manny Winfield at the ticket booth. I'll have him come and take you for a tour of the locker room and dugout during batting practice."

"Are you serious?" Ollie asks, his voice escalating in pitch with each word as Archie all but hops out of his shoes.

"Dead serious."

"Thank you, so much. That's very generous of you," Leo says putting his arms on both boys' shoulders. "Let's leave Mr. Wylder alone now. We've taken enough of his time."

"Not a problem," Easton says as Leo physically steers his boys to turn around and start walking the other way. "Ollie, try and keep your hands still before the pitch. It'll help with your bat speed. And Archie, close your stance up a bit so you can reach the outside pitch."

They both look back to him again and give eager nods before walking toward the infield, their infectious chatter floating back to us.

"What if one of those boys couldn't read? Do you think they'd think any less of you if they knew you had trouble too, or do you think they'd still think you were their hero? I know which one I'd put my money on."

"I never asked to be anyone's hero, Scout, let alone the poster child for illiteracy. There's a lot of responsibility that comes with something like that when I already have enough shit to deal with."

"Okay," I murmur. He's irritated, and I'm pushing when I shouldn't be, but I know this would help him. Not only would it give this selfless man a different kind of motivation to conquer his demons, it would also show him that the public still loves him regardless of what he deems to be his faults.

"Thank you for coming . . . for talking to me . . . but I kind of want to be alone right now."

I stare at him—at those conflicted brown eyes—and as much as I want to stay, sit with him and help him not feel so alone, I know I need to give him the time he's asking for.

I press a kiss to the backside of his shoulder. "Okay." Begrudgingly I start to walk away and then stop. "There are no conditions to my love for you, Easton. It's not that you play baseball or your ability to read or your public persona that attract me to you. Those things will come and go and change over time. It's your heart I love. It's your ability to open up to me even when you don't want to. The man you are makes me want to be a better woman, too. So, I'll give you time to think and be alone when I really don't want to as long as you understand I want you. All of you. Your flaws. Your mistakes. Your achievements. Your shortcomings. Your love."

He turns toward me and the look in his eyes tells me he understands.

It tells me he's coming home to me.

It tells me he knows I love him for him.

It tells me he loves me too.

CHAPTER TWENTY-NINE

Easton

"Hi, Momma." I slide into the booth beside her.

"Easton. Why are you here?" She looks around the dim bar like a scared rabbit. "Did Marty call you? I've been good. I promise I've only had a few drinks tonight."

I reach out and give her a hug. She still wears the same perfume I can remember from my childhood, and right now it's comforting. Sure there's cigarette smoke clinging to her clothes and alcohol on her breath, but that perfume makes me feel like I'm eight. When she patched up my skinned knees from crashing after trying to jump my BMX bike off my homemade ramp. Whenever anything happened, she pulled me in against her, kissed the top of my head, and told me it would be okay.

Is that why I came here when I left the Little League field? Is that why I drove an hour with Scout's parting words running through my mind and making me question how I deserve someone like her? Just to have my mom tell me it's all going to work out in the end somehow.

"Easton?"

"Yeah, I'm good," I say as I let her go and sit back to look at her. "I needed to take a drive to clear my head."

"Is something wrong? Did something happen?"

I stare at her and smile, wishing I could live in this oblivious, alcohol-induced make-believe world she lives in sometimes. Things would be so much easier.

"No. Everything is fine now."

"Oh. Good. I was worried maybe something happened to that nice young lady you brought here the other day." She takes a sip of her drink as someone changes the music on the jukebox. Johnny Cash starts singing about falling into a ring of fire, and I glance around this sad state of a bar before looking back to her.

"No, she's fine."

"Well, that's good. I like her." Her smile widens. "And she sure is pretty."

"I like her too. And she is pretty." I shake my head. "There's no way in hell I deserve her."

"I disagree," she says, tipping her glass to me and asking if I want any. I decline. "Everyone deserves somebody."

"Yeah?" I don't know why that comment strikes a chord with me. The woman's talking about deserving love, yet she's been waiting for years for hers to come. "Does your true love deserve you, Mom? Because he's left you alone all this time so I really don't think he does."

"Shush. Don't say that. He'll come back. He promised to fix things, and then it would all be better."

"Make what better? And if he hasn't come back now, why do you still think he's going to return?" I demand, taking my own frustration out on her maddening devotion to a lover who probably doesn't even exist.

"Because he's *the one*." She shrugs as if it's a proven fact, and there is no disputing it.

"Who is *he*?"

"A lady never kisses and tells, Easton. You should know that."

"You're frustrating as hell, you know that? You wait for a man who hasn't returned and you still think he's *the one*?"

"You'll understand in time." She squeezes my hand, a soft smile turning up her lips as she gets a faraway look in her eyes as if she's remembering something. "There will come a day, son, when someone will love the parts of you that no one else knows how to love. That's when you know they're the one for you."

After all the shit that happened today, I can't do anything but stare at her and absorb the wisdom that hits way too close to home.

"Are you going to stay with me tonight? A new sofa cover from the Home Shopping Network came today that I bought just for you." Hope fills her voice but it's got nothing on the hope she unknowingly just gave my heart.

"I'm sorry. I need to get back."

There will come a day, son, when someone will love the parts of you that no one else knows how to love.

"You're still up."

"Mm-hmm. I wanted to make sure you were okay." Her voice is sleep-drugged and it calls to every part of me. *I need her.*

The condo is dark save for the under-cabinet kitchen lights and the glow from the skyline beyond. I leave it that way as I make my way to the silhouette of her sitting in my chair looking at the world beyond.

"*Are* you okay?" she asks as I walk past her and step up to the windows. I stare at the city below, the darkened ghost of a stadium. Other people are facing much worse things than I am, and yet that fear is still there, holding me back as its hostage. After a while, I turn to face her. She has on one of my T-shirts, her bare legs are curled under her, and she has a glass of wine in her hand. I can't see her eyes but the compassion in her voice rings in my ears—*the sound of some-one loving the parts of me that no one else has known how to*—and I know how goddamn lucky I am that Doc didn't show up to take the Aces' PT contract five months ago.

I may have thought she was a prank, but right now I'm pretty damn sure the prank was on me. How could I have ever known?

"I had a lot to think about, so I took a drive to clear my head," I say as I lean against the wall.

"Go anywhere noteworthy?"

I think of my mom. Of her hugs. Of her unexpected advice. "Not really."

"Were you successful in clearing your head?"

"Yes *and* no."

She makes a noncommittal sound as she takes a sip from her glass. We stare at each other through the darkness for a few minutes as I work up the courage to say what I need to say.

"What if my shoulder doesn't heal?" I ask, her body startling from my unexpected question. "The surgery could have gone per-fectly, and I have the best rehabber in baseball on my side, but what if my shoulder doesn't cooperate? What if I can't make it back again?"

"Then we cross that bridge if and when we come to it," she says cautiously.

"There's this moment right before a game starts. Sometimes it's when I'm putting on my gear in the dugout, other times it's that mo-ment right before the first pitch when the stadium hushes for that split second . . . it's part rush, part adrenaline . . . it's indescribable . . ." Struggling with how to put something so real into words when it's not anything concrete, I turn to look at the ballpark's shadow to try and help.

"*It's the magic,*" she murmurs as she falls into step beside me, leaving me to do a double take because once again she gets it—*gets me*—when no one else does.

"There you go putting words to my thoughts again."

"I guess that means we're a good team."

"A damn good team." I hook my pinky with hers needing something to ground me as we wade through a room full of unspoken words. I feel like I can breathe for the first time since I got off the plane this morning. "I felt it last night."

Her pinky stiffens in mine and I know she's following my train of thought—because it's her—but she lets my comment settle before speaking. "Felt what?"

I clear my throat and second-guess myself, but I come up with the same answer I had driving back from my mom's. "There was a moment before the cameras turned on when I was sitting in that booth looking at the field before me. The energy in the air . . . and that magic—the feeling I thought was isolated to being *on* the field as a player before a game started—*I felt it, Scout.*"

"The magic," she whispers as she steps into me and slides her arms around my waist.

And after the day I've had, this, *her*, is what I need. The way she understands me. The way she doesn't push me but does. The silent reassurance. We stand like this for a moment. Me breathing her in and coming to terms with the fact that she's one helluva woman, and I do deserve her.

"There's more," she murmurs and presses a kiss to my shoulder. "What are you not telling me?"

And there she goes again. Stealing my thoughts when I believed it was only my heart she'd stolen.

"What if I blew my one shot, Scout? I've never thought of life after baseball—it's always been the focus of everything—but when it ends, do you know what I'd give to have a career where I can still feel that magic? To have the opportunity to remain a part of baseball? What if being a sportscaster is that chance and I just fucked it up because I can't read?" Frustrated that I'm not explaining myself very well, I step away from Scout and pace to the far side of the room before turning and facing her. "God, that sounds pathetic, but—"

"No, it doesn't," she says as she takes a step toward me. "It sounds mature and intelligent."

"You're making me sound like an old man." I chuckle, suddenly uncomfortable. It's one thing to think about life after baseball, but it's another thing to actively consider it. When there is no more showing up to the ballpark. No more locker room bullshit with the guys. No more jogging onto the field with the feeling of my gear clinking together at the knees. No more figuring out how to get my opponent at the plate to strike out.

"I think it's brilliant actually."

That comment stops the hand running through my hair. "What do you mean?"

"Fox Sports is still looking for their postseason commentator. What if you asked for another shot?"

This time my laugh is long and rich. "You actually think they'd give me another shot? You have seen the fallout on social media, haven't you?"

"Yes, I have. But what if Finn goes to them, explains the truth or if you're uncomfortable with that makes some reasonable excuse, and gets you a second chance."

The thought of having to tell Finn the truth, let alone the powers that be at Fox Sports, makes me want to choke on the air I'm breathing. I can stand in a stadium full of sixty thousand fans and not flinch, but this—people knowing my truth—makes my stomach churn.

"You're missing the biggest point of all."

"And that is?"

"I still can't read. I still can't decipher as quickly as the teleprompter scrolls, and it would just end up . . ." Jesus Christ. The thought alone drives me to walk into the kitchen and grab a beer from the refrigerator.

"Then Helen and I can spend double time teaching you. Trying to train your brain into seeing the words straight." She follows me into the kitchen, her voice insistent and tinged with optimism. "We practice, and we ask for the script ahead of time, and we make it work, Easton. Because you were hiding this before, you were only getting minimal studying in, but now, with me knowing and with you having downtime with your recovery, you don't have to hide anymore in your own home. And then once you nail it—because I have faith you will—you can choose whether to explain the truth to people about what happened the first go-round. Those kids, the ones who are scared to death they're going to be made fun of, will realize it's going to be okay. Their hero is just like them."

"Scout, I don't know . . ."

"I know you don't. And you might not see it for a while . . . but I can't imagine the pressure you've felt, having to hide this for so long. Can you imagine what it would feel like if you didn't have to hide anymore? The pressure to be something you're not would be gone."

I hate that the idea both excites me and scares the ever-loving shit out of me. I appreciate her unwavering faith in me. But more than anything I hate hearing the hope in her voice when I know I'll most likely let her down. But . . . she *loves the parts of me that no one else has known how to.* Is that enough?

Staring at her expectant eyes, the panic I've lived with my whole life resurfaces with a vengeance. I can tell the minute she sees it because she smiles softly and presses a soft kiss to my lips.

"I'm sorry. I know how capable and incredible you are. I know your fears are real and valid, but so is *possibility.* That's all I'll say. I won't bring it up again."

God, I love this woman and her rose-colored glasses.

Even at my worst, she still sees the best in me.

CHAPTER THIRTY

Easton

What the hell is he doing here?

I hang up the phone on Alec downstairs in the lobby and wait in my foyer for the elevator to ascend and the doors to open.

And when they do slide open I'm greeted by the hulking figure standing there. The man I was intimidated by as a child when I went to work with my dad. The man I've grown to respect as an adult playing for his team.

"Mr. Boseman," I say as he walks off the elevator and gives a cursory look around before shaking my extended hand.

"Easton. Good to see you."

"Likewise." I hate that my hopes surge momentarily from his unprecedented house call, but know there's no way in hell he's coming to offer me my job back. "To what do I owe this pleasure?"

"May I come in for a moment?" he asks, already walking into the open space, a man not used to waiting for others.

"Yes, please." I follow him and wonder what's going on.

He walks toward the wall of windows and spends a moment taking in the sight as most do. His hands are in his pockets, his suit jacket pulled tight over his shoulders, and he wears cowboy boots on his feet. He looks every part the oil tycoon that he is, less the cowboy hat that has left an indentation on his salt-and-pepper hair but is nowhere to be seen.

"Quite a view," he says with a nod as he turns around and faces me. We look at each other for a moment before he speaks. "I've done a lot of business dealings in my time, Easton. Some I'm proud of. Some I've been extremely successful at. A few that didn't sit well with me."

"Okay." I draw the word out, knowing that Ted Boseman likes to set the stage when he's working toward making a point.

"How long have I known you?" he asks before answering it himself. "Most your life?"

"Pretty much."

"I think of you like family. I think of all my players like family but you especially. In saying that, I hope you'll hear me when I say that what Tillman did to you is one of those things that didn't sit well with me."

"Thank you, sir." *What else can I say?*

"I was off pretending I was on Survivor in the Amazon trying to stave off a second midlife crisis, and he was here trying to screw up my organization." He clears his throat and looks back toward the stadium below. "I hired him because of his reputation. I've been preoccupied with business the past two years and things got a little out of hand in the front office. I talked to some fellow owners and heard about Cory Tillman and how he was able to cut costs and streamline other organizations. Trimmed the fat, if you will, as is needed every so often when running a business. I ignored the pissed-off players he had traded—their talk of him being unethical—and chalked it up to them being angry at being uprooted."

"Understandable," I say feeling like I need to participate in this one-sided conversation.

"As you know, I hired him. I gave him a budget I wanted him to be under and the authority to cut where he thought things needed to be cut to hit it. I even dangled a Texas-sized bonus for him if he could hit my budget by season's end. But see, that was where I was shortsighted and preoccupied elsewhere. You don't give a man carte blanche and then not expect him to cut your franchise player to make it easier to hit that budget in one fell swoop. Your salary is . . . *was* one of our largest. Our pockets are nowhere as deep as say, the Yankees, and so by trading you and bringing a catcher in at half the price, the budget becomes lower and that bonus a lot more attainable for Tillman."

"I appreciate you telling me," I say but don't understand why he's coming forward now and saying all of this. What has changed?

"Upon my return and hearing your agent's *numerous* messages, I was enlightened on the many things Tillman had done in my absence. Things that my other managers should have caught but didn't. Ethically questionable things. I called around to the other organizations he's worked for, spoke to the players who had been traded, and their answers—the ones I should have listened to originally—pissed me off." He runs a hand through his hair before taking a seat on the edge of the couch. "Why didn't you come to me after he made you sign those addendums when you were first hurt?"

Uncomfortable, I shift my feet. Do I tell him the truth? Admit that I can't read for shit and so I pulled Finn from pursuing it with him? That doesn't exactly make me look too bright. "You hired him so I figured you knew what was going on. It doesn't exactly look professional to complain to the owner when you don't like the new boss."

When I turn back around, his lips are pursed and he's sitting with his elbows on his knees and hands.

"I let Tillman go today. I had to pay a pretty penny to buy him out of his contract, but I couldn't let him ruin my organization any more than he already has."

His admission may stagger me, but it's a lot too late. *For me, anyway.*

"I can't say I disagree with your decision," I finally say.

His laugh rumbles as he shakes his head. "I didn't think you would, son. I know it doesn't change the fact that you're still a *Wrangler.*" He spits the word out as if it's almost hard for him to mention our rival. "And I apologize to you for that. But it's important to me that you know if I ever get the chance to rectify that clusterfuck and bring you home, I will."

He rises to his feet and takes a step toward me, hand outreached to mine. I shake it. "Thank you."

"What I'd give to have you back and Santiago gone," he murmurs as he makes his way to the door, "but contracts are contracts and I can't force other teams to negate theirs too. I don't think the Wranglers would take too kindly to me trying to steal you back, but God knows I'll try in the future." He turns to look at me one last time. "Sorry for the house call, but I thought you deserved this apology in person."

I've said thank you enough times I feel like a broken record, so I don't say anything at all. Rather, I nod my head and accept an apology I never expected to get.

It takes a lot for a man to face his mistakes head-on.

I should know.

CHAPTER THIRTY-ONE

Scout

Holy shit.

Boseman really did it. That's my recurring thought as I lean against the wall outside the locker room to gather my thoughts after the phone call I received. Sure I need to call Easton—let him know if Boseman hasn't already himself—but first I need a few seconds to process the ramifications.

What this might mean for me and what it means to Easton.

A crowded clubhouse is not exactly the place I can do that. And as if on cue, hooting and hollering rings through the closed door as it opens and closes. The sound startles me into action. I need to get my things and head home so I can celebrate with Easton this *come-to-Karma* moment with him.

Right when I grab the handle to pull open the locker room door, I'm startled to see two sets of shoulders hunched over, as they talk about something in hushed tones. Cal and Santiago. *What the?* Cal sees me first—wide eyes and mouth shocked into an O—and before he can say a thing, I slip into the locker room, uncomfortable and confused about whatever they're talking about. *Again.*

It's none of your business. Just grab your bag and phone and head home.

But I can't stop thinking about them and what they could be discussing. Then again, Cal works for the Aces. He could be telling Santiago the same news I just received. Tillman is gone, and he better watch his back.

But the thought doesn't sit right with me. *Wouldn't Cal wait and let Santiago find out once Boseman makes an official announcement?*

"Boys, let's hope like hell the Tampa score stays where it is because then it's a done deal." JP whoops, getting a rise out of the guys and shocking me from overthinking something that's probably nothing to begin with. Wondering who Santiago talks to doesn't deserve another second of my time.

"Playoffs, here we come," Riddell shouts to a raucous set of cheers.

"Great game tonight, guys," I add to the conversation as I enter my office, grab my backpack, and head out as quickly as I went in.

"You gonna come watch the rest of the Tampa game with us at Sluggers? Let's call East to meet us there, and we can celebrate."

"I'm not sure what his plans are," I say, although I know damn well he's not ready to face the public yet after the Fox debacle. Then again, maybe he'll want to celebrate with his ex-teammates after I tell him the good news. "I'll check when I get home."

"You know when she says it like that," Drew teases, "it means bow-chicka-wow-wow time."

"Oh please." I roll my eyes and laugh.

"Nah. I doubt it." Santiago's voice rings loud and clear. He must have come into the locker room when I was in my office. I keep walking to the exit, determined to *not* let him ruin my good mood. "Easton's too busy licking his wounds after making a royal ass of himself on TV the other night. Uh. Uh. Duh. Uh," he stutters, mocking Easton.

The ass. My feet falter. My anger riots.

"Fuck off, Santiago." I think that's Tino. Or maybe JP. I'm not sure because I'm too busy seeing red.

"You can't hide stupid." He follows the comment by a sarcastic laugh that grates on every one of my nerves. "That says a lot about your standards, Scout."

"Don't," I shout to Drew and his clenched fists. The last thing he needs with the playoffs looming is a team suspension for beating the shit out of Santiago.

But I'm done. So fucking done with Santiago's shitty comments. Good thing the suspension caveat doesn't apply to me.

"Hey, Santiago," I say loud enough to draw attention and shock the shit out of the guys. Towels stop drying and shirts get yanked over heads as I step up onto the bench. "Does this shtick really work for you? How you keep bad-mouthing the guy who was here before you to distract others from the fact that your numbers will never match his? You could only wish to hold his stats. I mean, there's a reason your contract is half the amount of Easton's. Does that eat at you? You and your big-ass ego? How much longer do you think that's going to fly? Do you think once Boseman finds a new general manager he'll put up with this?" I love the shocked look on his face. The startled heads of the guys around me. I guess I just made the announcement myself. "Oh, did you not know that? My bad. I thought that's what Cal was just warning you about in the hallway. Yeah. Your time is limited here. Boseman fired Tillman. Yep. The only person in your corner in this organization is now gone." My smile is smug as I shake my head in disgust. "So if you want to talk about being stupid, you might want to look in the mirror considering you've gone out of your way to *not* make friends here. And oops, the one friend you did suck up to is gone."

He takes a few steps toward me, his shoulders proud, his body language defensive, his face a mask of indifference. I know damn well I got to him and his sensitive ego. "You're a bitch, you know that?"

The guys rustle around me with clenched fists. I don't need punches thrown in here when reporters are right outside. Not on my behalf.

I jump off the bench and step up to him. Sure he has a foot on me in height and an easy fifty pounds in weight, but I'm so sick of his shit, I don't care. "I may be a bitch, but you're a wanna-be," I grit out. "It must kill you to want to be just like the man you'll never hold a goddamn candle to. You've tried taking him out, you've tried taking his spot, and lo and behold he's still better than you. That must really eat at you. His talent trumps your mediocrity any day."

The muscle in his jaw ticks and every part of him bristles at my words that hit a little too close to home. He steps into me, threatening me with his physical size. The guys take a step closer but I don't move. I just stare at Santiago, refusing to back down. *There are advantages to being raised among men, after all.*

"Touch me. *Pretty please.* I dare you to try it because I bet Boseman will forgive each and every one of them for beating the shit out of you if you lay a hand on me. He's a gentleman like that."

He just stares, Adam's apple bobbing as he reins in his temper and the buttons I purposely pushed before taking a step back.

"Coward," I mutter. One last button to press. The asshole deserves it.

He ruined my good mood.

"Scout?" He knows already. The excitement and all-around carefree sound in his voice tells me. "Did you hear?"

He meets me with a glass of wine and swift kiss as I come into the kitchen. I laugh as his good hand tries to roam freely over my ass.

"I did. I got the call right before I left."

"Son of a bitch deserves it."

"He does." I nod and take a sip, hiding my own concerns. "And did."

We're reviewing the moves Mr. Tillman made during his time in the position. He let a lot of people go and opened up the club to lawsuits, Ms. Dalton. Your position and probationary contract will be under review as well.

"Boseman came to see me."

"Like came here? To the house?" I ask, surprised he'd go that extra mile, but then again, it is Easton. And he did say he feared lawsuits.

"Yeah. Shocked the shit out of me, but he explained everything. How Tillman did what he did, and then he apologized for what he did to me."

"That's good, right?"

"It doesn't change a damn thing for me. The trade was still made. I'm still a Wrangler. He even said he'll work to try and get me back, but hell if it doesn't take some of the sting out of it."

"I'm glad then," I say as I step into him and accept the welcome-home kiss he gives me. This is so much better than last night. His laughter. His upbeat mood. The sound of a man vindicated.

I'll take it any day.

And I'll worry about how this affects me later.

How I may be out of a job.

CHAPTER THIRTY-TWO

Scout

I press my fingers to my eyes for a moment and take a deep breath before looking at the hospice paperwork. The doctor said it was precautionary, but after another stint in the hospital this week, he handed me the packet with my dad's discharge papers, and told me I needed to have a look at it. My dad's health is only going to decline more rapidly, so I need to mentally prepare myself for the next steps.

I flip through the pages and skim over the dos and don'ts and how to know when it's time to call hospice to come in. But it's too much for me right now. I don't want to accept this yet. I shouldn't have to.

And yet the doctor gave them to me.

I close the folder and push it away. Out of sight, out of mind. Do I really want some stranger there with us in his final hours? Wouldn't it be better if it were just Sally and me? Then again, death is a scary thing that I'm not sure I can face on my own. I'm petrified to admit it, but when the time comes, am I going to be able to hold his hand and talk to him as he takes his last breaths or am I going to want to run and hide and pretend it's not happening?

Both terrify me.

Easton's laughter rings through the condo. It's a welcome sound—the sound of hope cutting through my silent despair—and one I've heard over the past few hours since Helen's been here working with Easton.

"I'm heading out," Helen says to me as she pokes her head into my office.

"It's already that time?" I check my watch and can't believe I've been sitting here procrastinating and doing little for two hours.

"Yes." She lowers her voice, but her smile remains. "He's different now with the sessions. He wanted to learn before, but now it's like he has something to prove. When he gets frustrated, he powers through instead of wanting to end for the day. I'm pretty sure that's because of you."

"Thank you for telling me that," I say and she nods and heads to the door. *It's exactly what I needed to hear.* Tears well in my eyes and a lump forms in my throat. Her words mean more to me than she could ever imagine. I've spent hours dealing with something I have absolutely no control over or cannot influence in any way—my dad's health—to being told my support has given Easton new legs to stand on.

"Hey, you." Arms slip around my waist and pull me back against the hard length of his body.

"A good session?"

"Mm-hmm," he murmurs and presses a kiss to the back of my head. "I won't bore you with the details but it was better than good. Breakthrough kind of good."

The happiness in his voice warms so many parts of me.

"That's great to hear."

"Any news from Boseman yet?"

"No." I link my fingers through his that are around my waist and try not to think about my upcoming meeting with the owner of the Aces. Currently they're in the midst of reviewing all contracts Cory

Tillman initiated in an attempt to figure out whether he wants to keep them or void them. And of course that includes mine.

"Hey." He turns my shoulders so I'm forced to face him. "Boseman is a good man. Case in point, seeing the bastard that Tillman was and firing him even though he had a solid contract. I'm certain it cost him a fortune, but he knew it was the right thing to do . . . just like I'm sure he'll know that giving you the team contract is the right thing to do."

"I know. I just feel like the earth is continually shifting under my feet these days, and it's only going to get worse with everything to come." I think of my dad, of the hospice paperwork on the desk, and hate that I know this discombobulated feeling I have has nothing on what I'll be feeling sooner than I'd like.

"Go get some fancy clothes on," he says, shocking me to look up. I'm met with a wide smile and mischievous eyes. "Let's go out."

"But I thought you were still . . ."

"Screw the press," he says, waving his hand in indifference. "There will always be an asshole somewhere with a loud mouth calling me a dumb jock. I'm a big boy. I can handle myself. Besides, since the Aces made the playoffs, attention has shifted gears."

I love how this little bit of confidence he gained today has made him care less.

"Where are we going?"

"I don't know, Scout, but we're going to have some fun."

And the minute I buy into his infectious mood and turn to go get dressed, the buzzer on the door rings.

"Buzz kill," he says with a laugh as he heads over to it. "Go get dressed. I'll get rid of whoever it is quickly."

But for some reason, I don't move. There are a select few who have elevator access to the penthouse. Security didn't call to tell us there's a visitor so it has to be someone on the list.

"Dad. Long time, no see, Derek. How long has it been, man? What are you guys doing here?"

Cal steps off the elevator and gives Easton a pat on the back of his good shoulder and greetings are given all around between the three. I stare from where I'm standing in the kitchen at baseball legend, Derek Penbrooke. The man known for his bat in clutch situations, his three thousand-plus hit career, and his ten Gold Glove Awards for fielding.

"Derek was in town, so we had a late lunch together to catch up. We talked about the club, about that asshole Tillman, and then he asked how your arm was doing so I thought we'd stop by and check on you." Cal looks every part the proud father. I hate that I question if it's an act or if it's the truth.

Easton glances my way, an apology written all over his face and I just shrug. It's not exactly how I thought our night would unfold, but the smile on his face is sincere and I love seeing it there.

"Oh, Scout, I didn't see you there." Cal walks over to me, voice booming, chest puffed out. "Derek, are you familiar with Doc Dalton?"

"Very much so." He smiles. It's warm and genuine and draws me to take a step toward him. "He worked on my shoulder way back when."

"You mean back in the Ice Age?" Cal asks.

"If I was playing then, so were you, Wylder," Derek says with a laugh.

"This is Scout," Easton interjects. "Doc's daughter."

Derek narrows his eyes as he stares at me for an odd moment. "Well, what do you know? That is you. Last time I saw you, you were about this tall," he says, holding his hand at about three feet high. "You were chewing a wad of bubble gum too big for your mouth, had a bunch of freckles on your nose, and were giggling like mad with that brother of yours. Scout Dalton. My how you have grown."

"Good to see you again, Derek," I say with a smile and warm shake of his hand.

"How is that old man of yours? Rumor has it he hasn't been

working much lately. Has the retirement bug gotten hold of him?"

"Something like that."

"Scout's taking over the business if and when he does," Easton says, saving me from having to add one more white lie to the mountain I'm making.

"Come on in, gentleman," I say with a smile. "Can I get any of you a drink?"

"So there was a purpose to his little stop by." Easton laughs before bringing the bottle of beer to his lips.

"Your old man had ulterior motives," Derek says with an unabashed shrug. "Like that should surprise you. Two surgeries on this cuff, Easton, and the second was definitely harder to bounce back from, but once I did, wowee, it was perfectly fine. I won a Gold Glove and smashed forty-something homers that next season."

"Is this your way of trying to tell me it'll be okay, Dad?" Easton asks with a roll of his eyes as he taps the neck of his beer against Derek's.

"Just trying to give you a little positive reinforcement is all. Let you see that if you do what you're supposed to do, you'll return next season and kick some serious ass."

"Pushy fucker," Easton says but his lips are all smile.

"Someone's got to be."

I stand in the kitchen and listen to them drone on and on. The laughter is rich and continuous as the three men talk baseball and club politics and the upcoming match-ups for the playoffs. It's the most at ease I've ever seen Easton with his dad, and it's the most I've ever heard him talk baseball outside his teammates.

I pour more wine in my glass and when I turn around, Cal is standing on the other side of the island, head angled to the side, blatantly studying me.

"Did you need another beer?" I ask, suddenly nervous under his scrutiny.

"No. Thanks." He glances back to where Easton and Derek are laughing about something and then back to me. "So, Scout, are you living here now?"

I purse my lips as I contemplate how to answer, because for some reason, I feel like I'm being judged. "I have my own place still, if that's what you're asking."

"But this thing between you two is serious then?"

What's with the fifty questions?

"I'd say so, yes." I watch and wait for a reaction but his expression remains stoic.

"That's good. I'm really glad he has someone like you to help him through this tough time. Between the shoulder being reinjured and the damn broadcasting blunder, he needs someone supportive on his side."

Exactly. It's not like he can count on you, Cal, to be that for him.

I stare at him for a beat, hearing the words he's saying. However, I get the sense that he means something else. "He's a good man," I finally reply following Cal's glance to the family room where Easton listens intently to a story Derek is telling him.

Every part of Easton's smile is worth a missed night out with him.

"I know the next few months are going to be difficult for him. Itching to start rehab. Mentally readying himself so he doesn't fear injuring his shoulder again." He takes a sip of beer. "And whatever else life throws at him."

I murmur a noncommittal sound, wondering what *that* means. There can't possibly be more life can throw Easton's way to shock him after the year he's had.

CHAPTER THIRTY-THREE

Scout

"Sorry again."

"Don't be." I look up from the bed where I'm perusing my iPad and stare at Easton. He's fresh from the shower, jogging pants slung way too low on his hips—like it-should-be-illegal *low*—and his hair is still dripping wet.

Definitely don't be sorry if this is the view I get as a consolation prize.

"I'm the one who should apologize. I know this has been hard on you—all of it—but until I listened to the three of you talking tonight, I don't think I realized exactly how hard." I scrunch up my face because I know that sounds stupid. "I mean, of course I realized it, but after listening to Derek describe his injuries and recovery I kept thinking about you and how you must feel going through this for a second time in less than a year. It must be maddening."

"That's putting it lightly," he says and twists his lips in thought. "This time is different though. I don't feel as isolated as I did the first go-round."

"Why's that?" I'd think it would be the exact opposite. The

season's moved on. Teams have moved on. The postseason is here.

And he's basically missed all of it.

"Of course, I feel left behind. It's like I was with the cool kids and then all of a sudden I'm on the outside looking in on a life I used to have."

"You'll be back next season, though."

He shrugs. "Hopefully. But like I said, it's different this time."

"How's that?"

"*I have you.*" The words alone make my heart skip a beat, but the matter-of-fact way he says it causes me to melt in a way I never imagined possible.

I stare at him, our eyes hold, and I stutter over how to respond properly to a comment like that and not sound like an idiot, because that's how I feel right now. He's told me he loves me—and nothing can take away what those words mean to me—and yet for some reason these three mean more to me.

Maybe it's the setting, maybe the moment, but regardless I don't think I've ever loved him more than I do right now.

"Thank you," I finally say, touched beyond words.

"No need to thank me when it's true." That cocksure smile is back. "Tell me what else you learned tonight."

"How much you truly love the game."

He narrows his brow and chuckles. "I thought you had that part figured out by now."

"I do . . . but tonight. I don't know, listening to you talk . . . I could hear it in your voice. In your laugh. Your love for all things baseball was more than obvious."

"We talk baseball all the time." He shrugs.

"True, but not like that." I shake my head and look out the window for a beat before looking back to him. "Your voice tonight, the passion for the game in it . . . you had the same zeal that night in the press box before everything else happened."

"Hmm." He walks a few steps and stops in front of me, hands

on his hips, and eyes alive. "I can't remember the last time my dad stopped in just to talk. There was no criticism. No second-guessing. And then Derek. There's so much to learn from his experience. So much I can learn from him."

I smile. "Leave it to you to take a simple conversation and turn it into a chance to make you a better player."

"The minute you get content, is the minute you lose your edge."

"Does that pertain to all things, Mr. Wylder?" My tone is suggestive, my smile coy. He watches my finger as it trails up my inner thigh.

His tongue licks out to wet his bottom lip. "Are you telling me I'm losing my edge, Kitty?"

"Mmm." I glance down to where his dick is hardening against the loose fabric of his pants before scraping my eyes up his mouth-watering physique. *The view never gets old.* When I meet the amusement in his eyes, it takes everything I have to play the seductress when my patience is all but nonexistent. "I'm not sure. I might need you to demonstrate your skill set so I can judge for myself."

"I've got a damn good skill set."

"That remains to be seen, *Mr. Wylder.*"

His chuckle rolls over my skin and makes me think of how his tongue feels when it does the exact same thing. He takes another step forward and without warning drops his pants to the floor. His dick springs to life and the sight of it—and the knowledge of what it can do to me—causes chills to chase over my skin.

"Show me your tits, Kitty." His voice is an aphrodisiac.

I purposely make a show of biting my bottom lip as I reach for the hem of his shirt I'm wearing and pull it over my head. His groan is all I need to hear to know he appreciates that I'm braless and my panties are nothing more than strings holding a scrap of lace in place.

"That right there should be illegal," he says.

"Me?" I ask, feigning innocence as I spread my legs wider. "Or my panties?"

"All of it," he murmurs as he steps between them and runs a finger ever so softly over the heat of my sex.

My gasp is audible, the feel of his touch addictive as I look back at him. "Are you looking to get arrested then?"

"Any man worth his salt wouldn't hesitate getting arrested if it meant he got to taste you."

"Should I take that as a warning, then?" I moan as he slips a finger under my panties and slides it up and down my slit before pushing into me.

"You can take it any way you want so long as you understand when I say by any man, I mean *me*." He adds another finger and works both of them into me, moves them, and then slides them back out. He takes my arousal and rubs it over the length of his cock before stroking the full, hard length of it himself. "Only me."

God, he is sexy. His head is back, his bicep bulging as he pumps his hand over his shaft, and he groans in pleasure.

"Hey, Easton. You need to fuck *me* to show me your skill set. Not your hand."

And as quickly as I say it, he grabs my ankles, yanks me toward him, and then does some tricky move where he has me flipped over onto my stomach on the edge of the bed before I can even squeal in surprise. It's only when the palm of his hand lands firmly on my ass that I make a sound. And this time it's a yelp as the pleasure-versus-pain thrill races through my blood and ignites every part of me from within.

His hand fists in my hair as the stubble on his chin scrapes over my shoulder. "You want to be fucked?"

"God, yes." My answer is a breathless plea. This dominant side of him so very different than I'm used to. It's so goddamn hot.

He rubs the head of his cock up and down my seam, and I press into him to let him know how bad I want it. And oh, how I want it. His laughter is deep and rumbles through the room before it turns into tested restraint as he slowly presses his way into me.

"That okay?" he murmurs, heat on my ear, once he's seated root to tip inside of me.

"Mm-hmm."

That chuckle again. "Good, because that's the last time I'm going to ask. I'm not in the mood for soft and slow tonight, Scout. I want you. Plain and simple. And I'm going to take you. You got that?"

I grind my ass against him in response and knowingly ignite the fuse to his control.

And when he moves, there is nothing gentle about it. He sets a bruising pace I can't keep up with even if I wanted to. I'm so lost in the bliss of his cock and what it does to me that it takes everything I have to keep my legs from turning to jelly. Thank God, I have the bed beneath me or I'd collapse.

He drives me to my climax and instead of milking it out of me— slowing down so I can ride the soft waves of it—he keeps going, keeps thrusting, so before I know it I'm already primed for another one.

I slide my fingers between my legs and rub my clit to help bring me there. I know he's close too. He moves his hand from my hair to my shoulder to hold me in place so he can slam into me from behind.

He wages an all-out assault on my senses.

The sound of his groan. The slap of our skin connecting. My whimpers of pleasure. It feels so good it borders on painful.

The feel of his cock. Its head as it slides over every spot I need within me. The possessive grip of his hand.

The scent of his shampoo. The smell of sex. It surrounds me. Consumes me.

My name is on repeat with his every stroke. Each time it sounds more strained, more like his control is about to snap.

And when it does, I'm ready for it. For him. He bucks his hips and his fingers mark my skin from their grip.

"Jesus Christ," he says as he leans forward and lays his chest atop my back, his chin on my shoulder, his mouth by my ear. "Scout . . . you . . . damn . . ." he pants and presses a kiss to the nape of my neck.

"Mmm." I revel in the heat of his body and the feel of his skin on mine.

"See? Even with only one good arm, I haven't lost my edge," he says with a chuckle once he catches his breath.

"A skill set like that has to be illegal," I tease.

"Well, if we're going to jail, we might as well break the law again and again so we get our fill worth."

"Does that mean next time we get to use handcuffs?"

"I like the way you think, Kitty." I yelp as he straightens up and smacks my ass. "Teamwork at its finest."

CHAPTER THIRTY-FOUR

Scout

I glance around my apartment one last time.

Nothing here feels like home to me. Not the bed. Not the couch. Not the vanity in the bathroom.

Not the way Easton's place does anyway.

So it's time.

To walk away from this—formal surroundings that never really felt comfortable—and jump head first into what comes next.

Officially living together.

I laugh. It's not like Easton and I haven't been doing it already, but this next step will make it official.

I came to Austin—to this furnished apartment—to do nothing more than fulfill my dad's wishes before moving on to the next city. The next ball club. To keep living the transient life I've grown accustomed to.

I glance over to the last box to bring to my car. There is nothing significant in it. No mementos to hold close. No memories to remind me of a special occasion. Everything I have that's meaningful is already at Easton's or at my dad's house.

It's funny how I moved here six months ago, content with my life. With the constant travel. With the lack of permanence. And now, all I can think about is staying in Austin long-term. Winning the contract to satisfy my dad's wish all the while allowing me to remain in the only place other than my childhood home that I've ever really felt like I belong: Easton's place.

It takes me a second to remove my key from my keychain before setting it on the kitchen counter and heading to the door.

I came here closed off from the world, and I'll walk out open to the future.

I take one last look around. Give a half-hearted goodbye to the single life before willingly shutting the door on it.

I'm opening a different door now. One toward a new life.

To chances.

To possibilities.

To Easton.

CHAPTER THIRTY-FIVE

Easton

"**S**o whataya say, Doc?" Nerves rattle around as Dr. Kimble continues to manipulate my shoulder without talking. The little noises he makes to himself as he moves it here and there only add to my anxiety.

After his examination is done, he takes a seat opposite me. And fuck if I don't suddenly feel the need to throw up. A doctor facing you is never good. The whole needing to get on eye level to break the bad news is bullshit.

"I'm not sure, Easton."

"What does that mean?" My heart feels like it's going to pound out of my chest.

"It's healing on par with what I'd expect of it and the amount of days you're out from your surgery date . . . but I'd be remiss if I didn't tell you that your shoulder has suffered significant damage."

"I thought you fixed it during the surgery."

"I did, but sometimes what happens in surgery isn't always how the body wants to heal."

There's a buzzing in my ears. My head grows dizzy. "What are you saying, Doc?"

"I'm saying it's repaired, Easton. I'm saying with the proper rehab, you could report to spring training next year and hold your own. But with every ball you throw, you will risk permanent damage."

"I don't—"

"Let me finish." I nod and try to swallow over what feels like a baseball lodged in my throat. "Like I said, you can return. You can have a killer season . . . but the question is how much longer will it hold up? You need to think long-term here about your health and your life."

"Baseball *is* my life." I can hear the desperation in my voice.

He nods and the deliberateness of it tells me it's a practiced move. *Patience.* "I understand that, son. But you need to think of ten years from now. You'll be mid-thirties. You need to ask yourself *now* if you're okay living with an arm that doesn't do what you want it to *then*. Hold your wife. Play with your kids. Carry the groceries. That's a good forty years you'd have to deal with a damaged shoulder."

"That's bullshit." I reject his words immediately and shove off the medical table and pace to one side of the very small room and then back. "You're saying that to scare me. To make sure I'm cautious. It feels the same now as after I had the first surgery."

"And look what happened to it after that."

"It'll be fine." *It has to be.* And even though I say the words, the break in my voice betrays the conviction in its tone.

"I'm not trying to scare you. I'm letting you know the true ramifications to a shoulder that's been injured twice."

"But it's not a definite."

"No." He chews on the word. "But it's my job to let you know the possibilities when you play a position that uses your arm more than any other position on the field. You play a full game. Throw the ball back after every pitch and even though the pitchers change, three possibly four times per game, you remain behind the plate. Your shoulder bears the biggest brunt of any player out there."

"So what if I don't catch anymore?" The simple thought causes panic to close my throat. It's the only position I've ever known. It's *my* position. It's the one that controls the game. "What if I played first base so I didn't have to throw as much?"

"That would be up to you." His placating tone is like listening to fingernails on a chalkboard. I want to cover my ears and close him out.

"I could still play for ten years and my arm could be perfectly fine."

"You could, and it possibly could." His eyes say so much more than his mouth, though.

"Then why are you telling me this?"

"Because it's my job to tell you the truth."

I stare at him while disbelief and anger slam around inside me as I reject every single thing he's telling me.

"Fuck that, Doc. I'm playing. I haven't clawed my way back tooth and nail over two blown cuff surgeries to just lie down without giving it a good fight."

"Okay." He draws the word out only serving to irritate me further. "You have a lot to think about during the coming months."

"Are we done here?"

"Apparently."

Fuck that.

Fuck him.

I'm playing. No doctor is going to tell me how my arm is supposed to feel when I've been the one playing with it my whole life. I know my body better than anybody. I'm the best judge of if I can play or not.

But with each step, each corner turned as I walk through the city to clear my head, the anger morphs into disbelief.

I hit the sports complex, Little League fields all around me. Teams of all different ages are practicing in the afternoon heat. There's the clink of the aluminum bat. The laughter of kids. The stern reprimands of coaches.

The disbelief begins to shift into understanding.

And I don't want it to.

My feet slow down, and I begin to take in my surroundings. I've been here dozens of times. I've sat on my grassy knoll in left field and watched games and practices while I've cleared my head, but for the first time, I really pay attention.

To my left a dad does some kind of silly dance to make his daughter laugh before tossing the ball to her. She misses it, scrambles after it, and then when she throws it back, sends it sailing wide of him. But as he jogs after it, repeated praise is on his lips. How strong her arm is. How she'll be a great third baseman someday with that kind of strength.

There is no pressure. No expectations to live up to. Just a dad and a daughter playing catch. Bonding. Spending time together.

To my right is a team of older boys, junior high age. Three dads run the practice. Their instructions are a little harsher than the dad and his daughter but every single word is positive. I continue to watch them as they practice making double plays. Over and over.

My feet have stopped moving. I don't want to sit in the outfield today. I want to sit right here, in the middle of this. Things I don't remember experiencing with my dad but know I want to experience with my kids someday.

Kids?

What the hell am I thinking? I never wanted kids.

You never wanted Scout, either.

But the more I stand in the center point of four fields flowering off around me, the more I realize there is life after *playing* baseball.

There *are* things I want to be able to do.

It's top of the ninth.

"You have a big decision to make over the coming months, Mr. Wylder."

Full count.

Do I want to take the chance?

Bases loaded.

Or do I want a future where I can participate fully? Throw my kids up in the air. Make love to my wife in whatever position I want with two healthy arms. Work in the yard. Play catch with my son. *Or daughter.*

The pitch is thrown.

I look at everything around me. So many things out of focus before are now becoming crystal fucking clear.

What are you going to do, Easton?

I'm scared shitless. I have months to decide. Nothing is concrete. The love of my life may have shifted from a sport to the hint of possibility.

Strike out?

Am I just being a pussy?

Or swing for the fences?

Then again, I might not be.

And hit a homerun.

I tug my hat lower and look around again. Take it all in. The bitterness I felt earlier at Dr. Kimble is still there. The panicked feeling a constant tickle on the back of my neck.

I pick up my phone and stare at it a few minutes, scared to fucking death to make this call.

I hit send.

CHAPTER THIRTY-SIX

Scout

"Easton. What are you doing here?"

I fold Adler's patient file—a blown-out knee—and am so surprised to see Easton here, in the locker room, when I never thought he'd step foot in here again.

"I wanted to take my girlfriend out for lunch."

I eye him suspiciously because this does not sound like the man I know. "Is this a cover-up for some prank you're pulling on one of the guys when they come back from their road trip?"

"Who me?" He blinks innocently enough and yet there's always that mischievous little boy underneath who I don't trust but love knowing is still there. "Seriously, I know you're done with rehab for the day—I just talked to Adler on his way out—so come on. Let's go."

"Where in the world are you taking me?" I sip my chocolate milkshake while he swings our joined hands between us. The sun is out, the humidity not too horrible, and I have a belly full of all kinds of bad-for-you food Easton insisted we have.

"So you're a clue kind of girl, huh? You just can't jump right into a surprise, you have to prepare yourself for it?"

"There's nothing wrong with that. You say it like it's a bad thing."

"Isn't that the whole point of a surprise? The not knowing what is going to happen?" he asks and leans over and kisses my temple.

"Yeah, but you told me there was one, so now I know it's going to happen." I laugh. This line of conversation is ridiculous and amusing.

"What if I told you, there was no waiting because we're here?"

Startled, I glance at the lush greenery around us and take in the rows of cinderblock walls covered in graffiti. Beautiful, artistic graffiti but graffiti nonetheless.

"It's oddly beautiful," I say as I move toward the murals. They are amazing and profound in all their colorful uniqueness. As I walk through them, I can't resist reaching out to touch some of them and then standing back, trying to figure out what the others mean.

Easton follows me and his silent observation makes me nervous. "It's called the HOPE Outdoor Gallery."

"HOPE?"

"Helping Other People Everywhere."

"But it's graffiti. How is that helping people?"

"It started out as a movement to raise awareness about socially conscious issues. In reality, it's just a bunch of artists and musicians who come together to be active and donate their proceeds to certain causes." I walk a few feet as I mull over his explanation but don't understand what this has to do with these graffiti-covered walls. He must read my expression because he begins to explain. "These are murals made by some of the artists. They all deal with different issues close to their hearts."

"They're fascinating."

"Are you ready to add your mark to one of them?"

"What?" I whip my head toward him, eyes narrowed, and nose

scrunched up.

"We have a little section over here that's ours to do as we wish." He begins to walk to the backside of a wall.

"But wait—how—I can't paint for shit."

His laugh rings out and echoes off the walls around us. "It's art. Isn't it subjective?"

"Subjective, my ass." I stand with my hands on my hips trying to figure this out. "But I don't understand . . ."

"I did an event with the founder a few years back. I thought this place was pretty cool and since then have been a silent contributor to some of their causes. So in turn, I have a little section I get to screw up. On the backside of a wall. In the corner—"

"So no one sees it," I finish for him with a laugh.

"Exactly. So it doesn't matter how horrible we make it, it only matters that we make it," he says as he picks up a bucket full of spray paint that seems to materialize out of nowhere. "They knew we were coming." He winks but I just shake my head and stand my ground.

I look at the many walls around me. I take in their beauty and creativity and feel like I could study them for hours and still not decipher all their hidden meanings. And yet when I glance back at Easton, everything about him commands my attention. He stands in the tall grass amid walls painted in every color imaginable, and yet it's his true colors that shine the brightest—time and again—and steal every damn piece of my heart.

He smiles that crooked smile of his as he holds a can of paint out to me. "C'mon, Scout, you know you want to try it."

"I do," I say, fingers itching to, "but my skills are lacking in the creativity department."

"We're back on proving skills again, now are we?"

I roll my eyes and take the can from him. "So we can paint anything we want?"

"Anything."

"Challenge accepted."

"It looks horrible." My cheeks hurt from laughing so hard and my fingers are cramped and coated in a vast array of spray paint colors.

"Horrible is putting it kindly."

"Hey, be nice." I swat at him, but he grabs my hand and pulls me against him. His lips are on mine without hesitation. The breeze blows around us. The grass tickles my bare legs. We smell like the distinct scent of spray paint. But the taste of his kiss is the cherry on the top of this perfect day.

"Is that *nice* enough?" he asks when he ends the kiss.

"Definitely. I like nice. Maybe we can be even nicer later."

He rolls his eyes and shakes his head. "Pervert."

"And your point is?" I ask coyly.

"Nothing. You're perfect as you are." His smile is wide as his eyes leave mine and glance over my shoulder at our combined graffiti. "Just like that is."

I turn to face our wall. It's crude at best compared to the other skilled murals around us, but it's totally us.

"Have a day" is written across the top of the wall. Drips of paint, where I held the can too close make lines down the lettering. There's an open book on the wall. One page filled with letters going all different ways. The other page filled with the picture of a baseball diamond. There's a horrible blob of brown that was Easton's attempt at a fortune cookie. Just looking at it, I smile thinking of how hard we laughed as we tried to make it look better but only resulted in making it look worse. The same goes with my attempt at outlining a dog. At least the ears and tail can be made out. Then there's a crudely painted kitty cat in one corner with a number forty-four for our signature.

It's horrible at best but every single thing on it—all the way down to the round circles that are supposed to be Life Savers—reflects something meaningful to us.

I reach out and link my fingers with his, so thankful for this change of pace and reminder of what matters most. "Thank you for bringing me here."

"You're welcome." He stares at me for a beat before looking back to the wall, hesitating to say the words I can tell are on his lips. "I called Finn earlier."

"Okay." I draw the word out. He always calls Finn. What's the big deal?

"I asked him to get me a second shot at the World Series broadcast."

"You what?" Startled, I turn to look at him, but he keeps staring at the picture in front of us. I squeeze his fingers to let him know I understand how scary this is for him. How he's opening himself up to everything he fears . . . and doing so publicly.

"I'm proud of you, Easton."

CHAPTER THIRTY-SEVEN

Scout

"**M**en are on first and third," Easton murmurs to himself as he stares out the window to the stadium below. The ballpark's lights brighten up the sky, much like how the Aces being in the playoffs has brought the city to life.

I glance at the TV, see that Easton is right, and know that Tino is the fastest on the team. One long fly ball, and he can score to give the Aces the lead in this scoreless game.

"We can still go down and watch the game, you know," I say, checking my cell to make sure I have no texts from the team. After working nonstop for the past eight days, I decided to let Scott take the lead tonight so I could get a breather before what is looking more and more like the Aces going to the World Series.

"I know, but I need to get this nailed down," he says as he leaves the window and sits down at the table cluttered with papers. Papers that Finn was able to get from Fox in advance of the broadcast so Easton could learn them. The sponsorship information. The rehearsed commentary. Anything that needs to be read off a teleprompter. "I was just taking a break. My eyes burn from looking at this for so long."

He glances over to the TV as JP strikes out, and I know he would give anything to be playing right now. To be a part of his old team and clinching the National League title with them.

And maybe that's why he doesn't want to be at the game. It's a hard enough pill to swallow in general, but when the sights and smells surround you, it makes your reality tougher to accept.

"You and Helen have been working on this nonstop all week. I know you've got it pretty well covered, but if you want to go over it one more time, I'd be more than happy to help."

He cocks his head to the side and just stares at me. He looks tired—his eyes are bloodshot, his hair is all over the place, his favorite shirt has seen better days—but I'm so proud of him for how hard he is working. For studying his ass off and conquering his demons.

"What?" I ask, unable to read what he's saying in his look.

"What if I couldn't play ball anymore?"

Well, that's not what I was expecting, so it takes me a few seconds to clear the surprised look from my face and answer him. "Then you can't play baseball anymore."

"Would that bug you if I couldn't?"

"What kind of question is that?" *Where is he going with this?*

"You're obviously attracted to that side of me—the physical, the competitive, the everything about the game—so if I wasn't playing anymore, would that change things between us?"

I meet his eyes and my heart breaks for the uncertainty I see in them. "Easton, I love you for you. Sure all of those things are a part of you, but to me, there is so much more that makes up the measure of a man. More than anything, I'd be sad watching you say goodbye to something you love. But would I not want you anymore?" I ask as I stand and walk around the table, and set my hips against its edge so I can look at him. "Not a chance in hell."

That shy smile slides on his face and lights up his eyes as they roam down the length of my body. My thin camisole tank doesn't hide much and my little pajama shorts don't cover much more.

"Thank you for believing in me."

"There's no thanking needed," I say as he looks up from where my nipples are hard beneath my top and wets his bottom lip. "Do you want to go over these again?" I ask, trying to distract him—*half-heartedly*—from what the look in his eyes says he really wants.

"Did I ever tell you I always had a thing for teachers?" he asks as he pulls his shirt over his head, careful of his shoulder, and tosses it to the side.

"You did, did you?"

"Oh yeah. Their hair pulled back all prim and proper. The pencil skirts and buttoned-up blouses I'd stare at and imagine what was underneath should one of those buttons pop open when she was bending over the desk in front of me."

"Hot for teacher, huh?"

"Your hair is pulled up," he murmurs as he uses his good arm to slide my ass toward him so I'm now perched on the desk directly in front of him. "And I could pretend that your tank top has buttons on it."

"You could, could you?" My laugh fills the room above the muted roar of the crowd floating up to our condo from down below.

"Definitely."

"But I'm not wearing a skirt."

"Once I take it off you, does it really matter what you were wearing?"

"Good point." I follow the slow, sexy slide of his hands from my knees up the length of my thighs. "But I haven't taught you anything."

It's his turn to chuckle. "No worries there, I think I'll let you school me, right now."

I lean forward and press my lips to his, encouraging his fingers to find their way beneath my shorts.

We make love.

By the lights of the stadium he's played under his entire career.

With the roar of the crowd reminding him of the game he should be playing.

Under the spotlight he's lived his whole life.

We create something that's uniquely ours.

Our own magic.

CHAPTER THIRTY-EIGHT

Scout

Boseman's words ring in my ears. "Probationary contract, my ass. The guys respect you. Your work speaks for itself. You're a great fit for the club. I'll have the team contract for next season drawn up by tomorrow morning. That is if you still want the job with the Aces after the rigmarole bullshit Tillman put you through."

I *got* the contract.

I want to scream it down the tunnels. Let it bounce off the concrete walls and echo all the way to my dad so he knows *I did it.* I gave him his last wish. Doc Dalton has officially been contracted by every single clubhouse in the major leagues.

My heart is racing and my pulse pounds in my ears as I jog down the halls, sneakers squeaking over the concrete, to my office. It's early yet and we're not scheduled to board our flight to Los Angeles for game one of the World Series until tomorrow morning. So that means a day off.

A day with Easton. My calm amidst this madness.

And more importantly, it means I have time to go to my dad's and tell him the good news, face to face.

High on cloud nine, I say hi to a couple guys who've come in to work out or work with a coach on something giving them trouble—their swing, their backhand, you name it—but am oblivious to most everything as one of the weights that has been on my shoulders for the past, I-don't-know-how-long-it's-been is lifted.

Oblivious that is until I turn a corner and run smack dab into a conversation I shouldn't be privy to.

"A Wylder is a Wylder, right? I've gotten screwed out of that my whole li—" Santiago stops speaking the minute he sees me.

Cal snaps his head my way, his face paling as I start to backpedal.

And when I bump into a wall behind me, I turn despite Cal's protests and run to the exit.

I can't have heard what I just thought I heard.

It can't be true.

There's no way.

My hands are trembling and heart is pounding, but this time it has nothing to do with winning the contract. No. It's because of something I wish I'd never heard.

"Scout, wait up. It's not what you think."

But I keep jogging until I reach the doors that open to the parking lot. When I shove them open, the bright sunlight blinds me momentarily before I see Easton. He's leaning against his truck, preemptively waiting for me to give him good news about the contract. The huge grin on his face slowly slides into concern when he sees me out of breath and a little rattled.

"Scout? What happened? Are you okay?"

I struggle with words as the doors push open behind me and Cal emerges.

"Dad?" Easton takes a few steps forward, eyes swiveling from me to Cal and then back again. "What's going on?"

It's fight or flight time, Scout. Tell him the truth and derail his broadcast or shut your mouth and tell him afterwards.

What. Would. You. Do. Scout?

Nothing good ever came from a lie, Scouty-girl. I hear my dad's voice saying it but there's Easton in front of me and Cal behind me both waiting for me to answer.

"Nothing. I'm fine," I say as I gulp in a breath. "I got the contract."

"You did!" He whoops as he pulls me into a hug and squeezes me tightly against him.

I know Cal is there. Watching. Waiting. But I refuse to look his way.

I refuse to acknowledge that I lied for him.

Because I only did it for the sake of his son.

Someone has to protect him and it sure as hell isn't going to be Cal.

CHAPTER THIRTY-NINE

Scout

Guilt is a mean, nasty bitch.

Especially when it's guilt over lying to the man sitting next to you.

I try to rationalize what I overheard. I attempt to fool myself into thinking I really didn't hear what they said. I convince myself that I misinterpreted their meaning. And yet, when I add everything up—the various times I've seen Santiago, Easton's nemesis, with Cal, Easton's father—two plus two is definitely equaling four.

Then it hits me—Cal's warning the night Derek came over—when he thanked me for supporting Easton in his physical rehabilitation and *whatever else life throws his way.*

Was he telling me the shit was going to hit the fan? Was he warning me?

I glance over to Easton and he squeezes my knee. If my assumption is true, if Santiago is Easton's half-brother, it will rock his world, and I can't let that happen with so much riding on him going into this gig with Fox Sports.

"Don't be nervous," he says as he puts the car in park.

But I am nervous, just for things completely different than he thinks.

"I'm not. I just worry I won't be able to hide my reaction when I see him. What if he looks frail or is not the man I know? I'm afraid he'll see through me and know how bad he looks."

Easton turns my way and looks me straight in the eyes. "First of all, he already knows how bad he is, Scout. Just be you with him. And second, you're bringing him great news, so that will overshadow everything else that's worrying you."

He leans in and presses a tender kiss to my lips that chases the demons of betrayal away. For now, it warms me all the way through getting to the front door, introducing Easton to Sally, and then preparing myself to see my dad.

"You're holding back on me, Sally. I hear voices, and they're not you talking to yourself."

"Such a stubborn cuss," she murmurs but the warmth in her eyes tells me she loves that he still has the energy to be one.

"It's me," I say, preparing myself to see him before I stride in the room, "and I come bearing gifts."

"Gifts, eh?" he asks as he shifts in his chair to face me. He's much thinner now, gaunt, and his pallor is almost a grayish yellow in color. His eyes have sunken more, but the smile he tries to fight when he sees me is one hundred percent the old Doc Dalton. "Do they pertain to the whiskey and chocolate kind of gifts since Sally here has me eating all kinds of organic shit that tastes like cardboard instead of the crap I really want? Let the dying man eat the good stuff, already," he says loud enough for Sally to hear.

Tears well in my eyes as I lean down to hug him. It's so good to see him. To look into eyes so similar to my own and hear his voice in person. To deal with his ornery comments.

"No chocolate. No whiskey," I say as I press a kiss to his forehead and sit down beside him, keeping his hand in mine.

"I thought I was your favorite," he teases.

"You are my favorite. Always will be." My voice breaks.

"Don't you go crying on me, Scouty-girl," he warns.

I squeeze his hand. "If I cry it's because I'm happy to see you so zip it, old man, and let me be happy, will ya?"

His smile is back as he reaches up and wipes a tear off my cheek. I feel like I'm six years old and crying again because I miss my mom. He always sat beside me on my bed, wiped away my tears, and then told me some silly story until I was giggling and the sadness was overshadowed for a while.

"It's good to see you, Daddy," I whisper.

"It's good to see you, Scouty." I rest my head on his shoulder for a second and just breathe in the moment—the scent of his shampoo, the peace he brings me—thankful Easton let me have a few minutes with my dad before I introduce him.

It's so weird to sit here with my dad and feel like he's so whole and healthy, but know that beneath the surface, his heart is like a ticking time bomb ready to detonate at any moment.

He clears his throat and disrupts the silence. "Enough of that mushy shit. I want to know what my presents are," he says and then stops when he homes in on something over my shoulder. "Scout?"

I turn to see Easton standing there, his frame filling the doorway. He rubs his hands on his jeans and looks at me as if he's asking if it's okay to interrupt.

"Dad, this is Easton Wylder. Easton, this is my father, Doc."

"*The player,*" my dad murmurs quietly as he pulls his hand from mine and sits a little straighter as Easton crosses the distance and extends his hand to him.

"Such a pleasure to meet you, sir. I've heard so much about you from Scout and around the league . . . it's nice to finally get to shake your hand."

My dad eyes Easton's hand and then squints as he studies him. And for a brief second my nerves rattle around, wondering if this was a big mistake. Bringing home a man to meet my father for the first time under these conditions.

But I had to. I wanted my dad to meet the man I love.

My dad slowly extends his hand and shakes Easton's but doesn't relent on the scrutiny. "Hello, Easton. Nice to meet you too. *I think.* Please tell me running off and marrying my daughter is not the gift you come bearing. If that's the case, I think we should head to the garage where I can show you my safe full of guns." He plasters the cheesiest grin on his face while Easton's eyes widen and feet shift. "Big ones."

"Will you relax and be nice? He's not the gift." I swat at his leg. "I know you're joking, Dad. He doesn't. Sit down, Easton, and ignore my father."

"There is a safe full of guns though," my dad says with a wink.

Easton laughs nervously and takes a seat as I turn back to my dad. "I met with Boseman today."

"Poor bastard probably has every lawyer on his hefty payroll scouring that office to cover his ass after everything Tillman did. That's the problem with baseball these days. Too much corporate bullshit involved when it should be about a man and his love for the game." He briefly closes his eyes and smiles like he's remembering something. "No offense, Wylder, but contracts are out of control. No man deserves twenty-one million to play one season. The purity of the game is gone. The simplicity of a father and son"—I knock my knee against his, and he clears his throat—"*or daughter,* going to a game. The players are becoming soft with pitch counts ruling their playing time. It's horseshit. Don't get me started."

"You've already started." I laugh. "As you can tell, my dad is a throwback. He thinks business has ruined the sport."

"It has," Easton agrees and by the startle of my dad's head, surprises him. "The problem is it will never be able to go back to what it was—the game I remember watching as a kid—and that's a shame."

My dad stares at him for a moment and nods as if he's judging whether Easton is trying to impress him or if he really means what he's saying. I know he believes him when he lets the comment go and turns to me. "So? Boseman? What was it about?"

"He wanted to tell me he's yanking the probationary contract from us. He said probationary contracts are bullshit and a GM should know whether he wants someone on his team or he doesn't." I can't hide my smile any longer. "We got the contract, Dad. Boseman said he'll have it drawn up immediately."

My dad just stares at me for a moment, jaw clenched and eyes hard, before grabbing me and pulling me into him. He holds on as his body jars with the tears he's fighting.

I'm not sure what I expected to happen when I told him the good news, but it definitely wasn't this—*affection*.

After a few moments he leans back and meets my eyes. "Thank you," he whispers. *Two words*. They're only two words but the gratitude and love packed behind them erase the unending stress and anxiety I've endured to make this happen.

"Easton, why don't you let me show you around outside?" Sally asks from the doorway, saving Easton from feeling like he's eavesdropping and giving him an out.

"I'll be with Sally," he says giving me a soft smile before leaving.

My dad and I watch him leave the room, hear the screen door slam shut, and proceed to watch Sally point out things to Easton through the big bay window. Even though there are so many things to say, we sit in silence for a few minutes.

"I'm proud of you, Scout." He pauses and keeps looking at the long grass field where Easton is standing. "But you don't have to sign the contract if you don't want to."

"*What*?" The word is a shocked whoosh of air as I look to him but he continues staring straight ahead. Confusion and bewilderment riot inside me. "What are you talking about? It's what you wanted? The cap on your career. Dad, talk to me. Please tell me this wasn't all for nothing."

"Not all for nothing, no. Sometimes accomplishing something is the success itself," he says, reaching out to grab my hand.

"What the hell does that mean?"

"It means I needed you to love something more than you love me. I needed you to do something that seemed impossible from the start and succeed at it so *you* would know you could do it on your own. So *I'd* know you'd be okay when I'm gone." I shake my head as I try to grasp what he's telling me. "I'm so sorry for pushing you away, Scouty, but your whole life you looked to me to help you when things got tough. And there's nothing wrong with that." His voice breaks right along with my heart. "But I needed you to know that you didn't need me to fix anything. You're strong and capable and had the tools to fix it yourself. I needed you to realize you didn't need me at all."

"But I do need you, Dad." My voice hiccups as I fight back the threatening sobs.

He looks at me for the first time and I watch a tear slide down his cheek. "Do you have any idea how hard it was to push you away? I may be a hard-ass, but pushing my little girl away was the hardest thing I've ever had to do. I wanted to be selfish. To pull you near and keep you in this bubble of ours and never let you go . . . but I couldn't. I pushed—no shoved—you toward the contract because if you could handle those hard-ass, sexist, stubborn men, then I knew you'd thrive at whatever it is *you* wanted to do. I could give a rat's ass about the contract, Scout. I couldn't care less if you continue the business or not. I just needed to know before I go that you're going to be okay. That you'd believe in yourself enough to know you're going to be okay too."

I put my arms around my dad, and he holds me as I cry.

"I'm so sorry I have to leave you."

I can't stop the huge, heaving sobs.

"I'm so very proud of you. Never doubt that."

I refuse to let go as he strokes his hand over my hair again and again and tells me things I need to hear but wish he didn't have to say.

"You're my heart, Scouty. I love you more than anything in this world, and I don't want you to ever forget that."

After some time, when the tears are all cried out and the emptiness has been filled with his unquestionable love, I lean my head on his shoulder like I used to do when I was little and watch the world outside. The grass moving with the breeze. The clouds sliding across the sky. The big tree Ford and I used to climb—where my dad has already chosen as his final resting place.

"I say we go sit on the porch and enjoy this nice weather. What do you say?"

My breath is still hitching—the fallout from my sobs—and I'm sure my eyes are swollen, but it sounds like the best idea in the world.

Like we used to do when I was little.

"I'd love to."

"Can you help me make it out there?" he asks.

"Of course." I wrap my arm around his waist and stand up with him. He's so light. This hulking man of my childhood has been reduced to skin and bones. "You okay?"

"I'd be a helluva lot better if you slip some of that whiskey in the cupboard above the fridge into my cup. Sally would never know."

I laugh. "I'll see what I can do."

"That's my girl."

The sky is purple and orange as the sun sets, and my dad and Easton talk all things imaginable—my childhood, his shoulder, baseball— even about the safe of guns in the garage. Sally and I have chatted for the first time in forever about topics that don't have anything to do with my dad's illness and it feels so damn good. Dare I say, almost normal.

"Are you sure you need to head out?" Sally asks.

"Unfortunately. I have an early flight to Los Angeles in the morning," I say glancing at my father again and the dark circles of exhaustion under his eyes.

"Game one of the World Series," my dad murmurs, and I love that there is still that nostalgic look in his eyes when it comes to the game. I'm grateful his sickness hasn't taken that away from him.

"Yep." I nod. "The only thing that would make it better is if Easton was playing in it." I look at him and smile, knowing he feels the same way.

"Remember what I said, Easton," my dad says with a nod. "Your body knows its limitations. Listen to what it tells you and you'll make the right decision."

"Yes, sir," Easton says and I wonder what exactly they were talking about while Sally and I had gone inside to refill our drinks. Was my dad giving Easton advice on his shoulder? "It was a pleasure meeting both of you." He steps forward and gives Sally a big hug and then shakes my dad's hand. My dad leans forward and says something in Easton's ear I can't hear. Easton meets his eyes in an exchange of unspoken words. He holds it a bit longer than normal and smiles with a nod as if he's thanking him for things only they understand.

"Maybe we can do it again sometime soon. Get together. Once the series is over, and you're both around more."

"I'd love that," I say, my heart hoping I get to have a lot more of these moments with them now that everything is out in the open.

"Can you guys give me a minute with Scout?" my dad asks.

"Let me walk you to the car, Easton. You may have lost your way, considering it's right in front of you," Sally jokes as I turn to my dad.

"I just wanted to remind you that you can take or leave the contract. That contract was my dream and my goal, and I want you to have your own." He squeezes my hand.

"What if mine are the same as yours? What if I want to carry on your legacy?"

"I'd like that," he says with a soft smile as his eyes close momentarily. When he opens them up, there's a clarity there I don't expect.

"Thank you for my gifts."

"Gifts? I only had one."

"Nah, you gave me two of the greatest gifts I could have ever asked for: knowing you'll be okay . . . and seeing you in love."

I hug him as tight as I can to let him know those words were the greatest gift he could have ever given me in return. Knowing that *he* knows I'll be all right.

"I love you, Daddy."

"Clear mind. *Full* heart, Scouty-girl. Never forget that."

"Never."

CHAPTER FORTY

Scout

When I walk in the press box of the stadium, Easton sits with his head down studying the papers spread all over the counter in front of him. Not wanting to disturb him and ruin his concentration, I lean against the doorjamb and wait for him to notice me.

"You done with work?" he asks without looking my way.

"Yeah. Adler's coming along and I completed my reports for Griswold," I say referring to the interim general manager until Boseman finds a new one.

"You heading home? You've been here all day, you must be exhausted."

"I am, but I figured I'd sit here with you awhile if you don't mind."

"You don't have to."

"I know," I say as I close the door and approach him. He remains focused on what he's working on so I take in the view of the field from our position at the club level. The grass is in pristine shape, the World Series logos have been painted on the infield, and strings of plastic flags have been hung along the left and right field lines. There are a few guys on the field—it looks like JP, Guzman, and Santiago, taking a few extra cuts at the ball. Getting some additional batting practice in before the next game tomorrow.

The Aces are tied with the Anaheim Angels, one game all, so the city is abuzz with the knowledge that they'll be in front of the hometown crowd for the next three games.

"You couldn't have asked for a better location to have your broadcast, huh?" I put a hand on his back and scratch it softly.

"The second best thing to playing in the series is broadcasting it." I hear the bitterness and sarcasm in his voice and let it go without commenting. I'd feel the same way if I were in his shoes. "Sorry."

"Don't be. I get it. All I meant was at least you're familiar with this booth and its layout since you've broadcast here before. Besides, this stadium is your second home of sorts so that might help combat the nerves some."

There's a crack of the bat below. Some whooping as the ball hits the upper deck beyond the right field wall.

But it's Easton who demands my attention when he reaches out to pull me to him. When I step between his parted knees, he wraps his arms around my hips, pulls me into him, and rests his head on my abdomen. My hands automatically thread through his hair to reassure him that I'm here, still rooting for him, still the one who wants the best for him.

"I'm nervous," he admits after a few silent minutes, the heat of his breath seeping through the fabric of my shirt and warming my skin.

"I know you are," I tell him, trying to imagine what he's going through—the pressure he's put on himself and the fear of public scrutiny if he messes up. As soon as he was announced as part of the broadcasting lineup for tomorrow's game, the assholes behind their keyboards started their bullshit.

He holds on for a few minutes as the sounds of baseball below filter up to us when I get an idea. Something to make him a little more at ease. Something for him to remember when he's feeling nervous during the commentating.

"Hey, you know what they say to do when you get nervous, don't you?" I ask, pulling away from him and walking toward the door. The stadium is far from vacant with the game tomorrow and the postseason preparation, but I'll take the risk that no one is going to come knocking on the press booth door.

"Picture everyone naked," he says.

I flip the lock on the door and turn around to face him, a more than coy smile on my lips. "You *can* do that." I take a step toward him and lift one of my eyebrows. "Or you can imagine me standing here naked."

One corner of his mouth turns up in disbelief as his eyes narrow, curiosity owning his expression. And so I make good on my comment. I pull my tank top and sports bra over my head, the weight of my breasts falling when they're free of the restrictive fabric.

His eyes widen. "*Oh, fuck.*"

"Exactly. Oh, fuck."

I toe my shoes off and shimmy off my exercise pants so I'm standing in the broadcast booth of the Austin Aces, completely naked, with an audience of one.

He wets his lips and shifts in his chair.

"You know what's even better than imagining me naked?"

"What's that?" I love that he can't keep his eyes from roaming all over my body as if it's a treasure map he can't wait to explore.

"Imagining me sucking you off in the exact same chair you'll be broadcasting from."

"Imagining you doing it or *remembering* you doing it from first-hand knowledge?" he asks as he shifts again in his seat, his erection tenting his shorts.

"That depends," I murmur as I step between his thighs again, lean down, and press my lips to his. I make the kiss soft and slow, so that when I break from it, he sits forward to try and take more.

"Depends on what?" He chuckles.

"Why your shorts are still on."

In a flurry of movement, he has his gym shorts shoved down to his ankles and has one foot out of their leg.

With my eyes on his, I drop to my knees, lower my head, and ever so slowly slide his cock into my mouth. I press my tongue to its underside as my lips suction around him and am rewarded with a guttural groan when he hits the back of my throat. His eyes break from mine as they close and his head falls back.

I take my time, letting the warmth of my mouth, the suction of my lips, and the pressure of my tongue work him up the ladder of ecstasy.

"*Goddamn*," he groans.

Music to my ears.

Holding him as deep as I can take him, I bring my hands into the mix. First with fingernails scraping gently over his balls. His thighs tighten. His feet flex. And then as I slide him out of my mouth, the release of the suction making a popping sound that fills the booth. I grab his shaft with my other hand and twist it gently as I begin to work it up and over his length while my mouth pleasures its tip.

Easton's hands are everywhere. First on the armrests. Then on his thighs. Then one fists in the back of my hair and holds my head as he lifts his hips and fucks my mouth.

It's erotic as hell.

The sound of his groan. The pop of the suction when he breaks from my lips. The crack of the bat down below. Knowing people are right there while we're doing this in here.

Intoxicating.

The groan he emits. The possession in his grip. His stilted praise between pants of breath.

Empowering.

Knowing I can give *this* to him. Not just the climax, but something to recall and put him at ease when he's here tomorrow night. A little private moment to make him smile right before the nerves kick in when the teleprompter starts rolling.

"Scout." It's a dirty moan as he bucks his hips up, and I suck harder. "*Scout.*" His dick swells and his muscles tense. "Scout." And then he's lost as I suck and swallow everything he has to give me. "Oh. God. *Scout.*"

His grip loosens from my hair but he pulls back on it so I'm forced to look up to him. I bring a hand up to wipe my lips when he slips from my mouth.

His disbelieving grin reaffirms the risk was definitely worth it.

"You're bad."

"Would you rather I be good?"

"Hell, fucking, no." His laugh fills the booth as he helps me rise from my knees. "Look at you. I didn't even get to take advantage of all of this." He runs his hands up and down the sides of my torso and murmurs in appreciation.

I bat his hands away. "You can take advantage of it later. I've got to get dressed before we get caught."

I love the sound of his laugh. "Not so brave now, are you?"

"You got what you wanted, didn't you?" I ask as we begin to put our clothes back on.

"Damn straight I did." He looks like the cat that ate the canary right now. *Smug as hell.*

"Don't ever say I'm not a team player," I tease.

"You sure as hell just took one for the team." He shakes his head and looks at the many papers in front of him before looking back to me. "And I'm more than certain that your generosity for *the team* will help ease my nerves tomorrow night."

"Good to know."

The love in his eyes is overwhelming and makes me unexpectedly uncomfortable. I avert my eyes and focus on tying my shoes, but when I look back up, he's still there, still looking at me.

"Are you done?" I ask.

"Nah. I want to run through this a few more times. You going to head home?"

"Do you mind if I stay here with you instead? I have my book to read so I promise I won't bug you."

His smile is soft. "I'd like that."

CHAPTER FORTY-ONE

Easton

"**I**s Helen coming back tonight?" Scout asks as she dries her hair with a towel.

"Nah," I glance over to the kitchen clock and then back to the papers I'm shuffling through. "We're done for the day."

Crap. Where are my notes?

"You have to be exhausted. You've been practicing in the booth all day."

"Not *all* day." God. Damn. Her sucking me off earlier was unexpected but fucking perfection.

"Let's not talk about that." When I glance her way again, her cheeks are flush with embarrassment.

"Don't even . . ." I roll my eyes. "I know you, Scout Dalton. You don't get to act all shy when I know the sexy vixen you are in private."

She laughs and that visual of the top of her head, the heat of her mouth, the suction of her lips . . . I'm one helluva lucky guy.

"What are you looking for?" she asks, purposely changing the topic and drawing me back to the matter at hand—finding my cheat sheets for the broadcast tomorrow.

"I think I left them at the stadium."

"Left what?"

"My notes. I've got to run back and get them."

"Ah . . . just when I was going to let you take advantage of the rest of me."

"You were?" *Music to my ears.*

"I'll be in bed." Her smile tells me she's damn serious. "Naked. And waiting."

"I'll hurry."

Yep. I'm one lucky son of a bitch.

With my notes in my hand and thoughts of exactly what I want to do to Scout when I get home on my mind, I jog down the halls of the club level feeling damn good about life in general.

Things with Scout are incredible.

I'm more than prepared for tomorrow.

My shoulder is coming along.

The Aces are in the series. And fuck, I technically may be a Wrangler, but my heart will always be with the Aces. At least I get to call the game. It's not playing but it's better than nothing.

I round the corner.

And stare.

What the hell?

"You have to stop talking about this here. People will start noticing."

"Let them talk." Santiago throws his hands up. "See if I care. It's your image you're trying to preserve by keeping this all secret. *Not mine.*"

"Keep your voice down, will you?" my dad says with a resignation

I've never heard from him before.

I can't move even though every part of me tells me I don't want to know what they're talking about.

"Where do you want to discuss this then, *Cal*? You refuse to talk to me at your house. You won't meet me anywhere else because God forbid someone sees us out in public together—the father and the villain—and starts asking questions. Here we're expected to talk to each other. Here we'll get overlooked. Here your precious fucking son might not question it."

My shoes squeak and both of them snap their attention my way. I shake my head as I look from Santiago then to my dad.

Oh my fucking God.

"Are you kidding me?" I think I say it. I'm not sure because my head is full of so much white noise right now I can't even . . .

How the hell have I never seen . . .

Fuck.

Santiago is my dad's son?

My half-brother?

"I can explain." My dad steps forward but I take one back, head still shaking and mind still wanting not to believe.

"No. Just . . ." I blink my eyes several times trying to unsee what I'm seeing. The same shaped eyes, the same chin. It's barely notice-able with the difference in their skin colors, but I can see it. And now I can't not see it. "Is it true?" I ask, my voice a croaked whisper.

My dad's mouth pulls tight as he meets my eyes. *And nods.* "Easton, let me—"

"Fuck this." I turn on my heel to escape as he calls after me. Walking to jogging to full-on sprinting. Anything to get out of this concrete maze that feels like quicksand pulling me under.

I need fresh air.

I can't breathe.

I can't think.

I shove open the door to the parking lot. My hands are on my knees as I suck in air.

Scout.

I need Scout.

I jog home. Fidget restlessly in the elevator pushing the P button several times as if it will make it ascend faster.

The door opens.

"Scout! Scout!"

She runs out from the bedroom and stops in her tracks when she sees me.

"Easton." Her voice is calm, her eyes are cautious. "Your dad just called. What happened?"

"What did he say?" She takes a step toward me and I take one back. I just . . . I need . . . *what is happening here?*

"Oh shit," she says, voice cracking. She takes a deep breath and looks back at me.

"You knew?"

"Not for sure. I still don't," she stutters in argument. My chest constricts from her words. "I ran into your dad and Santiago the other day—"

"What? When? Where? *Christ.*" It dawns on me: Scout wide-eyed and out of breath when she slammed open the doors to the parking lot. "Was it when my dad followed you out of the stadium?"

She nods.

Fucking hell. Why would she keep it from me if she thought . . .

Anger slowly creeps and seeps into every part of me. "You *knew* and *didn't* tell me?"

She holds her hands up. "I overheard them whispering a few words and drew my own conclusions, but I didn't know for sure. And I sure as hell didn't ask."

"Why didn't you tell me?" I want to shout at her, shake her, get some kind of reaction out of her because I have so much anger and confusion eating at me from the inside out that I don't know what to do or say or how to feel.

But I can't. This isn't her fault. Not a damn fucking thing. No, Santiago *isn't* her fault. *He's my dad's.*

"I was going to tell you—"

"But you didn't. Were . . . were you going to?"

"After tomorrow night." Her voice is so soft compared to my shouting. Day to my night. Light to my dark. Fucked to my fucked up. "I didn't want it to affect you and the broadcast. You've been studying so hard and I wanted you to have a clear head and—"

"Yeah, well, that's shot to hell now, isn't it?"

"It doesn't have to be."

My dad has another kid. How long has he known about him? How long has he kept him a secret? Does my mom . . . Shit. My mom.

"Santi-fucking-ago." I bring both hands to the sides of my head and walk from one length of the room to the other. So many thoughts. So many questions.

"Easton." She reaches out to me and as much as I want to back away, to shrink into a hole and pretend this isn't happening, I don't. She's the one person I trust right now when I feel like I can't trust anyone.

Even myself.

"I feel like I'm drowning. Like I can't breathe. I've got to go. To think. To . . . I don't know what."

I grab my car keys from the basket and push the button for the elevator.

"Stay. Talk to me. Please." The break in her voice nearly kills me. Begs me to stay here when right now I know I can't.

I close my eyes, take a deep breath, and wish this all away. When I open them though, nothing has changed. She's still here, and he's still my half-brother.

The two things I know for sure.

"I won't do anything stupid," I say as a tear slides down her cheek. "I just need some time to think."

She nods. *She gets me.* She understands.

And yet I understand nothing.

"Open up." The door rattles as I pound on it. "C'mon, Mom, open up."

Lies upon lies. So many lies.

Anger. Confusion. Hurt. Betrayal. All four crash head-on inside me.

"Mom. I need you to answer the door." *Bang. Bang. Bang.*

My dad's the reason my mom is broken. His lies broke her.

"Easton? Easton, are you okay?" her slurred yet muted voice comes through the door before the distinct sound of the locks opening can be heard.

"Yes. No. I don't fucking know," I say as she opens the door, her face a picture of confused concern.

"What's wrong?"

I walk right past her into the depressing house of hers—stuck back in time with more empty bottles cluttering the counter than I've ever noticed before—and try to hold back my rage that she doesn't deserve. This isn't her fault.

"Mom . . ." I don't even know how to say this. "I know the truth. I know why you and Dad broke up."

Her face pales and her hands grow shaky as she ambles unsteadily to the kitchen and unapologetically takes a huge gulp from her glass tumbler. Her back is to me but I can see her shoulders rise and fall as she takes in a fortifying breath. When she turns around to face me, she suddenly looks twenty years older.

"Why did we break up, East?"

"No. Don't." I walk over and take her glass out of her hand and toss it in the sink. She cries at the loss, but I'm so goddamn sick of her addiction I don't care.

I need her more than she needs the alcohol right now and I don't think she sees that. *She never has.*

I wonder if she ever will.

"We were young."

"Bullshit. Everyone was young back then." I run a hand through my hair and catch a glance of a picture on the wall of the three of us, and I fight the urge to smash my fist into it. "He cheated on you, didn't he? He was in different cities every night with the team, and he was so goddamn selfish thinking only about himself instead of his family that he couldn't keep his fly zipped."

Her chin quivers as she braces herself on the counter and slowly lowers herself to a chair. I see the tears well. Notice her hands shaking. Hear her whisper, "*Oh God.*"

"And then he got someone pregnant."

"No. *Stop.*" My mom covers her ears and a violent sob escapes from deep in her chest. She shakes her head back and forth, repeating the word *no* over and over again. She's unhinged, much like I feel right now, but I desperately need to reach her. I need confirmation.

I need to hear her say it.

"Is that what happened? Is that what you've kept from me? You led me to believe he's a good man when in reality he's a piece of shit who loved himself more than he loved us?"

She starts rocking back and forth, her eyes flicking to the half-empty bottle within reaching distance, and she cries harder.

"No. He was . . . he's going to—"

"Don't make excuses for him. Don't you ever make—"

My words fall flat as my thoughts finally align and fall into place.

He's going *to* . . .

Present tense.

I'm across the room in a flash and shake her shoulders so she snaps out of it. I need to see her face when I ask the next question. The one that's currently making me sick to my stomach.

"*Who's the love of your life, Mom?*" Panic is all I see on her face.

226

"Who? Is Dad the true love you've been waiting for?"

She doesn't respond. Her lips open and close. She looks to the bottle again and then back to me. Need versus duty. Addiction against love.

It all makes sense now.

"That's why you always kept those pictures of the three of us up on the wall, isn't it? I thought you did it so I'd see our family wasn't always broken. So that I'd know I was loved by two parents long after I was only allowed one parent at a time."

"You were loved."

"But that wasn't it at all, was it? You left them up because you still love him. Because he loved the parts of you no one else loved."

Her bloodshot eyes are glassy and her smile lopsided despite her tear-stained cheeks. "He said he'd make it right and come back for me."

I stare at her. Disbelief owns every part of my soul when I thought I'd been shocked enough for one day.

And for the first time in my life, I wish I could be her. Addicted to something that has such a hold over you that you live in the past. Believe things that aren't true.

Hold on to the lies you've told yourself just so you can get through the next second.

The next minute.

The next day.

The next bottle.

CHAPTER FORTY-TWO

Scout

"**H**e's not here."

Cal stands in the foyer, a defeated man. "Do you know where he went? I need to talk to him."

"I think your actions have spoken loud enough."

Did he make a mistake in his past? Obviously. Do I feel sorry for him? On the I'm-a-human-being level, *yes*. On the I-love-and-want-to-protect-Easton level, *absolutely not*.

"What do you want me to say, Scout?" He scrubs a hand over his face.

"You know what? He's tried to live up to your perfection his whole damn life. He's tried and failed and hated himself because he's fallen short in more ways than you could ever imagine . . . and you let him believe that. You let him think he was less than your pristine image."

"I did no such thing." He says the words but there's no conviction there. A proud man uncertain how to be humble.

"You don't have a leg to stand on, Cal." Agitated and worried about Easton, I pull on the back of my neck with both hands to try and calm myself. "Did you think this little secret of yours would never come out?"

He hangs his head for a beat before looking back at me. "Do you know the odds that someone I had an affair with way back when, would have a son who would also become a major league baseball player? The odds are so slim to even make it, let alone two kids from the same father."

"How long have you known?" I ask. "Years? Months? How long have you been hiding this from Easton?"

"Santiago never knew I was his father." He shakes his head as if he's still trying to comprehend all of this. "After his mother died last year, he found some newspaper clippings she'd saved on me. He connected the dots and approached me in March."

Eight months.

"You've had months. You weren't going to tell Easton, were you?" My tone is not half as bitter as I feel.

"I don't know." He pauses. "Yes. Eventually."

I'm not sure if I believe him or not. "So in the meantime you were going to what? Stand on the sidelines and watch Santiago continue to sabotage Easton's career?"

He stutters. The words he wants to say don't make it past his lips. "I'm—I'm still in shock."

"Shock or no shock, Cal, it's *him*," I yell unable to get the words out fast enough. "The guy who deliberately hurt your son. The one who ruined his career. Do you not care? Did you not think to protect him from—"

"You have no idea what—"

"Did you know before he hurt Easton?" My stomach churns at the thought.

"No. I swear. I didn't. Santiago was hurting. His mom had just died for Christ's sake, and he'd spent a lifetime without a father. So he was alone and left to realize the one guy whose career he envied the most was none other than his half-brother."

He was hurting. The sentence sticks in my head. The familiarity in his tone. The excuse for the inexcusable. Well, Easton was hurt too—then and now—more than I think Cal will ever fathom.

I stare at him, mouth agape, and head shaking as if I'm trying to believe what I'm hearing. "Please tell me you're not excusing Santiago for hurting Easton." My voice is ice cold.

"I'm not. It's just . . . Jesus Christ." He walks to one side of the house and then back to the other. He's got to know he's in a no-win situation here.

"There's nothing you can say to dignify what Santiago's done. How can you even let him into your life knowing what he did to Easton?"

"But he's my son." His voice is whispered disbelief.

"For the past twenty-five years, *Easton* was your *only* son. Funny thing is I've yet to see you cut him any of the slack you sure as hell have shown Santiago."

Tears well in his eyes. I can see his pain. His uncertainty over what to do. The chaos inside his soul.

And a very tiny part of me feels sorry for him.

The other part of me despises him for destroying so many lives. His wife's with his infidelity and then condemning his son to be her caregiver year after year—watching her suffer and stumble. His son's by constantly making him feel less than he ought, and then bringing his bastard child into his face as if to taunt him.

CHAPTER FORTY-THREE

Easton

It's late.

The lot is a ghost town.

I'm not sure how long I sit in the truck staring at the gray concrete walls of the parking garage to my building, but I can't bring myself to go upstairs just yet.

So many goddamn lies I can't wrap my head around them all. What to believe. What not to believe. How my mom can be so fucked up she still thinks my dad is going to come back for her. How I share the same blood with Santiago when I fucking despise him.

I climb out of the truck. The looks on my dad's and Santiago's faces etched in my mind. And then my mom's. Her pitiful love for a man who'll never come back for her. And my pathetic hope that this is all a dream.

"Easton."

I'm halfway toward the elevator. I stand there in no man's land— *so close to home*—and grit my teeth.

I don't want to do this right now.

I don't want to see him.

I don't want to face this.

"Easton."

I snap.

"You couldn't keep your dick in your pants, could you? Big, bad, on-top-of-the-world baseball player had to fuck anything with two tits, a hole, and a heartbeat to keep your god complex at full speed."

"It wasn't like that. Can we go upstairs? Somewhere private?"

"Oh, of course. You want to keep this on the down-low so we don't ruin the image you have of being Mr. Fucking Perfect . . . Well, you're not so goddamn perfect after all, are you?"

He takes a step toward me. "We need to talk, son."

"Don't you *son* me!" I turn to face him for the first time, and just like my mom did, he looks like he's aged one hundred years tonight. He looks old. Tired. Broken. And the fact that I care only pisses me off further and fuels my fire. "How many other siblings do I have, *Dad*? Maybe I have a sister in Dallas. And another brother in New York. Hell, maybe there's one in every city you've ever played in. *Lucky me.*"

"It wasn't like that, Easton. His mother never told me more than she was pregnant. I didn't even know that there was a *him* to begin with."

"Let me guess. She told you she was pregnant, and you wanted to get rid of 'the little problem' so you shelled out some cash to shut her up and for her to get an abortion. Anything to avoid ruining your reputation. And, lo and behold, she didn't do what she was told."

"Easton." His eyes narrow as he takes a step toward me. "Who the hell do you think I am?"

"I don't know anymore." The words are the calmest ones I've spoken, but by his grimace, I know they cut the deepest.

"It wasn't like that. I promise you it wasn't." He runs a hand through his hair and looks around to make sure we're still alone. "She told me she was pregnant but didn't want me to have any part of the baby's life. That it wasn't fair to my family and it wasn't fair to her and the baby. For each of you to get half of me."

"How convenient."

"I'm serious. I didn't even know about him until he sought me out earlier this year." *He's known for months and didn't fucking tell me?*

"So what? You told Mom you had a baby momma on the side and you ruined our family anyway?"

"It wasn't like that," he repeats for what feels like the hundredth time.

"Then what was it like? Enlighten me. Why don't you tell me what it was like to throw away a normal life for your son because you were too goddamn selfish to put him before yourself."

"I'm not proud of what I did, but—"

"Big of you to take some ownership, *Cal.*"

"I tried to hide your mom's drinking from you," he says, talking right over my sarcasm.

"She didn't drink until after you left us."

"You didn't know she drank until then because I sheltered you from it. Hid it from you."

"That's a fucking bullshit cop-out, and you know it," I shout at the top of my lungs.

He's going to blame this on my mom? Fuck him.

"Think about it, Easton. Think back to when you were a kid, but look at it through the eyes of an adult."

I stare at him and reject the words he's saying, despite the random memories they trigger that never made sense. Surprise pickups from school where he and I would spend the night at a hotel even though it was a school night. The garbage can that clinked like glass bottles when I had to help drag it down to the edge of the driveway for the trash pickup. His only explanation being that they were beer bottles from the guys coming over to play poker, except I never remembered any guys coming over. Last minute road trips with the team when I was supposed to stay home because I'd already missed too much school.

I don't want to believe any of the memories because that would mean he's telling the truth, and right now, *his* truth is not something I trust.

"Your mom had two loves. You and her alcohol. She became married to the bottle and had no room left for me." There's hurt in his eyes that I refuse to acknowledge. "Maybe I'm the one who caused it. Maybe my traveling and leaving her with a young and energetic little boy was too much for her to handle. I'll never know, Easton. But in a period of six years, we went from being this loving household to one where she shut me out. It's no excuse, but I was lonely. My affair had to do with so much more than sex. It had to do with companionship. It was having someone to talk to at the end of the day. Was it wrong? *Yes.* Were there better ways of handling it? *Definitely.* But I held on to our family for as long as possible and then Maria became pregnant."

So she has a name. "Maria," I whisper, hating the way it sounds in my head.

"Yes," he nods. "Your mom found the letter Maria had written, telling me goodbye and that she didn't want me to ever contact her again or the baby after it was born. Your mom and I fought over it. I told her I'd make things right and earn her trust again and she agreed to get clean. We agreed to spend some time apart, but I promised I'd come back for her. Fight for her. When I did, it was obvious that our separation only served to strengthen her love for her alcohol."

"But she loved you. She still does."

"And I'll always love the woman she was. The one I chose to see when I'd pick you up for my scheduled days. The sober one who'd get all dressed up with her red lipstick on to let me know she was still interested. And I did go back some nights after you'd fallen asleep. I'd beg her to go to rehab. To get treatment. And she tried—that summer you road-tripped with me and the team for two months—but in the end her addiction won."

I try to digest everything he's telling me. "What about Maria?

You just let her walk away without a fight?"

"No. I tried to find her but she was gone. Picked up and moved without a forwarding address."

I'm at a loss what to do here. My stomach churns and my chest hurts from the anger eating me whole. There's so much more I need to know but am too afraid to ask. In the hour it's taken to get from Mom's shitty trailer, so many things have crossed my mind.

"I have a shit ton of questions. So many my head's fucked up, but I need answers. Can you give me that? Can you be the man everyone else thinks you are and answer them?"

He cringes at my dig, but fuck decency. "Yes." His voice is barely a whisper and I know he fears what I'll ask next.

"Did you know Santiago was your son before he took me out?" I clench my jaw and wait for the answer.

"No."

He starts to say something and I raise my hand to stop him. I need to get through these to keep my calm and fight back the rage.

"Is he blackmailing you?"

His eyes flash to mine, the question startling him. "Not really."

"Yes or no, *Cal*. You can't *sort-of* blackmail someone."

"He was distraught over his mother's death. Angry at the world because he lived a life trying to make ends meet without a father. Everything was a struggle for him, and then he found out he's *my* son. And while he was struggling day-to-day, you, the guy whose stats he chased for years, had it all. He felt robbed. He questioned why you led a life of privilege when he'd lived one of poverty . . . yet you both share my blood."

"That's not *my* fucking fault."

"You're right. It isn't. And I tried telling him that, but resentment is a hard thing to let go of."

It's no *excuse.* That's all I think over and over as my dad talks. None of this is a valid excuse for fucking up my career.

"Blackmail, Dad. Yes or no?"

"All he wanted was the same privileges and opportunities you had."

"And all you wanted was to keep your dirty, little secret quiet, right?" The sarcasm falls second to the disbelief as he hangs his head momentarily, eyes looking at his feet.

Who the fuck is this man? I don't even know him anymore. How many other lies have there been?

"What was I supposed to do, Easton? *What?* Deny him something I had no control over his whole life? Wouldn't you think less of me if I walked away from him? I'm struggling to figure out how we go from here."

"*We?* There is no *we*, here."

He nods. "I meant me and Mateo."

Mateo? I don't want to think about him being on a first name basis with him. And fuck if that correction wasn't what I wanted but at the same time only makes the sting a little stronger.

"Did you have any influence, play any part, in bringing *him* to the Aces?"

The sudden slump of his shoulders makes me take a step away from him. "It wasn't supposed to be like this."

Every part of me begs him to say no.

But he doesn't speak.

"Yes or no?" I shout.

"Yes." I can barely hear the word. It rings in my ears.

He knew.

He organized for the asshole who ruined my career to play for the Aces. With his fucking son. His fucking *first* son.

"You were never supposed to be traded. I didn't have a clue what Tillman had up his sleeve. Not a fucking clue."

"Convenient." I snort. "You felt the Aces could give *him* the same thing *I* had? What *he* wanted? Just to ease your guilt?" *What about me?*

"I know you have no reason to believe me right now, but please, believe this, it wasn't intentional. Tillman was looking for a back-up catcher—at least that's what he told everyone. He said he wanted to bring someone on board to help ease your transition back. Of all of the available catchers, Santiago had the best stats of the lot."

"You can sugar coat it any way you want to make it easier for you to swallow, but let's face it, you talked the asshole GM into bringing the guy who fucked up your son's arm to the club he plays for out of guilt."

"Yes. No. I was desperate, Easton."

My laugh is anything but humorous as I try to wrap my head around everything. As I try to put myself in my dad's shoes but know they reek of bullshit.

"All he wanted was my time, Easton. A chance to get to know the father he never knew—"

"He got a contract that doubled his goddamn salary. You can't tell me money wasn't a motivating factor here, Pops."

"He only wants more—"

"Spare me your excuses, Dad."

We stare at each other. The fury coursing through my veins makes it impossible to listen to any more of this.

"When you were traded," he says after a moment, "I went to Boseman and told him what Tillman did. I told him about the rumors going around about what he did to other players. I'm the one who helped to get him fired—"

"You expect me to thank you for that?" *Jesus fucking Christ.* "He's an Ace. And I'm not. He took *my* position. *My* team. So fuck that, Dad. Fuck you. Fuck this whole fucked-up situation."

"It was a perfect storm of coincidence between Tillman's and Santiago's—"

"He's the one who fucked up my shoulder," I shout at the top of my lungs to break through the fog he seems to be operating under. The sting of betrayal real and raw and unwelcome. "Why can't you acknowledge that? Santiago *purposely* took me out and singlehandedly ruined my fucking career."

"It's far from ruined, Easton."

"Don't you dare defend him." My shout thunders across the concrete space and echoes back to us. "He wanted what I had and you gave him the keys and opened the fucking door for him to take it." I chuckle condescendingly. *He may have stopped playing baseball years ago, but he's still playing a game, now it's with people's lives.* "You two deserve each other."

"Easton . . ." He takes a step toward me.

"Don't. Just don't." His eyes plead with me to understand him while my heart and head riot with rage from his betrayal.

Why did I ever want to be like him?

Fuck this.

Fuck everything about it.

I need to go home.

I need Scout.

CHAPTER FORTY-FOUR

Scout

"Easton? Is that you?"

It's late. The room is dark.

"Shh."

The sheets lift.

The bed dips.

He slides in behind me and pulls me into the curve of his body.

"Are you okay?"

"Just let me hold on to you, okay?"

I hate the hurt in his voice. The pain. It breaks my heart.

"I'll be whatever you need me to be," I whisper and slide my hands over his, resting on my abdomen.

"You already are."

CHAPTER FORTY-FIVE

Scout

I'm startled when I wake up to an empty bed. The sky is gray in that time of dawn where it's not light and it's not dark . . . but just is.

I hear the rattle of keys. Smell the beginnings of coffee. And I wonder how he's doing.

"Easton?"

"In here."

I find him in the kitchen, running shoes on, gym shorts darkened by sweat, and skin flushed from exercise. He's at the stove fixing scrambled eggs.

"Hey." My voice is cautious, uncertain what he's thinking after yesterday and what I swear were his quiet sniffles as he held me tight last night.

"Good morning." His voice is cheerful, seemingly unaffected, body still turned to the stove. "I just found out this building has an official kennel downstairs. An actual place where, if you have a dog, you can take them there like a daycare center—doggy daycare they call it—so those of us who want a dog can have one."

"I didn't know."

"I was thinking since I'm injured and we're about to officially be in off-season . . . it might be a good time to get that mutt you were thinking about. What do you think?" He turns toward me for the first time since I walked into the kitchen.

I study his face before he turns back to the eggs. There's nothing there that hints to the drama of last night. "Easton . . ."

"We can go next weekend if you want. After the series is over. We can adopt one from Pet Haven or we can go somewhere else. You should start thinking about what kind of dog you want."

"Do you want to talk about last night?"

For the first time I see a break in his chipper demeanor, but it's only a momentary stiffening of his shoulders. "And I think we should take a trip. Somewhere tropical. Or Europe. I've had my life on hold for so long for baseball, and I need to stop being a slave to it and start living, don't you think? I was talking to your dad this morning and—"

"My dad? This morning? It's not even seven o'clock."

I feel like I've stepped into an alternate universe.

"I texted him about something—needed an opinion from what he's seen over his years—and he texted back. So then I called and . . ." He shrugs. "We talked."

"Okay." I draw the word out. "Does it have anything to do with what he whispered to you before we left that night?"

"Nope."

Mr. Talkative.

I watch him dish the eggs onto two plates and place one of them in front of me. "Thank you."

"Of course," he says, walking around me and pressing a kiss to the top of my head before sitting beside me with his own plate.

"Easton," I repeat. "Do you want to talk about what happened last night?"

He's quiet as he chews his food, and I wonder if he's going to say something profound. "No."

"No?" I ask. "But—"

"What time are you headed to the stadium today? I don't have to report in until five but will probably get there at four thirty for one more run-through. We can walk over together if you want."

My fork is midway through the air, eggs perched precariously on its tines, but all I can do is stare at him and wonder if he's in denial. Classic avoidance at its finest.

"I think we should address everything . . ."

His shoulders drop and he closes his eyes momentarily. He draws in a breath as if *I'm* the one frustrating *him*. "I don't want to. Not now. I can only handle one thing at a time, Scout. And today I'm handling the broadcast. After that, I'll handle getting a dog with you. You moved into my home and this is all me . . . so if we have a dog together it would be like creating something together. Maybe make here feel a bit more like yours too."

I'm not sure if going along with his avoidance is healthy or if forcing him to talk about everything is better.

But at least his head is where it needs to be, on the broadcast to-night. That's half the battle.

And after the battle is won, it appears like we're getting a dog.

Together.

Taking the next step.

CHAPTER FORTY-SIX

Easton

I t's game day.

I can feel it in my blood even though I won't be touching the field.

There's excitement and energy and *magic*.

Scout's beside me chattering away about who she needs to stretch first, and how she's concerned about Dungey's elbow.

"Everything good, Easy E?"

"Manny-Man." I turn to find the one face I've seen more times in my career other than my father's and grab the old fucker and give him a hug.

"You're still pretty." He smirks.

"And you're still ugly," I reply with a lift of my eyebrows.

And just like that, the little bit of nerves I had walking through these tunnels tonight vanish.

"Someone has to be." He steps back and looks at me. "I'm proud of you for giving it another shot tonight. I'm sure they have those teleprompters in perfect working condition." He glances over to

Scout and smiles with a nod before looking back to me.

I swallow over the lump in my throat, hating that I'm lying to Manny of all people—the one guy who probably wouldn't judge me—but it's not the time or place to explain.

"I've been assured they are." I hold up my folder full of notes. "And if they aren't, I asked for cheat sheets ahead of time so I'd know what to say."

"I always knew you were smart."

"Yeah, yeah." I laugh. "You sticking around to watch the game?"

He eyes me for a second. "Yeah, I think so."

"Really? Which greats are you hoping to watch tonight?"

"*You.*"

I stare at him for a beat, too many emotions whirling around after all the shit last night. I don't trust my voice to respond so I just nod.

Scout steps up and gives him a hug. He's startled by it, but when she says something in his ear, his smile widens and he laughs as she steps back.

"See you after the game, Manny-Man."

"Not if I see you first," he calls as we walk down the hall toward the locker room.

"You don't have to walk me in," Scout says as she turns to me. I know she's nervous that I'll see Santiago.

"Bullshit. He doesn't exist to me, Scout."

We enter the locker room and they're all there shooting the shit and relaxing so they can get in the zone. The calm before the storm. I fist-bump some of the guys, wish them luck, and razz them a bit as Scout heads to her office.

And I might have even slipped a couple of packs of trick bubble gum into Drew's stash.

I miss this.

And the longer I stand here the harder it is to know I may never have this again.

Too much fucking shit all at once.

"Hey," I say to Scout from the doorway of her office. "I'm going to head up."

Her smile is wide as her eyes flick over my shoulder to where I'm sure all the nosy fuckers are watching us to see if they should make kissing noises like eight-year-olds before landing back on me.

"Have a game, Wylder." Her smile says everything her kiss would have.

"You too, Kitty."

When I turn he's right there. Standing in front of me. No smirk. No arrogance. Just him. A dozen pairs of eyes wait for a confrontation. They have no fucking clue how much has changed.

Walk away, Wylder.

They know he fucked me over, but they have no idea how bad.

You've got a game to broadcast.

I stare at the fucker, standing in my locker room with my uniform on.

Don't let him get any more of you than he already has.

He deserves what's coming to him. Every. Fucking. Thing.

Walk. Away.

And I do. I take two steps.

That's all I manage.

Fuck ignoring him.

Fuck. Him.

I do everything I told myself I wouldn't. My fist is cocked back and then flying forward before I even have a chance to think.

I hear Scout yelp. I hear one of the guys say *let them have it out*.

"You fucking asshole," I grit, hand still fisted as he stumbles against the wall behind him. "You got exactly what you wanted, didn't you? My job? My city? My fucking everything. *What did I ever do to you*? Not a goddamn thing. If you want to be pissed at the world, fuck up someone's life, then do it to his. He's the reason this all happened, *not me*."

Santiago stares at me with a look so very different than I've seen before. His hands are fisted and his smile taunts me. "Why should you get it all?"

My blood roars in my head and blocks out all reason. There is a room full of guys listening to us right now. Assuming. Concluding.

And I don't fucking care.

My fist flies again and glances off his cheek. His laugh fills my ears and ignites a rage I've never felt before.

"You're a spineless piece of shit," I shout.

"Like I care what you think of me."

"You should, you fucker." My hands are fisted in his shirt and I slam him back against the wall. "*What*? Not going to fight back now?"

I twist my hands tighter into his shirt and slam him again. The guys close in around us. My hands itch to punch him one more time. My fury crashes around inside of me.

"No need to. I got what I wanted."

"Yeah. You did. *Our daddy* sure as shit noticed you. First by taking me out and fucking up my shoulder. Such a dickhead move. And then by the bullshit you pulled when you came here." I lean in closer. "I shouldn't expect any less from a *bastard* though, should I?"

"You motherfucker," he grits out as he throws a fist.

It barely hits me because the guys are on him, holding him back before he can get enough behind it to do some damage.

I stare at him, hands trembling and body tensing as every part of me begs to punch him again. *Asshole.*

"You're not worth it."

He's not.

I've gotta get out of here.

I glance to Scout on the way out but don't stop.

The guys nod as I walk past them. *Looking more than shocked.*

The secret is out in the open.

Can't say that I fucking care in the least.

CHAPTER FORTY-SEVEN

Scout

The sounds of the game go on around me. The last-minute player rushing in for some eye black. Manny picking up the trash left behind. The voice on the PA echoing down the tunnel and into the locker room.

But I'm glued to my computer screen where I have Fox Sports streaming so I can watch the game in real time.

My knee jogs up and down as I wait for the known jingle to end while praying Easton does well. After that confrontation with Santiago, I need to know he's okay, but the few times I braved my way to the press box, he was surrounded by others and I didn't want to interrupt.

But he seemed good. And after the shitstorm during the last twenty-four hours, that's what concerns me more than anything.

"Good evening, baseball fans. You are in for an incredible night of baseball here in game three of the World Series. The Austin Aces against the Anaheim Angels. The battle of the A-teams. Both have one win apiece going into tonight's game, but it stands to be seen, can the Aces wrap this up while here on home turf over the next three games or will we be heading back to Anaheim without a victor? The man next to me might have something to say about that. Longtime Austin Ace, Easton Wylder, sits beside me in the booth tonight ready to help call the game."

"Good evening, Bud. Thanks, everyone, for joining us. Can you feel that energy in the air tonight? That's the magic of baseball, folks, and we're about to watch it come to life with the first pitch coming up shortly."

I let go of the breath I'm holding and feel like that little added comment, the *magic of baseball*, is his little way of telling me he's got this under control.

And he does.

He makes it through the starting line-ups without even a stutter.

He ends the segment with a lead into their sponsorships before the commercials.

Everything he was fearful of appears to be nonexistent this time around.

Bud and Easton banter for a while about the strengths and weaknesses of each team.

"Drew Minski is on fire with his bat right now," Easton says. "He's batting five hundred for the first two games and four hundred for the entire postseason. Look for him to be pitched outside tonight in the hopes he'll chase the slider and strike out instead of crank it over the fence and add another RBI to his tally."

Bud chuckles as the camera zooms in on Drew finishing his warm-up in the outfield. His face is scrunched up and he's pulling what looks like a black gob of gum from his mouth. His teeth and tongue and part of his lips are stained black also. "It looks like someone has fallen prey to a prank today."

"Nothing like a little fun to ease the nerves." Easton laughs as Drew, still on camera, shakes a fist toward the press box.

And I know. *Easton strikes again.*

"You wouldn't know anything about pranks now, would you, Easton?"

"Not. A. Thing," he says, but those who know him, also know that tone of voice. *And* that he's lying.

The silly prank is nothing on the grand scheme of things but it does wonders for me. He's going to be okay. He's wrestled his demons, and he's going to be okay.

I'm not sure how he's compartmentalizing it all, but he is. And I applaud him for it.

By the time the first pitch is thrown, Easton has more than redeemed himself from the last time and proven he's a natural at adding color commentary.

CHAPTER FORTY-EIGHT

Scout

I fight against the crowd as I make my way to the press box. There is chaos in the masses—strangers giving high fives, people whistling, the drunk ones stumbling, the kids in parents' arms struggling to stay awake—as people make their way out of the ballpark to celebrate the Aces' decisive win over the Angels.

I'm excited for the Aces too, but I'm more eager to celebrate with Easton on *his* incredible success tonight. He was flawless and funny and charismatic and engaging. I couldn't be prouder.

Upon entering the press box, I laugh, but am not surprised to see the spotlight has turned to Easton. He can't seem to escape it. At least this time though, it's in a positive light. Cameras are angled his way and a sports reporter is holding a microphone to Easton's mouth.

"We're so thrilled to catch a moment with you, Easton. How does it feel to be back working in some capacity in the city of Austin?" the reporter asks.

"Austin will always be my home, Chris, so of course it feels great to be here contributing in some way to this excitement. Once an Ace, always an Ace."

"Can you tell us how your shoulder is doing?"

"It's getting better little by little, day by day. Patience isn't exactly my strong-suit."

"Understandably. Is that why you took a shot at broadcasting?"

"Something like that." Easton flashes his megawatt smile.

"I hate to bring it up, but what made you do it again? Your attempt last month resulted in a lot of disparaging comments. Did you work the nerves out and want another shot? Why knowingly invite potential criticism again?"

Easton looks away from Chris for a second and somehow amid the bright light of the camera, he finds me. There's a confidence in his eyes I haven't seen in a while. There's also pride. He nods his head subtly before looking back to the reporter.

"That's a good question, Chris, and one I struggled with for quite a while. Most people don't know this about me but I'm dyslexic and up until this last month, I struggled to read anything. Case in point, how bad I botched my first broadcast with Fox." He blows out a breath while Chris just looks at him stunned and more than willing to let him speak since this startling confession will most likely end up as a trending sound bite on all sports and social media channels. All I can do is stare at Easton, feel immense pride, and hold a hand over my heart to send him silent support. "I've skated through my whole life by faking it, making excuses, what have you . . . and that broadcast was a wake-up call for me. The teleprompter worked just fine that night. The fault lay with me, not a tech. I was too embarrassed to ask for help but that night was the dose of reality I needed to seek help. So I had my agent approach Fox and ask them to let me have another shot at it. Understandably they were reluctant, but in the end they agreed to give me another chance."

"What made the difference this time around?"

"Owning my problem instead of running from it. With the support of my tutor and my girlfriend, I've studied like hell to prove to myself that I could do this. That I could overcome the one thing I've been ashamed of my whole life."

"Well that definitely wasn't the response I was expecting when I asked that question," Chris says.

"You and me both." Easton laughs nervously. I can tell he's suddenly uncomfortable and I love him all the more for it.

"Needless to say, you did a great job tonight."

"Thank you. It was a lot of fun. Who doesn't like to talk baseball?"

"True. So is this something you'd like to pursue at some point after your playing days are over?"

"With my shoulder this year, I'm sure to some it looks like that's already the case."

"But you are planning on returning, aren't you?"

"You never know what the future holds. Thanks, Chris."

Easton ends the interview.

But never provides a concrete answer to the question.

CHAPTER FORTY-NINE

Easton

"**W**hy didn't you tell me?" Finn's voice searches for answers. There's a trace of hurt there too.

"It's not exactly something you brag about."

"It's me, East. The one who knows you better than most." And he's right, he does. "I could have . . . I don't know."

"There's nothing to say. Signing that addendum and fucking this all up was a huge wake-up call with serious consequences. I mean, it is what it is, so just know I'm still a work in progress."

"You're always a work in progress," he jokes.

"Fuck off. I'm the best client you've ever had."

"Speaking of being my client . . . Why is it you went on national television and alluded to the fact that you might be hanging up your gear for good when you haven't even told me, your agent?"

I shrug, although he can't see it, and laugh at how very different this same conversation went last night with Scout, long after *our* celebrating ended when she asked a very similar question.

"Is there something you're not telling me, Easton?"

"Nothing set in concrete, no."

"What about set in mud?" The way she looked at me. With narrowed eyes and a tilt to her head said she knew I was contemplating stepping away from the game.

My only response was to chuckle softly, pull her closer against me, and kiss those perfect lips of hers.

"That's what I thought," she responded to my non-answer. "There's something to be said about going out on top."

"Easton. Are you there?" Finn asks, shocking me from remembering what happened next. Laughter. Kissing. And then me being on top. *Of her.* "Your silence is telling me you're actually considering it."

"People are going to hear what they want to hear, Finn. You know that."

"Well, Fox heard you all right," he says.

"I hope so since it was their reporter asking the question."

"Don't be a smart-ass."

"I'm not trying to be one," I say but don't say much more.

I've seen the papers this morning. The headlines. The next biggest story in the baseball world besides the Aces taking one game up on the Angels in the series is whether or not Easton Wylder is retiring.

"Like I said, you sure made a statement without saying shit. And Fox heard you loud and clear, but they're not the only ones."

"What do you mean?"

"I've received two phone calls this morning. One from Fox Sports offering you a contract as the regular sportscaster on their telecasts. The other from Boseman himself. Asking you to come home to the Aces, where you belong—his words, not mine—but this time as their permanent on-air commentator for all their games."

"What?" My head spins with the news.

"You heard me. For a man who hasn't even announced his retirement yet, you have two incredible offers if you want to take them.

Ones anyone in their right mind would kill for."

"Wow." It's part sigh, part *holy shit*.

"It seems you have some serious thinking to do during the off-season."

"I do." *I feel like thinking about my future is all I've been doing lately.*

It's all fun and games to think about retiring, but when it could be a reality it's scary as fuck.

But I now have options.

Ones that allow me to stay in the game I love. Keep that magic in my life. And give me the other opportunities I still want out of life.

I think back to that little girl playing catch with her dad at the field.

That's what I want.

With Scout. I definitely want her there too, sitting in the dugout with a little boy named Ford in her arms.

A family.

Our family.

One I can be around for.

Be a part of.

Not miss out on because I'm always on the road.

This game can be rewarding. I know that better than most. But it has nothing on having a family.

I hang up and look at the world outside my windows, and for the first time since I met Scout, I know exactly what I want.

Funny how my decision has been there all along.

I was just looking in all the wrong places.

CHAPTER FIFTY

Scout

Easton uses the remote to turn the TV off. The room is bathed in darkness except for the lone foyer light.

I called it ambiance for the romantic comedy we just watched.

Easton called it perfect let's-have-sex mood lighting.

"We should go to bed," I murmur but make no attempt to move from where I'm snuggled perfectly in his arms. He doesn't respond and yet I know he's not asleep because his finger is tracing aimlessly up and down my bicep.

"Hey. You okay?" I ask, curious about where his thoughts have been.

"Yeah. I'm fine."

"You sure?"

"Mm-hmm."

We fall back in silence as my mind races a million miles an hour to try and figure out what's made him so preoccupied. I can list several things—his dad, his mom, Santiago, if he's retiring or not—but remain quiet, lulled slowly to sleep by his even breathing and warm arms.

"I don't know how to fix this."

"Fix what?"

"My fucked-up family."

"Oh." He's avoided talking about it for over a week and just when I've given up trying to make him so he doesn't keep it all bottled up inside, he says this.

"The movie was all about family and how it makes you crazy but you kind of have to go with the flow or in the end you'll end up all alone." He pauses as he links his fingers through mine. "And it got me thinking about things. About you and how well you are taking everything with your dad in stride. I know it's tough and I know at some point you're going to break while I stand by and hold all your pieces, but you appreciate every single second of the time you have with him. You have one parent who will be gone soon and I'm sitting here with two parents I haven't even talked to because I don't know how to move forward."

"It's two totally different circumstances, Easton," I say to try and redirect the discord in his voice. "You can't compare them."

"I know but at the same time, I feel selfish . . . but I don't know where to go from here."

"You've had an awful lot thrown at you in the past couple weeks. Unfortunately, there's no guidebook on how to handle it or what steps to take."

"I know." He sighs and presses a kiss to the top of my head.

"Your mom," I prompt in the hopes that I can somehow help him. Although I'm the furthest thing there is from a therapist, I tackle the easiest one first. There's no hope for any type of relationship with Santiago—*as there shouldn't be*—and his dad's a tough one I'm not sure he's ready to deal with yet . . . so, his mom, it is.

"What about her?"

"What's changed for you with her?"

"Nothing really, I guess. She's still her. She's still in love with her bottle, and she's more convinced than ever that my dad is going to come back for her."

"So you don't love her any less than you did before, right?"

He falls silent as he mulls over my question. "No . . . but I'm angry with her. According to my dad, *her* drinking is what drove him away. It was the catalyst for him to look outside their marriage and ultimately break it apart. She's an alcoholic—that will never change. I have a lot of resentment for both of them right now, and I'm not sure how to deal with it."

"If she called you right now and needed your help, would you go?"

I feel his body tense and know he's trying to figure out where I'm going with this. He's hesitant to answer but he finally does. "Yes. Of course."

"Then nothing has really changed there. She *is* your mom, Easton. It's her you love and her addiction you hate. Give it some time. You just found out a lot of things, but that doesn't change anything between you."

"Blood is thicker than alcohol," he murmurs with a sigh followed by a disbelieving laugh.

"There's that," I say, thankful he still has his sense of humor.

"My mom is the easy one. Things get a little more complicated from there."

It's my turn to chuckle, knowing he's talking about his dad. "That's a whole mess of complicated."

"You've got that right." He sighs deeply. "How do I forgive him?"

"No one said you had to."

"But isn't that the only way to move forward?"

"I wasn't aware you wanted to," I say, leading him.

"I don't know what I want. Can I partially forgive him? Can I empathize with the lonely husband who had an alcoholic wife? In recent years, I've been the one who has taken care of her like he once had to. I know firsthand it's a lonely place to be."

"That's a huge first step," I murmur. "It's very mature of you to think that way."

"Well, hold that thought because the immature side of me is going to come out now. I don't know how I can move past him being so blinded by his need to keep his reputation intact, that he brought his problem to my doorstep."

"True but—"

"Better yet, let's not talk about this," he says as his hands run up the sides of my ribcage, thumbs strategically placed to graze over my nipples.

"Mm. Talking is overrated at times," I murmur, appreciating his knack for changing the subject. It's his way of telling me he's not ready to figure out what to do about his dad yet. And that's perfectly fine.

"It sure is," he says right before his lips meet the curve of my neck.

"Then I suggest you put those lips of yours to good use, Mr. Wylder."

"I've got a whole lot more I can put to use than my lips." He nips my earlobe. "But they sure are a good start."

CHAPTER FIFTY-ONE

Easton

"That one is so ugly. Are you serious?" I think she's lost her mind. I stare at the picture on the computer and just shake my head. The dog is a mess. A rescued pit bull used as a bait dog in dogfights. One ear is half torn, the other almost gone; her face is covered in scars with one eye permanently closed. She's so damn ugly she's adorable.

"We've both been battered and bruised in this lifetime, but that doesn't mean we're not worthy of love, does it?" she asks with tears welling in her eyes; reinforcing every word she's said.

I put my arm around her waist and pull her into me. She's going to need this in the months to come. Something to comfort and hold. To snuggle with as she watches her dad slowly slip away. I plant a kiss on the tip of her nose.

"She's perfect," I say, knowing I'll never be able to resist giving Scout what she wants. "What's her name?"

"Daisy."

"Daisy?" I laugh. "She does not look like *a Daisy*."

"Everyone deserves some pretty in their life regardless of the scars they bear."

Damn woman.

"Daisy it is, then."

She yelps and jumps into my arms. Legs around my waist. Kiss on my lips. God, this woman is going to be my welcome undoing.

The buzzer sounds and we both groan. "Just ignore it," I say then begin to kiss her again.

"What if it's important? What if it's Finn with contracts to look over so you can make your final decision?"

"He would've called." I go back in for another kiss, but she drops her legs from my hips and steps back despite my good arm trying to hold her near.

"You don't answer it, we don't have sex. You answer it, we have sex." My arms drop. "Good sex. Hot-for-the-teacher sex." Now, she's talking. "Baseball-cage-net sex." Definitely fucking talking. "Or maybe we invent an *all new* kind of sex."

"Like what kind?" I say as I take a step toward the elevator.

"Hmm. I could be your bat girl and make sure I handle your balls just right."

I throw my head back and laugh. "Oh, Kitty . . ." My words fade off as does her laughter when the door slides open and I see my dad standing there.

Oh, how the mighty have fallen.

"Cal," Scout says with a nod, acknowledging him. I'm not quite sure how I feel seeing him here. "I'll leave you two to talk."

I hear her feet pad down the hallway and hate that I don't know what to do or say or even how to act. The hurt comes back instantly. The confusion not far behind it. The feeling of being sacrificed to save him.

"Can I come in?" he asks.

"Sure." I step back but don't invite him farther into my home. We stand and stare at each other. He looks tired. Old.

"I've come here almost every day for the past two weeks. I've walked into the lobby, then I'd second-guess myself—that you might want to see me and talk about things—and then I'd leave. Today, I told myself I was to talk to you whether you wanted to see me or not."

"You're seeing me now. You satisfied?"

His face falls at the disinterest in my voice. And I hate that I care. Other than talking briefly about it with Scout, I've successfully pushed this out of my mind for the better part of two weeks. I've tried to anyway, but hell if my daily runs through the city haven't turned into all-out sprints to ease it eating away at my insides.

"Are you going to the victory parade today?" he asks. The nervous shifting of his feet tells me he's stalling, needing something simple to talk about before diving into the deep shit.

"Yep. Scout's a part of the team so she'll be there. I'll get to watch from the sidelines." Yeah. *That's a dig meant for you. A little reminder why I'm on the sidelines.*

"I never knew about your reading problem, East. Why didn't you tell me?"

I shouldn't have had to. "Because you weren't around much when I needed it to matter."

He nods, accepting my comment. "I deserve that. I could give you more explanations to why and that your well-being was my greatest concern, but it doesn't matter. They don't matter. I'm your dad, and I should have known. I should have been there for you. I'm sorry, son."

All I do is stare at him and hate that my throat feels like it's closing up. Words I've never thought I'd hear him say, he just said.

"How did you . . . high school, college–you know what, it doesn't matter why or how," he says. "All that matters is that you did. I'm proud of you for working on it, trying to fix it, but I'm also proud of you for admitting it. People are still talking about it. Boseman has proposed that I spearhead some community outreach projects between the Aces and your charity to—"

"Enough, Dad. *Enough.*" Enough with the small talk. Enough with the *I'm proud of you.* Doesn't he get I used to crave his approval and now I could give two shits what he thinks of me?

I should invite him in, offer him a seat, but I can't. Not yet. So we stand like strangers, face to face, a few feet apart, in the entrance of my home.

"And you did great in the booth. Rumor has it they might offer you a guest spot next season."

"Not a guest spot."

"No?"

"No. A permanent place with their on-air team." I wait for his reaction and *hate* that a small part of me hopes to see that he's proud of me. *Still.* The other part of me watches to see him connect the dots.

"So the rumors are true then?" He looks surprised.

"I haven't decided anything yet."

"Well, it's always good to have options. Good for you. You'll do great at whatever it is you de—"

"This isn't what you came here to talk about is it, Dad?"

"No." He looks down for a beat and takes a big breath before looking back up. "I can't change the past, son. I can't undo the things I've done, and I don't ever expect you to forgive me for them, but I'm hoping in time, maybe we can be *okay* again."

There are tears in his eyes and I can't remember ever seeing him cry. It makes me feel like a little kid, flailing around in an adult world when I have no clue what to do there. When I don't speak, he continues.

"I went to visit your mother the other day."

"*What*? Why?" Fuck. Will she drown herself in alcohol now that the love of her life resurfaced just to end up leaving again?

"I felt I owed it to her to tell her face to face. About Santiago finding me. About all the hurt it's caused you. To apologize again to her." He looks out the window and then back to me. "She's still beautiful."

"She always has been." My voice is unforgiving because even

though I can forgive him for his reasons why he left her, I can't forgive him for leaving me. Old wounds are hard to heal once they've been busted open.

He looks over his shoulder, back to where Scout went. *She's not going to save you.*

"I don't know how to fix this, East. Tell me what you need from me, and I'll do it," he pleads, desperation owning his voice.

I've thought about what to say to him while on my runs. How I'd scream and yell and blame him for everything, but seeing him here, like this, the fire has burned out.

"The things you told me, about Mom being sick back then, I never knew. And knowing that, I still blame you, Dad, but at the same time I can't blame you. I know what it's like to love her but to be disappointed that she loves alcohol more. It's damn lonely at times. I don't know how to feel and that's the hardest part."

"I understand."

"No, actually you don't. I didn't have an out like you did. I was left behind to deal with it all while you continued being you. And now . . . now I'm left to deal with a whole different kind of fallout that again I have no control over and yet completely controls my life. And once again, you will continue being you."

"There's nothing more I can say than I'm sorry. I screwed up."

"Yes. You did. This can't be fixed with an apology. Don't you see that, yet? He ruined my career, Dad." My voice escalates in pitch with each word. "He ripped my shoulder apart because he hated me for something I had nothing to do with. Because we share the same blood. He didn't get a *raw deal* because of me. He's a piece of shit as far as I'm concerned, yet for the life of me I still can't fathom why *you* gave him the opportunity to do more damage to me. You opened the door. You saw firsthand the damage he caused and yet you let him in. And . . . want to *know him. This* son got screwed in the deal. Not sure how if you love me, you can be okay with him, knowing what he did. Talk about twisting the knife in my back. So have a relationship with him if you must to ease your guilt and curiosity. Find out if there is anything redeeming in him. Just never fucking talk to me or Scout about him."

His expression is stoic but his eyes reflect a resigned devastation.

"As for you and me, it's going to take time. So yeah . . ." I move around the space to work out the anger inside me. "I need time."

"Okay." He nods again, compliant when he's never been that before in his life. "I know it doesn't seem like it right now, but I love you, son."

Without another word, my dad walks to the elevator and steps inside. When the door shuts, it takes everything I have to not go after him as the familiar feelings return. *Love and loathing*. Side by side.

I love you too, Dad, but right now, it feels like hate.

Love and loathing.

Now just on a whole different scale.

CHAPTER FIFTY-TWO

Scout

"Look at her. She fits in perfectly." I stare at Daisy sitting between us on Easton's truck's seat; the windows are down, and what's left of her scarred ears are flapping in the wind.

"After the life she's had, I'm sure a soft seat under her tail, the treats you're feeding her nonstop, and your hand constantly on her is like hitting the lottery."

"True. I thought she might be sad leaving Pet Haven but she's doing great."

"It's only been thirty minutes." He laughs but runs a hand over her back and rests it atop mine already there. "It's not that far out of the way, I think we should stop by your dad's and let her run around a bit."

"Really?"

"Really."

"What are you two—*three* doing here?" Sally laughs as she steps out of the house and closes the door behind her before squatting down to give Daisy—who is sitting so patiently—some love. "Who's this?"

"This is Daisy. We just adopted her and were on the way home. Easton suggested we stop by so I could see Dad and let her run around for a while before heading back to the city."

"I love her," Sally says. "She looks like she's had a hard life. I'm sure she'll eat up all the attention."

"She already is." Easton nudges me. "Scout has already given her a box of milk bones."

"So what?" I laugh. "She deserves them for surviving everything she's been through." I look over her shoulder to the door and then back to Sally. "Can we see him?"

"He's sleeping right now." She twists her lips as she puts her hands on her hips. "Have you guys had lunch yet? Let me fix you some lunch, and you can go eat in the field. I'm sure he'll be up by the time you're done."

"Sally, that's so generous but we couldn't impose on you."

"Nonsense. Give me a few minutes, I'll bring it out."

Easton tucks a flower behind my ear to add to the dozen others he's been annoyingly sticking in my hair. "I think Sally knows how to spoil you," he says.

"I think so." I giggle as I look at the picnic basket she handed us full of more food than we'll ever eat. "She's so used to feeding my dad who eats nothing nowadays that she's grateful for a big, strapping man to feed."

"Big, strapping man?" he asks as he leans forward and presses a kiss to my forehead.

"Yeah, I'm not sure when he's going to arrive but we can sit here for a while and wait for him. I'm sure Daisy won't mind."

And before I can finish the last words, Easton yanks me toward him so I sit between his legs, his arms wrapped around my torso holding me against him.

"*We'll wait for him?*" he growls playfully.

"Yep." I try to wiggle away.

"You've got all the man you need right here."

"Oh please." I roll my eyes.

"Are you disagreeing?"

I stop struggling. "No. I've got all I need right here."

His arms holding still soften, and he hugs me affectionately. "It's beautiful here," he murmurs. "It's very romance-novel worthy."

"Romance-novel worthy?" I roll my eyes and shake my head.

"Can't blame a man for trying." He laughs. "Seriously though, I can see why you like it so much."

"It's one of my most favorite spots in the whole world. I can still see Ford running over there thinking he could be a human scarecrow but failing miserably since he couldn't stand still for more than a minute. Or my dad teaching me how to hit a baseball right over there." I point to our left where Daisy is chasing a butterfly that seems to be toying with her. "So many memories here. So much good happened here."

"I love that you have that."

"Me too."

The long grass rustles as the breeze blows across the field like the memories of happiness that continue to ghost through my mind.

And then I remember something.

"Are you ever going to tell me what my Dad said to you on the porch when we left a while back?"

"Nosy. Nosy. Can't two guys keep a secret?" he teases as he turns me so he can see my face.

"No. Not from me."

"We'll see about that," he murmurs as I swat at him. He catches my hand and in an unexpected move, presses a kiss to the middle of my palm. When he looks back at me, there's an intensity in his eyes that makes the fun words on my lips die.

"Your dad told me to take care of his little girl. To let her be stubborn but know how to bend her will. To let her be girly but make sure she sticks her toes in the mud every once in a while. To let her run through a field with flowers in her hair with as much passion as she applies to healing her patients. And most important, to let her love with a clear mind and a *full* heart."

I'm a sobbing mess. I can't even hiccup out a sound as Easton leans forward and kisses the tears from my cheeks while every emotion in me is a mess of contradictions.

"I promised him I would, Scout. I want all of those things for you. The flowers in your hair, the mud on your toes, the stubbornness that puts me in my place, the sweet, the sexy, and everything in between. The first time we went to my place, you stuck a bookmark in my heart and then you ran away. And I think it's the perfect time to move to the next chapter and start a life together. I love you, Scout Dalton. I love the parts of you no one else knew how to love just as you do me. So there's this question I want to ask."

My heart is pounding and tears are falling and hands are shaking but I can hear his words. I can see the ring box he opens up with a simple diamond band that is perfectly me.

"Will you marry me?"

"Yes," I whisper as I bring my hands to his cheeks and press my lips to his over and over between saying yes.

He wraps his arms around me and holds me tightly before whooping and yelling, "She said yes!"

I'm startled by the sound of cheers from the house. I look at Easton and then over to where Dad and Sally are eagerly staring our way from the patio.

"I wasn't sure he was going to make it to the wedding, so I wanted him to be here for the second best thing, the proposal. It was important for him to have peace of mind knowing I was going to take care of you when he couldn't."

And then I get it.

He planned this.

My dad wasn't asleep.

The picnic basket was ready and waiting.

I look at him as the tears fall again.

"Thank you." He has no idea how much this simple gesture means to me. I don't think he ever will.

But I'm up and running toward the house.

Daisy barking her way behind me.

Through the field of grass.

With a full heart.

And flowers in my hair.

To hug my dad.

EPILOGUE

5 years later

"Throwing out the first pitch tonight, we have one of our hometown favorites, Easton Wylder."

I watch from the on-deck circle as Easton walks toward the pitcher's mound with Ford and Fenway in each of his arms. The sold-out crowd whistles and cheers as he crosses the infield, his smile a reflection of the love being showered on him.

The love he deserves and then some.

When he reaches the mound, he squats and sets down Ford with his miniature Aces uniform on and then Fenway with her Aces cheerleading outfit. He kisses both of them on the tops of their heads as he picks up the ball.

"Okay, ladies and gentlemen, let's see if Easton still has the magic touch."

When he throws it with perfect aim to the catcher, the crowd goes wild and it makes me wonder if this is bittersweet for him.

"And he does. That was a strike. But oh, hold on. It looks like little Ford wants to throw out a pitch too."

Not really understanding what's going on, and since he's used to being the one Daddy plays catch with, Ford runs toward the catcher to get the ball. The catcher, Wingar, hands the ball to Ford who then throws it to Easton, the ball bouncing a few times before he picks it up.

"And that was a great throw by the little man. And oh"—the announcer laughs along with the crowd—"here comes Fenway to get her turn and by the looks of her hands on her hips, she's not going anywhere until she gets it."

Wingar squats back down behind the plate as Easton walks Fenny closer. She throws the ball and even though it stops well before home plate, she throws her arms up in the air in victory before waving them animatedly in excitement at all the people watching her.

"Great job, Wylders. It looks like there may be another future hall of famer—*or two*—in the family."

Easton starts to head back toward me, Fenny in one hand and Ford running my way already. My dad would have loved to see this. His two grandchildren—one named after his son and the other named after his favorite ballpark—taking charge in the infield of the Aces' stadium.

Choking back the tears, I think about how proud he would be. I look toward the dugout and imagine him sitting there, a huge grin on his face, and flashing the thumbs-up sign like he used to when I was a little girl.

And when I look back to Fenny and Ford and then to Easton, I couldn't be prouder of the three of them, even though it's also a bittersweet moment for me. Four and a half years. Fifty-four months since I lost him, and I still miss him every single day.

I notice Easton glancing toward the stands to where Cal sits in his official capacity for the team. Their eyes meet briefly, a quick acknowledgment of each other, before he glances to a seat above the opposing dugout where his mom sits nervously in a rare outing from her trailer.

It took a lot of work to convince her to come and sit in the crowd, but the effort was worth it because Easton deserved to have her here tonight. To have both of his parents here, regardless of the status of their work-in-progress relationships.

"Hold up a second, Easton," Boseman says as he heads to the infield. There's a curious look on Easton's face. "While we have you here, we thought we might do a little something for you."

Easton looks over to me, eyes searching to see if I know what's going on. All I do is shrug and give him a big smile. Ford reaches up and holds my hand as Boseman continues to speak.

"We had you for most of your career. Even when you left us for a short stint, we still considered you an Austin Ace. And then you came back to play your final season with us, and we couldn't have been happier to have you end where you began so long ago. When you retired, we knew you did it for a good reason, so you wouldn't miss a single day of your twins' lives, but the city of Austin still hated seeing you go. And now that you're the lead baseball analyst for Fox Sports, we couldn't be more proud. And so to remind you that you'll always have a home here, that you'll always be an Ace, we'd like to officially retire your jersey number."

I love the shocked look on Easton's face. The wide eyes and smile so big it's infectious. I love that Ford and Fenny are here to be a part of it even though they'll never remember it.

And then a green strip on the outfield wall is pulled down and there, next to his dad's number twenty-two, is Easton's number forty-four.

"Let's take a look back at his incredible career. Congratulations, Easton."

Boseman shakes Easton's hand as the crowd cheers loudly and then he points to the jumbotron where a highlight reel of Easton's career plays.

But I don't turn to watch it. Instead I watch my husband as he stares at the centerfield wall with tears in his eyes, truly touched by Boseman's gesture.

The highlight reel stops and Fenny claps her hands in that unco-ordinated way two-year-olds have before planting a kiss on his cheek. Boseman hands Easton the microphone and then steps back.

"Thank you. That was totally unexpected. I'm a little speech-less to be honest." He shakes his head and takes a big breath. "There has only been one thing I've loved more than baseball and being an Austin Ace, and that is my family. Scout and Fen and Ford. I knew it would be hard to leave the game. I knew I'd pushed the limits with my shoulder. And then when these guys were born, I wanted to make sure I was present for every part of their childhood. I wanted to be home to tuck them in every night instead of traveling from game to game. That was important to me. So I struggled with the decision to quit the game I love before my time, leave behind the records I had chased, and walk away while at the top of my game to be the only other thing I was meant to be, besides a ball player, a dad. I thought I'd regret walking away. I thought my days of playing would be for-gotten . . . so this truly is a surprise. I am honored to have played most of my career here and now I'll always be a part of the Aces as they will always be a part of me. Thank you to everyone for your love and support over the years. Thank you."

The fans begin standing one by one. The cheers grow louder. More people stand. And before you know it, the whole stadium is standing and paying tribute to Easton.

I have chills on my skin and a heart overflowing as Easton takes his hat off and tips it to the crowd before setting it on Fenny's head. Her face disappears under the cap and all you can see are her curls sticking out from the back.

With the same grace he had when he played the game, Easton walks off the field, one more time. And when he reaches me, there are tears in his eyes. He struggles to hold them back.

"Surprise."

"You knew?"

"Of course I did. Congratulations, Hot Shot."

He sets Fenway down and pulls me in close for a hug.

"Thank you," he whispers just above the noise of the crowd. "It's because of you, Scout. Because of you I don't regret a single thing."

And when I lean back, his lips are on mine.

He doesn't care about the thousands of people around us.

Or the two-year-olds clinging to our legs wanting attention.

Or the cameras clicking over our shoulders.

He kisses me as if I'm the only person in the world.

He kisses me with a clear mind and a full heart.

THE END

ABOUT THE AUTHOR

New York Times Bestselling author K. Bromberg writes contemporary novels that contain a mixture of sweet, emotional, a whole lot of sexy, and a little bit of real. She likes to write strong heroines, and damaged heroes who we love to hate and hate to love.

A mom of three, she plots her novels in between school runs and soccer practices, more often than not with her laptop in tow.

Since publishing her first book in 2013, K. has sold over one million copies of her books and has landed on the New York Times, USA Today, and Wall Street Journal Bestsellers lists over twenty-five times.

Stay tuned for her upcoming series—the Everyday Heroes. This three book series will focus on three brothers: a police officer, a firefighter, and a medevac pilot.

She loves to hear from her readers so make sure you check her out on social media or sign up for her newsletter to stay up to date on all her latest releases and sales: http://bit.ly/254MWtI

Connect with K. Bromberg

Website: www.kbromberg.com
Facebook: www.facebook.com/AuthorKBromberg
Instagram: www.instagram.com/kbromberg13
Twitter: www.twitter.com/KBrombergDriven
Goodreads: bit.ly/1koZIkL

Made in the USA
San Bernardino, CA
29 June 2017